THE EMERALD HORIZON

THE STAR AND THE SHAMROCK - BOOK 2

JEAN GRAINGER

For my Family

CHAPTER 1

erlin, April 1944.

ARIELLA BANNON STRAINED to hear what was happening, her mouth suddenly dry. Men's voices came up through the floor, muffled but definitely there. Why were there men downstairs in the middle of the day?

Herr Braun never got home from work at the Sturmabteilung's Berlin headquarters before six, usually much later. Life at the official paramilitary wing of the Nazi Party was increasingly busy, and he was much in demand, according to his wife. Ariella was used to hearing him come back; it was the signal to not move for the next twelve hours.

He was often loud and she was used to hearing him shout at his wife from the moment he came through the door, so at least she always knew when he was there. Once he was in the house, she lay, barely breathing, never moving. Thankfully, and much to Ariella's relief, he was frequently called to the SA High Command in Munich, and it was as if the house could breathe when he was gone.

1

The Brauns never had visitors, and Willi, the Brauns' only son, was away at the front, proudly serving the Reich, so it couldn't be him. They'd had lodgers at one stage, but they'd both been called up to the services.

She tried to check the time by looking through the gap between the end of the slats and the wall of the house and judging the level of light. It seemed bright, but it was hard to know what time it was. She tried to keep track of days, marking each long sleep on the wall with a pencil that Frau Braun had provided. She smiled. Erich and Liesl would always count how far away things were in sleeps. Fifteen sleeps until a birthday, five sleeps until Grandpa's visit – at least before Peter's father died and left a big hole in their family. She'd been up in this attic for over 1,600 sleeps. It felt like forever. No conversation, no real communication, no news, no idea of what was happening in the world...nothing.

Her interaction with Frau Braun was minimal; they didn't chat. Her saviour tapped the trapdoor when the coast was clear, and Ariella would lower a bucket on a rope, into which the other woman placed a small amount of food and bread, a little cheese sometimes, soup if it was very cold. Ariella pulled it up and then lowered another bucket, the one she used as a toilet. Frau Braun took the bucket and emptied it. Most days, no words were spoken. The water tank was the only other thing in the tiny attic, so she had access to water at least. She kept herself as clean as she could and drank enough to stay alive.

The bed, which she'd made out of a few planks of wood she'd found up there, left over from some carpentry job in the house, lay across the joists. It was made a bit more comfortable by blankets and a cushion Frau Braun had given her the day she rescued Ariella off the street. Her whole world was that three foot by six foot pallet. She slept, she did her daily exercise regime, trying to stop her muscles from wasting, and she lay, hour after long hour, thinking.

Ariella lay there now, terrified that the sound of her heart pounding in her chest would be enough to alert whoever was downstairs to her presence. *Calm down*, she berated herself. *It could be anyone – a friend from the post office, a neighbour, anyone. It doesn't mean anything is wrong.* She focused on stilling her racing mind and drumming heart.

But Frau Braun never invites anyone into the house, a voice in her head argued. In all the time Ariella had been hiding in her attic, there had never been anyone but Hubert and Katerin Braun, and once or twice their son when he got leave, in that house.

The last time Willi came home, Frau Braun had hissed at her to remain extra silent, as he would be at home during the day. Ariella had been given rations for a few days that time – bread only, no soup – and she'd had to wait until he went downstairs before using the bucket. It had been full to the point of overflowing by the time he rejoined his regiment.

She could hear Willi moving about in his bedroom on his short leave periods, and once she overheard a conversation between him and his mother during which he begged her to leave his father. Willi loved Frau Braun and she adored him. Ariella remembered him as a sweet boy, full of fun, and she knew he couldn't bear the idea of Hubert being violent with his mother. Katerin had shushed him, telling him that she could handle Hubert, but Ariella knew differently. She heard it all – the crying, the blows.

Once Willi had gone back to the front, normal service resumed, but for weeks afterwards, Frau Braun was in very low spirits. Ariella had no idea why the monosyllabic Frau Braun was helping her. Never once since the day the old German postwoman confronted her in the street, more or less dragged her back to her house and shoved her unceremoniously into her attic had she given the slightest indication of her motivation. But here Ariella was, a Jewess, surviving the war in a German attic, her children safe, having got out on one of the last Kindertransports.

A letter lay beside her pillow, torn on the creases from being read and re-read over and over. Her few letters and cards were the only physical thing linking her and her children, who, with their lovely childlike handwriting, told her that they had moved to Ireland because Elizabeth's house was bombed, and that they were happy.

Frau Braun had explained at length how she had taken a huge risk intercepting the letter at the post office, but the Irish postmark made her think it might be important. She went to great pains to explain that if anyone had seen her, she would have been in a lot of trouble – all the Jews were supposed to be gone – but she did it nonetheless.

The day she delivered it with the food was the happiest day of all spent in the attic.

The gratitude Ariella felt towards Peter's cousin Elizabeth transcended words. Elizabeth was an angel, nothing less, and Ariella knew she would endure anything, survive everything, because one day she would see her precious children again.

She tried to focus on their faces in her mind's eye...anything to distract from what was going on below.

The voices continued. Were they angry? Friendly? It was impossible to tell. What were they saying? She strained to hear. The men were on the ground floor, in the hallway, she thought.

Oh no! There were heavy footsteps on the stairs. That creak on the step – she heard it each night as the Brauns went upstairs to bed. The attic ran the width of the house, over both their and Willi's bedroom as well as the bathroom. Someone was opening the bathroom door. Why would visitors go into the bathroom? One person might need to answer the call of nature, she supposed, but the footsteps indicated more than one person.

She felt nauseated. Bile rose from her stomach, and she clamped her hand over her mouth. She couldn't swallow and exhaled raggedly, sure the sound was audible. The voices were clearer now.

'Do you have any other beds, ones that could be placed in here? This room could accommodate more than one person.' A man's voice. What was he talking about?

'I don't.' Frau Braun sounded calm. 'My son is an only child, so we never had cause to have another bed in here,' she replied, her voice neutral.

'And you just have the two bedrooms and the downstairs parlour?' Ariella heard the same man's voice again.

'Yes, that's right,' Frau Braun replied.

Why was he asking about the house? It was a typical Berlin house, in a terrace, a small yard to the front and two floors. It had two bedrooms, a bathroom, a living room and a small kitchen and pantry at the back. The Brauns' house was much more modest than her and Peter's big bright apartment just two streets away, but it was a solidly built house.

'What about the attic?' This time Ariella heard a different voice.

She held her breath, not daring even to move her head in the direction of the trapdoor, just a metre from her head.

'It is not a proper attic. The floor is just joists. My husband was going to floor it properly but never got time, as he is so busy with Party business. Also it's not even high enough to stand up in – you have to crawl around up there. All that's up there is the water tank, so it wouldn't be suitable.' Ariella marvelled at how she stayed so calm.

'Can I see?' the man asked.

This was it, the moment of her discovery. They would find her. There was no way they could not if they opened the trapdoor, even if they never came up. She couldn't move. There was nowhere to hide anyway, but even if she tried, the noise would give her away.

She lay there, trying to visualise Liesl's face first, then Erich's, then her darling husband Peter, long dead now for trying to defend an old Jewish lady in the street. If it weren't for her children, she would have longed to join him and given herself up, faced whatever the Nazis had in store for her, but she wanted to see her babies again, to hold them in her arms, smell their hair, feel their fingers intertwine with hers. She had endured it all – the long hours, days, weeks, months, years – just to see them again. And now it was over.

CHAPTER 2

allycreggan, County Down, Ireland, April, 1944

LIESL BANNON GAZED CRITICALLY in the mirror.

'You look lovely,' Elizabeth reassured her, placing her needles and thread in her sewing basket.

'I look like a crow, a hard angular old crow, all dark and threatening,' Liesl replied miserably.

Elizabeth fought the urge to laugh. Liesl was growing into a beautiful young woman, but she was tall, and as of yet, her bust was small and her hips had not taken on womanly curves. She was neither a child nor an adult. Elizabeth remembered that age, and wouldn't go back to it for all the tea in China.

Liesl's lustrous dark hair was in the very fashionable victory roll – all the girls wore it like that these days – and her brown eyes expressed her disappointment. Elizabeth knew Liesl had hoped the red dress that had been altered to fit her would work a miracle in the bust department, but it hadn't.

There was a gentle knock on the bedroom door, and when Elizabeth called, 'Come in,' Daniel stuck his head around it. She smiled at his reaction to Liesl.

'Oh, Liesl, you look beautiful, and how clever Elizabeth is to make this dress fit you so perfectly.'

Liesl seemed to cheer a little. She looked up to Daniel and trusted him completely. He never lied to them, ever, so if he said she looked beautiful, perhaps it wasn't all that bad.

'Should we go?' Elizabeth asked her husband.

'Yes. Erich is getting anxious, and he doesn't want to be late. He's convinced himself he won't remember his piece from the Torah, though we've gone over it about a hundred times.' He smiled as Liesl passed him and went downstairs.

'Nerves,' Elizabeth whispered, kissing him on the cheek as she passed.

'Well, his bar mitzvah is a big thing. I just wish his parents could see him. They would be proud,' he said sadly.

'Well, we'll have to do,' Elizabeth replied quietly as she went downstairs.

Erich was dressed impeccably in a dark suit and tie, and he was holding both his and Daniel's tefillin. Elizabeth had grown accustomed to the trappings of Judaism, but at first she'd admitted being confused by the tefillin, the black leather boxes attached to straps that had to be wrapped around the head and arms of the men. Daniel explained that parchment scrolls of handwritten Hebrew texts were contained within the boxes and that they were an important part of their faith. In lots of ways, her gradual reintroduction to the faith was made easier because even though Daniel was Jewish by birth, he didn't know he was a Jew until the Nazis arrived at his door. Rudi, her first husband, had been a Jew as well, but he'd kept it to himself and she'd been a young girl, busy with her career as a teacher, so she didn't recall his faith impacting their lives at all.

With Daniel it was different, as he was learning. His parents had lived as secular Catholics and he and his brother were raised as such, so his true identity came as a total shock.

She watched as Daniel adjusted his own kippah and then Erich's, before smiling broadly. 'Well? Shall we do this, family?'

Liesl and Erich gazed up at him, nothing short of adoration in their eyes. Unlikely as it might have been, Elizabeth and Daniel had made a family with Liesl and Erich, the son and daughter of a first cousin she'd never met. Peter Bannon was the son of Elizabeth's uncle, a man who'd left Ireland for Germany and married a German woman. She remembered Christmas cards and the occasional letter, but there had been only minimal contact with her father's brother in Berlin. She suspected the hand of her mother in that; Margaret Bannon wouldn't have had much truck with foreigners. Elizabeth could still hear her voice now, her nose wrinkled in distaste at anything foreign. Erich and Liesl were Peter's children, sent to Elizabeth by their mother, Ariella, who was a Jew. At the time she sent them on the Kindertransport, Peter was missing. It had all sounded terrifying, and Elizabeth had agreed immediately to help. Technically, she and the children were cousins, but she felt like their mother.

'Let's go,' Liesl said, holding her brother's hand. She wouldn't embarrass him with such a gesture in front of his friends – he was thirteen now and very conscious of what his peers thought of him – but in the safety of their own home, they were affectionate and loving to each other.

The 1929 Morris Minor that Daniel got in return for fixing a farmer's tractor had seemed like a dead loss when he and Levi towed it to the farm. The farmer had been embarrassed to pay such a great engineer with a battered old car that hadn't fired for years, but Daniel assured him he would get it moving again, and with Erich's enthusiastic help, he had. It was a four-seat two-door fabric saloon with a four-speed gearbox, Erich explained proudly to anyone who would listen.

They were one of the few families in Ballycreggan with a car of their own, and though petrol was severely rationed and travel was accordingly restricted, they'd decided today was a red-letter day and they would drive to the farm.

The farm was a refuge for the Jewish children of the Kindertransport and their adult carers, and it had since 1939 become part of the fabric of Ballycreggan. The children attended the local school, and the European refugees were well known about the village by now.

Erich sat in the back and Elizabeth sat beside him, allowing Liesl to take the front seat. Normally Liesl sat behind, but Elizabeth felt the boy she thought of as her son needed some reassurance.

'Rabbi Frank is giving me a tallit. Normally men have their own, but we don't, so there are some that anyone can use,' Erich explained, though Elizabeth knew this already. The rabbi had popped in for coffee at the school during the week and addressed her class, explaining everything about the upcoming bar mitzvah.

'It will be a lovely day,' she reassured him. 'And after the ceremony, there will be cake and sandwiches, and Bridie from the sweetshop has made a donation of some lollipops, so it's going to be really special.' As she put her arms around him and pulled him close to her, she felt his thin body relax. He had grown so tall and gangly since he first arrived as a small anxious boy, determined to be brave. He was almost as tall as her now, and his dark hair was like silk. His features were different to his sister's, and Elizabeth wondered if he looked more like Peter or Ariella. She'd never met either of them, and she never would meet her first cousin Peter now. They'd had notification of his death. They'd not heard from Ariella in such a long time, but Europe was in chaos, so that might explain it. The children wrote to their mother each week religiously, and Elizabeth encouraged it, but they'd not heard a single thing from Berlin for four years.

CHAPTER 3

The Braun house was still and silent once more. The men were gone. They seemed to accept that there was nothing worth seeing in the attic because soon afterwards, Ariella heard Frau Braun bid them good day or something like that – they were two floors down, so it was muffled, but she definitely thought the voices were cheery – and then the front door closed.

She lay there, afraid to move. She needed the bucket as her insides were twisted with anxiety and terror, but she dared not stir. The sunlight slipped in under the slats, so it was still daytime. She and Frau Braun were alone in the house once again.

Frau Braun was a postmistress now, having been elevated from a mere delivery woman a while ago. When she announced her promotion, Ariella congratulated her but secretly presumed two factors precipitated the promotion: first, her husband's rise within the Party, and second, the lack of anyone else to do the job. It was hardly her charming manner or her love of the postal service. For want of something better to talk about, Ariella tried to engage her on the subject of her job, but according to Frau Braun, the work was too hard, the hours too long, the pay terrible and her colleagues morons. It was such a negative way of going on, but it was all Ariella had as conversation, so she sympathised and tried to draw her out, so acute was her longing for human contact. The long hours she spent alone dripped so slowly.

The occasional positive thing Frau Braun did say was how well Hubert Braun was doing in his career. She boasted about how they were now being invited to Party functions, though to Ariella's knowledge, Frau Braun never went out in the evenings. She also spoke of how Germany was winning the war by way of each person throwing themselves wholeheartedly into the war effort. She relayed stories of German victories, all on the excellent authority of her husband who was so high up these days. The fact that he was a violent brute didn't enter these conversations, and of course, Ariella never let on that she knew anything about their marriage.

She assumed it was not going to be long before Germany was victorious, based on her only source of information, and she lay awake at night wondering what that would mean for her and her children. She was a Jewess, and the Nazis hated the Jews. Her children too were Jews because of her, though Peter had been a Christian. According to Frau Braun, there were no Jews left in Berlin. When the war was over, what then? How quickly could she get to Ireland?

She thought about her apartment. How would she go about reclaiming it? Perhaps when Germany won, they would allow the Jews to come back from the work camps. There would be no further need for them surely at that stage.

She spent hours planning their future. Berlin would have too many sad memories for her; there were so many places she'd gone, firstly with Peter, then with Peter and the children as a family. She decided she would sell their apartment. They had some investments in America, so she could hopefully realise their value as well, and she thought she might buy a place in the country. She'd hidden the papers relating to their bank accounts and American investments under the floorboards in their apartment after Peter was taken and once she heard of Jewish assets being seized, just in case, so she could go back and retrieve them once the war was over. Peter had believed they were safe – he thought her Jewishness would not be a problem

11

because he was a Christian and held a position of influence at the bank. He was wrong.

Despite Frau Braun's snippets of war news, of how Germany was winning, the Allied planes dropped bombs every night. Someone was fighting back. Britain, she assumed. It was terrifying lying there, wondering if the Braun house would be the next hit, and if it was, praying it would be quick.

She longed to do her former daily exercise regime. She was determined to stay strong physically and mentally. She would need all of her wits about her when the time came to find her children and restart their lives after all of this madness.

Sometimes the long hours played with her mind; she felt like she really was losing all sense of reality. Was this really happening? Was she dreaming? Would she wake up to find Peter sleeping beside her, and would she tell him over breakfast about her horrible strange dream? But no, it was real all right, so all she could do was focus on the future. To occupy her time at night if she couldn't sleep, she translated poems into as many languages as she could. She did mental arithmetic; she designed their new house.

During the day, when she was sure Herr Braun was at work, she would read the letters the children had written.

She knew one by heart. It was from September of 1940.

Dear Mutti,

We hope you are well and that you can write back to us. We have moved to Ireland because Elizabeth's house was bombed. Not just her house, but lots of houses, and the school she worked at too and the baker's. Her mutti *is dead, but she had a house in Ballycreggan in the north part of Ireland, and so we have come here and it is lovely. It is very green here, and we live near the beach, so Elizabeth says when it warms up, we can swim there. Irish people talk very fast, and it is hard to understand them sometimes. There is a lady called Bridie, and she has a shop that sells sweets. She is very funny and friendly. She said she remembered Papa coming to visit when he was a little boy with Opa. Opa's brother was Elizabeth's papa, did you know that? Elizabeth is our teacher, and she is so nice. She treats us the same as everyone else in school, but at home, she is like you.*

We miss you and we love you.

Liesl and Erich xxxx

All Ariella ever felt was gratitude, not jealousy, that it was Elizabeth who was kissing them goodnight, or putting bandages on their cut knees. If Ariella had not put them on that train, if she hadn't written to Elizabeth, who knows what fate would have awaited her precious babies.

She longed for another letter, but Frau Braun said there were none. She didn't know if that was true or not, but when she pressed, the postmistress explained how dangerous it was to even smuggle that last one out. She said that Ariella was lucky to know that her children were fine and should be happy with that.

She tried to imagine Liesl, as she was now. She was only a child when they left and Erich her adoring little brother. He would have his bar mitzvah soon, if life had gone on normally. She supposed he had no idea about his Jewish faith if he lived in Ireland.

She hoped they didn't think her silence was because she was dead. She would hate them to be upset and worrying, and if there were any way to get a message to them, she would. She once asked Frau Braun to send a telegram, but the woman had exploded and asked her if she were mad. Did she want to be discovered and both of them put on a train to the east before their feet hit the ground?

Instead, she composed letters in her head every week, and she translated them into English, French, Hebrew, Italian, Russian. One for Liesl and another for Erich. In these, she poured out her heart, her love for them, her love for their father, the pain at being apart from them, her gratitude to Elizabeth, to Frau Braun.

In the many hours she lay silently still, she speculated as to why the German woman, a dedicated follower of Hitler – at least on the face of it – had taken her off the street that day and hid her in the attic of their home. Surely if her husband found out, he would kill them both.

The prospect of discovery by Hubert Braun terrified her. He stayed out late, and she thought he sometimes came home drunk, as often very late at night, there would be the sound of crashing and things being knocked over. She had known the Brauns by sight before the war – her apartment wasn't far from theirs, though in a much nicer part of the neighbourhood – and she'd had Frau Braun as her postwoman for years. She'd seen her husband a few times but had never spoken to him.

Frau Braun only spoke of him in terms of his role in the Party. But Willi was a whole other matter. If she spoke about anything, it was her son. On that subject, her face lost the hard angular grimace she habitually wore and she looked young. Her love for the boy shone.

Willi was twenty-seven years old and her only child. He was with the Infanterie-Regiment Großdeutschland, the unit that had, according to Frau Braun anyway, brought about the capitulation of Western Europe and were now doing the same thing in Russia.

Ariella remembered Willi as a schoolboy. She recalled a cheerful lad with a mop of dark curls and flashing eyes. She would see him sometimes on his bicycle going to or from school, and he also delivered their newspaper for pocket money. He was always singing or whistling. It struck her, even then, how unlike his dour mother he was.

Frau Braun had shown her a photograph of Willi in his uniform, and she replied dutifully that he looked very handsome. In truth, the sight of that uniform made her feel sick with fear.

In turn, she had offered a photograph of her and Peter with Liesl and Erich that they'd had taken professionally in a studio. It was the only thing she had in her purse when Frau Braun rescued her off the street. They were so happy then. They'd gone Christmas shopping after the picture was taken. She felt joy flood her heart when she looked at her beloved family. That day, swapping photographs, the two women were not a Nazi postmistress and a Jewess; they were just mothers. Mothers missing their children.

The house was still quiet. Had Frau Braun left for work?

No. There was a tap on the trapdoor.

Ariella realised she was holding her breath again, so she exhaled slowly and opened the trapdoor, peering over to see down to the landing below.

'Come downstairs. We must talk.' Frau Braun's face was ashen.

From the day Ariella had arrived, she had never left the attic, not once. One time, Frau Braun had fallen off her bicycle and broken her leg. She was in the hospital for two days, and once she was home, she couldn't get upstairs. Ariella thought she might starve, but once the house was empty, the German woman managed to drag herself upstairs and Ariella leaned down from the attic to receive some bread. She asked if she should come down at that time, to help her if nothing else, but her offer was rebuffed bluntly.

'You can never leave there! The attic is where you live or where you die, but you never come into my house,' the other woman said firmly, the pain of moving on her broken leg causing perspiration to bead on her forehead.

Now, Ariella moved her stiff and weak body to the edge. She managed to get her feet through, and she gripped the rope she used to lower the buckets down. She'd tied knots at intervals so it was easier, and she was sure it would bear her weight. She gripped the rope and allowed her weak body to slide down. She fell in a heap at the bottom. Instantly, Frau Braun dragged her to her feet, half pulling, half pushing her into a darkened bedroom.

CHAPTER 4

*L*iesl sat at the kitchen table, having finished her homework. She should, by rights, be attending the secondary school in Strangford, but she didn't want to. She and the other Jewish children from the farm opted to stay in Elizabeth's class in Ballycreggan National School, and nobody objected.

They had all grown up together and had shared a classroom for four years, so they all wanted to continue as they had done. The older children helped the younger ones, and they had become such a tight-knit group that the idea of going anywhere else to attend school was unthinkable. There had been a meeting, and the decision to let them all stay together was made. In their short lives, they had each lost so much – they needed each other in ways others couldn't understand. Rabbi Frank called in once a week and gave them some instruction in the Judaic faith, and of course, they all attended services at the synagogue on the farm.

Elizabeth taught them all she could – maths, English. They were all fluent by now and spoke with a hybrid accent of whatever country they were from mixed with County Down. Some of the local colloquialisms and phrases out of the mouths of Poles and Germans caused the people of Ballycreggan to smile. The previous week, Liesl had told

Viola to 'catch herself on' when she was saying she should not use her sweets ration because she was putting on weight. Bridie in the shop had pealed with laughter, saying that Liesl was 'one of their own now'. It felt nice to hear.

'What's up?' Daniel asked Liesl as he prepared their dinner and she chewed her pencil, deep in thought.

Liesl looked at him and smiled sadly. 'I'm just writing to *Mutti*, and each time I do, I wonder, is it time to stop? She's obviously not getting our letters because she would reply if she was. I kept it up for Erich, but he's had his bar mitzvah now, so he's a man, even if he's a very annoying little one.' She grinned to show she was joking. 'So I wonder if we shouldn't just stop.'

Daniel put the knife down and placed the potato he'd been peeling on the table. He pulled out the chair beside Liesl, sat down and faced her. 'Why would you do that?' he asked gently.

'Well, it just feels pointless.' She was trying to sound matter-of-fact, but saying those words still hurt.

'But you don't know if she's getting them or not. Maybe she is and can't reply.'

'I watch the newsreels in the cinema. I read the papers. You know as well as I do what's happening. They are gathering all the Jews and sending them away somewhere. *Mutti* didn't have anyone to help her, and Papa isn't there, so maybe it's even crueller to Erich to keep up the pretence?'

Her eyes searched his kind, handsome face. Liesl loved Daniel, and though she would never forget her papa, Daniel was, in every way imaginable, their father now. He was kind and funny. He never talked to her like she was a child or treated her opinion as silly, and she loved that about him.

'I don't think so. I know it's hard not knowing, but Europe is not as we left it. Communications are severely disrupted, and the military will be using any systems that still work, and civilians are far down the list when it comes to using infrastructure in wartime. There is a chance that your mother is getting your letters. But nobody I know, Jew or Gentile, has had a letter out of Germany for years, so perhaps

17

it's just not possible, I don't know. But I do know this – hope is not a bad habit, Liesl. You know your papa is dead, and we said Kaddish for him. He is with God now, watching over you and Erich. But your *mutti* did not look Jewish – you always said that – so there is a good chance she wasn't picked up. Perhaps she managed to live somewhere else, maybe she is living on false papers or hiding. We just don't know.' He tucked a stray piece of hair behind her ear.

She hoped he was right.

'Look, I'm not trying to fob you off, and of course we all know what has happened at home, but until we have some information, I think a little hope cannot hurt. You write each week to her, and even if she doesn't get the letters, I think, wherever she is, she knows you are thinking of her. And in those letters, you can talk to her, share what you want to with her, and that's a good thing, isn't it?'

Liesl shrugged. 'I suppose so.'

'And for Erich too. He needs to talk to his mother, as do you. So why stop?' He smiled and ran his hand over her thick, dark-brown hair.

'Do you ever write to anyone back in Vienna?' she asked.

He shrugged and shook his head. 'Nobody there for me any more. My family is here now. You and Erich and Elizabeth are my life now, and I'm a lucky man.'

'I miss my papa.' The words came as a surprise to her, but she felt his loss so keenly in that moment. She swallowed the lump in her throat as tears leaked from her eyes.

'Of course you do.' Daniel put his arm around her, wiping her tears with his thumb. 'But you can talk to him too, you know? I think he can hear you.'

'Really?' she asked, uncertain but longing to believe him.

He nodded. 'I talk to my parents, and my brother, Josef, who died in a car accident, all the time. I understand why my mother and father didn't tell us about our Jewish heritage. They thought they were doing the right thing, that we'd have an easier life if people saw us as Christians, so I'm not angry with them but I do have some questions. I love my faith now – I love being a Jew. It feels right. I realise that something was missing before, and now it makes sense. I know Elizabeth talks to her parents, and Rudi, her first husband.' He smiled at the look of confusion on Liesl's face.

'Don't worry. I love Elizabeth and she loves me, but Rudi was her first love and a part of her heart will always be his – that's fine with me. But my point is, those we love don't die, not really. They are in our hearts, in our heads.'

'All right, Daniel.' She grinned. 'Maybe you should become a rabbi, as you are so wise.' She winked, and he chucked her on the chin affectionately.

'I think I'm not learned enough for that, but I do know you should finish your letter to your *mutti* and then get on with your homework!'

'I've everything done. I was leaving the letter until last.'

Daniel returned to peeling potatoes. 'And of course you can tell your mother things you don't tell me or Elizabeth without fear of judgement.'

'I tell you and Elizabeth everything,' Liesl replied, her eyes wide and innocent.

'Hmm...everything?' Daniel glanced over his shoulder at her and raised a sceptical eyebrow.

'Yes, of course.'

'Even about a certain Jewish-Irish boy from Dublin with blue eyes and a cheeky grin who always waits to talk to you after Shabbat?'

Liesl coloured to the roots of her hair. She didn't know Daniel had noticed Ben waiting around to speak to her. He was from Dublin, and his father was one of the people who had set up the farm in the first place. Ben had arrived a few weeks ago, having finished school, to work on the farm. He was lovely, and her heart fluttered when she caught his eye, but she was much too young to be thinking about boys in that way. She knew Elizabeth and Daniel would not allow her to keep company with him, so a brief exchange each week after Shabbat would have to be enough.

'I...I don't know who you mean,' she muttered, dropping her head and focusing intently on her letter to her mother, hoping he couldn't see how much she was blushing.

19

Daniel stood up, his tall, broad frame shadowing over her. 'He's a nice boy, and clever too. He's working hard on the farm and is very interested in engineering, though I suspect his interest in my work has more to do with you than me. You are a little young yet, so we will keep an eye on that situation, but Elizabeth and I don't mind you sharing a friendly conversation now and again. Is that all right?'

Liesl was mortified, but a warm glow filled her chest. Daniel wasn't sanctioning anything more than a friendship, but it was something.

'That's fine,' she managed, and began her letter.

Dear Mutti...

CHAPTER 5

Frau Braun went to the other bedroom, leaving her alone. Ariella took the woman's absence as an opportunity to take in the surroundings. On that first day, more than four long years ago, she'd been so distraught, confused. She was so hungry, having given Liesl and Erich all the food she had left for the journey, and she'd been too terrified to go out onto the street for days following their departure. She had no ration book so couldn't get food, and she'd been warned that the protection she'd enjoyed by being married to a Christian was at an end. Peter was dead, and her children were gone… There was no hope. She'd left her Jewish identity card in the apartment in case she was stopped, and she had not one penny in her purse. She had nothing but the photo of their family.

When Frau Braun insisted brutally that Ariella follow her home, she was terrified but had no choice. The woman had never been friendly – she'd never even seen her smile in all the years she delivered the mail. She may well have been taking Ariella to hand her over to the authorities, but ravenous and terrified, Ariella was almost past caring.

But that day she didn't hand her over. Without a word of explanation, she shoved her in the front door, checking that nobody was watching, and directed her upstairs. Then, using a stool, she pushed her into the attic. Ariella wanted to ask what was going on, why she was doing this, what her plan was, but for some reason, she couldn't. Silently, she did as the woman bade her and pulled the bedding up behind her. She made her bed and that was that.

Frau Braun disappeared, only to return a while later with the rope and two buckets, one for food, another as a toilet. Ariella would never forget the food that day – some bread and cheese and a cup of hot coffee. She thanked Frau Braun and fell on the food gratefully, as she'd not eaten for days. The coffee was like nectar, and Frau Braun refilled the cup once she'd drained it.

'Thank you for doing this,' was all she managed to say at the time. 'Why are you helping me?'

Ariella remembered the older woman fixing her with a steely gaze. She was hard in every way, thin and lacking any womanly curves. Her hair was cut short, the colour of salt and pepper, and her skin was leathery and prematurely wrinkled. Ariella had never seen her dressed in anything but her post office uniform. Frau Braun stood on the stool, her head poking through the access to the tiny attic.

'It doesn't matter. You just make sure that you do not make a sound once my husband gets home. He leaves each morning at seven fifteen and returns around seven in the evening. If he knew you were here…well, you know. So stay absolutely silent. During the day, I will bring food and you can relieve yourself in that bucket.' She pointed to a metal pail. 'I'll empty it.'

'But I don't understand. Am I to hide here?' Ariella felt braver with the food inside her.

'You don't have any options, Mrs Bannon. You are a Jew, your husband is dead, your children are safe now that they are out of Germany. This is your only chance.' She nodded as if that were enough of an explanation and promptly disappeared, shutting the trapdoor behind her.

That was so long ago, it felt like forever.

Now, back in the house proper, Ariella tried to stretch her limbs. Her legs ached painfully, having borne her weight for just a few moments. Her hair was to her waist now. There was a mirror attached to the dressing table on the other side of the room, and even if she could have walked over to see herself in it, she doubted she wanted to.

Frau Braun returned with some clothes over her arm. 'Those men you heard earlier, they were from the housing office. They say that anyone with space in their house must provide accommodation for those who are bombed out. They say we can take four people. Our address is on a list that will be handed out to people who are destitute, or soldiers on leave, or whatever.

'Keeping you here is too dangerous. Someone might hear or see something, and it's too risky. You have to go. I've done my best for you, but it's just too dangerous now. I thought it would just be for a few weeks, and I've lost count of the number of times I was sure I'd been found out. I can't live like this any more. No, it's time for you to go.'

Ariella fought the swell of panic. 'But where can I go? I don't have any papers, nowhere to go. I can't...' She tried to keep the hysteria out of her voice.

'Look, that's not my problem. I've taken a huge chance keeping you here, and now it's just not possible any longer. You'll be fine. You don't look Jewish with that red hair and so on. And there are no Jews left now anyway, so they are not so busy seeking them out. We'll tidy you up, cut your hair.'

'But Frau Braun –' Ariella tried to reason with her, but the other woman went on.

'Now, we don't have much time. Hubert is in Munich for three days, but someone could appear at any moment looking for lodging. Go, quickly! The bathroom is across the landing. Wash thoroughly, and then I will cut your hair.' She shoved Ariella out of the bedroom.

Walking was still excruciating, and her back and shoulders protested painfully at her newly erect movement, but she did as she was told.

Once in the bathroom, she had no choice but to see what she'd become, and it shocked her. She didn't recognise the woman who stared back at her. Her normally lustrous curly red hair was matted and dull, and it hung limply. Her skin was dry and flaky, and while she had always been pale, now she looked malnourished and ill.

She ran her hands through her long hair. Peter had loved her hair, had told her she looked like a wild Irish princess. His father was Irish, and he'd told Peter stories of the folklore of that country. Peter in turn told Liesl and Erich. His father had taken him to Ireland once when he was a little boy, and Peter spoke so fondly of the place, it sounded almost mystical. He wouldn't see a wild Irish princess if he could see her now; she looked like a frightening old witch.

She leaned into the mirror, examining her face for the first time in years. Her skin was grey, as were her lips and cheeks; her face was almost monochrome. Her dress and cardigan, the same ones she'd been wearing the day Frau Braun rescued her, were worn and had holes. She had taken them off and washed them in the bucket, using the water from the tank as often as she dared, but that only helped a little.

She ran a bath.

In the summers, she sweltered in the hot attic – there was no respite of a breeze from the dead heat – and in the winters, she froze. Frau Braun had given her the only spare blankets she had, but still she shivered, desperate for warmth. Each year, each season brought its own conditions, and she'd endured it all, wearing the same clothes, the same underwear, because she was determined. No matter what it took, she would see Liesl and Erich again.

She stripped off her clothing and stepped into the bath. The water was barely tepid, and in the spring air, she shivered. She managed to lower herself in, every muscle and joint resisting movement after such a long time immobile.

She took a bar of soap – tiny and obviously used many times – from the shelf and began to wash herself. She tried her best with her hair, but it was matted and her scalp hurt when she tried to untangle it. She washed as best she could and then pulled herself out of the bath, wrapped her thin frame in the towel Frau Braun had thrust through the door and returned to the bedroom.

The other woman was there, and on the bed were a brassiere, some underwear and a pink and blue floral-patterned dress. It was actually quite pretty, though Ariella suspected it would be too big for her.

'Put those on,' Frau Braun demanded, and Ariella once more wordlessly did as she was told.

As she suspected, she swam in the dress, and it came to her mid-calf rather than her knees as it was intended, but Frau Braun produced a slim white leather belt and buckled it around her waist, cinching the dress in. Then she left and returned with a navy blazer and a pair of low-heeled court shoes. Again, they were too big, but they were better than nothing.

'I thought I was slim when I wore that dress, long ago now. I suppose I was wrong.' A sad little smile threatened as the memory of herself as a younger Katerin Braun in a pretty dress seemed to cross her mind.

'It is lovely,' Ariella said shyly.

'Yes, well, it may be, but you most certainly are not with that mop of hair. And we'll have to stuff the toes of those shoes.'

She pulled Ariella, sat her at the dressing table and placed the discarded towel around her shoulders, grimacing as she pulled up the red tresses. 'I'll have to cut it off, most of it anyway, and see if I can't shape it a little better.'

Ariella watched in silence as the other woman used kitchen scissors to chop her hair off. Once she had cut it to Ariella's jaw, she set about shaping it a little, and Ariella had to admit the end result wasn't too bad.

Frau Braun fetched some pins and pinned the remaining hair up and back off Ariella's face. Then she produced a little silk bag, which contained some foundation, a pot of rouge, mascara and lipstick. Ariella tried to hide her astonishment at the dour and utilitarian Frau Braun ever owning such frivolous things.

Once the older woman was finished, she stood back and didn't exactly admire her handiwork but at least seemed satisfied.

'Now, go. You need to get out of here. And don't come back.' She paused and looked straight at Ariella's reflection in the mirror.

'But I don't have anywhere to go. They'll pick me up for sure without papers...'

'Look.' Frau Braun stood and, grabbing Ariella's elbow, manoeuvred her out the door. She practically shoved her down the stairs with a hand on her back, and Ariella almost stumbled.

Ariella stopped before the front door and turned. 'Please, don't do this. I can't survive, and what was all of this for, all the risks, if you're just going to put us both in danger like this?' she pleaded. 'If they catch me and find out where I've been –'

In an instant, she found herself pinned to the wall. The older woman's face was inches from hers.

'Don't you mention my name, do you hear me? If you do, we'll both suffer. I took such a chance, I've made such sacrifices for you – don't you throw that back in my face.'

The mixture of terror and panic was frightening. Ariella realised she'd come to think of Frau Braun as her protector, but she was just a frightened old woman.

'Why did you do it?' Ariella asked. Suddenly it was important to know.

A shadow crossed the other woman's face, and it was impossible to know what she was thinking.

'It doesn't matter now. I just did, and now I can't any more.' She seemed to soften a little.

'But where should I go? I don't know anyone now and...'

Frau Braun exhaled impatiently. 'Look, there was a man – Wilhelmstrasse – the house had a black door, I think. He was suspected of making false papers, ration books, that sort of thing. He was arrested but let go. I don't know, but he might be able to help. Hubert and some of the others were talking about him.'

'Can you remember what number? Or a name?' Ariella was

focused now. She was being thrown out either way; she needed to get as much information as she could.

'I don't, but it's the one beside the shoe shop, I think. Maybe the name was Olfson or something like that.' Frau Braun seemed relieved that Ariella was making plans to leave. It could all be a lie, of course, anything to get rid of her, but it was all Ariella had to go on, so she memorised the details.

As they stood beside the front door, Frau Braun pressed a purse from the hallstand on her. 'Here. There's some money inside – it's all I can spare. It's enough to get you some food. I…I hope you make it. Don't come back here, please. I can't do any more for you, not now. If someone found out, Hubert… And Willi isn't here… You have to go now.'

She opened the front door and glanced up and down the street. She held her hand up, indicating Ariella should remain inside. Ariella saw the shadow of someone pass the front door. Then Frau Braun turned and said, 'All right, go quickly. The street is empty.'

'Thank you,' Ariella managed to say, despite her heart thumping wildly.

'Good luck.'

Did Ariella mishear it, or was there a slight softness in her voice? A kindness? Her actions and her demeanour didn't match. She was hostile, borderline aggressive in her dealings with Ariella, but then she had taken a huge risk helping her, and Ariella had no idea why.

'What date is it?' Ariella asked.

'It's the 30th of April. Please…' Frau Braun was pushing her out now. 'Anyone could come any minute.'

'What year?' Ariella persisted.

The other woman let out an exasperated sigh, as if Ariella were being a particularly annoying child.

'It's 1944. It's the 30th of April, 1944. Now go.'

Ariella left, her head down, staying close to the buildings as she walked through her old neighbourhood. She wrapped her hands around the purse, hardly able to breathe. Her limbs hurt and she was terrified.

All she had were the clothes she wore and the small wad of notes in the purse in her hand. She'd left the photo and her letters from the children behind in Frau Braun's haste to be rid of her. She longed to return to the safety of her attic, the comfort of that picture and her children's handwriting, but she couldn't. Luckily, it was warm and she didn't need more than the dress and blazer. She tried to look inconspicuous by pretending to walk calmly and not scurrying with her head down.

The street was at once familiar and also totally alien. The rubble everywhere was shocking; the water mains were leaking and spurting. For four years, Frau Braun had told her how Germany was winning, how the victory was going to be glorious. But this was not the capital city of victors. It was totally decimated. She'd heard the bombers, felt the shuddering vibration of the blasts, but nothing could have prepared her for this carnage.

Several houses on the street where she'd lived were without glass in the windows. She walked purposefully to the corner, where once there had been a baker's where Peter often stopped to get pastries for the children on his way home from work. It was closed now, the windows boarded up. Turning right onto the main street, she crossed over and saw that there was no point in waiting for a tram – the tracks were buckled and twisted, so nothing could run on them. Her old apartment was only two blocks up, but she didn't dare turn in that direction. What if someone recognised her? She needed to get away from these streets.

These people, these Nazis who stood by while the Jews were rounded up, weren't strangers. They were her neighbours, people she and her family had interacted with all the time. She could recall the shocked horror she felt as one by one the Germans around her joined the Party. Had they hated her and her children all along? It seemed inconceivable, but seeing Frau Loss and her daughter Heidi – from the greengrocer's on the corner – in the uniform of the women's and girl's Nazi organisations made it real. Frau Loss had always been so nice, giving Erich and Liesl an apple or a plum when Ariella shopped there. Or Herr Krupp with the handlebar moustache, who had a bicycle repair shop and who mended the wheel of Liesl's pram when it came off one day in the Tiergarten. He made funny animal noises to entertain the children, and they would giggle at him, but then he put on a Brownshirt uniform and became a different man.

Surely they couldn't all believe it? Maybe they were like Frau Braun? She was a loyal Nazi, a *hausfrau* with medals from that despicable regime for being such a fine example of German womanhood, her husband a card-carrying Nazi and proud of it, their son wearing the uniform of the regime that had killed Peter.

But she was also her rescuer. Ariella wouldn't have stood a chance alone in the city in 1939 with no money, no ration card and a notice to vacate their apartment. Frau Braun took her in. The risk was unfathomable. She would no doubt have paid the ultimate price if she were caught helping a Jew, but she did it, and though Ariella had no idea why, she would be in her debt until the day she died.

She passed the railway station on Friedrichstraße, the place she'd dropped Liesl and Erich that day. It had felt like someone reached into her chest and squeezed her heart as she saw their little backs retreat down the platform onto what became one of the last Kindertransports out of Berlin, but every day she thanked God that she'd had the strength to do it. And that her husband's best friend, Nathaniel, had arranged it. She thought of him and Gretel. They were the only people she could conceivably go to. But should she put them in danger like that? They were such good friends. It had been to Nathaniel and Gretel's she went the night she put Liesl and Erich on the train, and sobbed for her husband and her babies.

Nathaniel was Lutheran. He'd worked at the same bank as Peter, and he and Gretel had a beautiful house overlooking the Tiergarten. Ariella and Peter often went to supper there, long before either couple had children. They would drink wine and eat delicious food – Gretel was a fabulous cook – and they would laugh. How innocent they all were, never imagining for one moment that life could ever turn sour. They married the same summer, each couple attending the other's wedding, and when Gretel became pregnant a few months after her, it was perfect. Their son, Kurt, was five months younger than Liesl. She wondered where he was now? They had two daughters in rapid succession before Erich was born, and Ariella remembered how Kitti and Elke could wrap their father round their little fingers.

She wondered if Liesl and Erich would just slip into the old easy friendship with them if they were reunited. Could that ever happen? That life would go back to normal? What was normal any more?

CHAPTER 6

*L*iesl and Erich walked up the hill to school. Other siblings they knew bickered and didn't like to spend time together, but the promise Liesl had made to their mother to care for her little brother was something she took seriously, and so they rarely had a cross word. The Bannon children were totally united, and everyone who knew them was aware of it.

'Sean and Barry are going fishing after school – there's trout in the Shanagadeen River. Barry's brother caught two beauties yesterday, and Levi said the kids from the farm could go too if we liked, but I'd better ask Elizabeth, do you think?' Erich asked.

'Yes, ask, but I'm sure it will be fine,' Liesl responded absentmindedly. Her thoughts were on Ben. After Shabbat, he'd stood outside the synagogue, now a beautiful building on the farm thanks to Daniel and Levi and the others, and she knew he was waiting for her. Her friend Viola nudged her when she saw him standing there.

He was dressed appropriately for worship, dark trousers and a white shirt, his kippah sitting neatly on his head, but to Liesl he was like a god or something. Viola was such a great friend that Liesl knew she wouldn't laugh at her, so she told her how she felt about him and what Daniel had said about it being all right for them to be friendly but nothing more as she was too young.

Liesl and Ben talked about her schoolwork, and he told her a funny story about his maths master at school in Dublin. He was so easy to talk to. His gorgeous Irish accent, creamy skin lightly dusted with freckles, piercing blue eyes and dark hair haunted her dreams. More than once, Elizabeth had caught her daydreaming about him in class when she was supposed to be concentrating on conjugating verbs or learning the rivers of Europe.

'Did you have a nice talk with Ben after prayers?' Erich asked, a slight smirk on his boyish face.

'Yes, I did.' Liesl stopped and looked into her little brother's eyes. Erich was almost as tall as she was now, and filling out almost daily. It both broke and warmed her heart to see him looking so much like her beloved papa. 'But don't be going on about it, will you? I don't want the teasing to start and then the rabbi to hear about it and think something was going on. But he's very nice and I like him.'

'All right, no teasing, I promise.' Erich smiled, his brown eyes warm. 'He is a nice fella actually.'

Liesl smiled at his Irishisms.

'He fixed the puncture on Marcus's bike last week even though he had so much to do to reroof the chicken coop after the high winds.'

Liesl smiled. She was glad Erich liked Ben too.

'Did you write to *Mutti* about him?' Erich continued as they walked along.

'Yes...well, a bit. I...' She paused, wondering if she should go on. She decided Erich wasn't a baby any more, and anyway, she wanted to share Daniel's wisdom with him. Even if Erich never said anything, he must have had the same thoughts.

He looked quizzically at her.

'I was going to stop writing...well, because I thought there was no point, as she probably isn't getting the letters.' Her voice was quieter now. She wanted to tread carefully with this conversation.

'Do you think *Mutti* is dead, Liesl?' Suddenly Erich wasn't the tall rangy boy whose shirttails were always hanging out and shoes scuffed from kicking a football. He was her little brother, looking up to her for everything. What she said next was crucial.

'No, of course I don't. But maybe she's not getting our letters, or maybe she is and can't reply. Daniel was saying nobody can get letters out of Germany since everything is so disrupted.' She deliberately kept her gaze on the path ahead.

'Do you think it's true, that it's as bad as they say on the news? Or is it our side making some of it up to make the Germans look worse and make people more enthusiastic about winning the war?' Erich asked.

'I don't know. I think some of it's true. I know it's hard to imagine,' she confirmed quietly.

'And so do you think they took *Mutti* to one of those horrible camps?'

She heard the catch in his voice, though he was trying to sound calm. He was kicking a pebble, his eyes not meeting hers.

'We have to face facts that there's a chance they did.' She wanted to prepare him, but she also wanted to at least give him a little hope as Daniel had given her. 'But we don't know for sure. And even if they did, then after the war, Elizabeth and Daniel will help us find her.'

'Some of the others are saying we'll be put back on trains when the war is over, just sent back where we came from. I...I don't want to go back to Berlin unless *Mutti* is there to meet us, Liesl. I can't even speak German properly any more, and what if the Nazis are still there but hiding?' His eyes were wet now, and she put her arm around him.

'Elizabeth and Daniel won't ever do that, silly. Of course they won't.'

'But what about the others? Will they send them back? And what if they can't find their parents?'

'Nothing like that will happen, I'm sure of it. Tell them not to worry – we'll be looked after.'

He nodded, believing her as he always did.

'So are you going to keep writing?' she asked.

'Well, if you write, so will I,' he said, and the sadness in his voice broke her heart.

Later that evening, as Erich was in the bath, Liesl followed Elizabeth to the kitchen after dinner. She started drying the dishes that Elizabeth washed.

'I talked to Erich today. He was worried that we are all going to be put on trains and sent back once the war is over.'

Elizabeth looked aghast. 'Of course you won't. How could he think that?'

'They all think it, all the kids at the farm. That was the arrangement – that we'd have to be returned when the war is over.' Liesl was almost sure Elizabeth wouldn't allow that, but she needed to be certain.

Elizabeth put down the soapy serving platter and turned to her. 'Liesl, you and Erich are staying here until such time as your mother comes to claim you or she instructs me to send you to her. Not a minute before. And as for the others, well, we'll have to start the process of finding their families, but it won't be easy or quick. In the meantime, of course we'll take care of them.'

Liesl nodded, relieved to have this confirmed. 'Perhaps you should tell them that, save them worrying?'

'Of course I will, and thanks for letting me know.' Elizabeth gave her a quick squeeze.

'I can't ever imagine going back, even if *Mutti* were there,' Liesl said. 'Ballycreggan is our home now.'

Elizabeth smiled. 'I'm so glad you feel like that. And when your mother turns up, I'm hoping she'll be happy to come here too so we can share you both. I can't imagine our lives without you two.'

Liesl hesitated but then said what was on her mind. 'It feels wrong to say this, and of course I love her and my papa too, but you and Daniel feel like our parents now, and it confuses me. I feel so disloyal to *Mutti* and Papa, but then it's just how I feel.'

'My darling girl.' Elizabeth placed her hands on Liesl's shoulders. 'No wonder you feel confused – so much has happened in your short life. What you feel is normal. Daniel and I feel like your mum and dad, we really do, and I never imagined I'd have children of my own, so this is such a blessing. But there's enough love in that big heart of yours for all of us. When your mum turns up, and I'm sure she will, we'll work it out. She wants you to be happy, otherwise she would never have put you on that train, and so do we. So nobody is going to force you or Erich to do anything or go anywhere you don't want to go.'

Liesl sighed and relaxed for the first time in ages. Everything was going to be all right.

CHAPTER 7

*A*ll the way across the city Ariella walked, not with her head down, but not up either; she tried to look like someone with someplace to be. She hid her shock at the state of her city. Everyone else seemed to be used to it. She'd grown up in Berlin and saw it as home even if the current regime saw her as an alien. Berlin was a beautiful city – at least it had been before it was flattened by Allied bombs.

She didn't dare walk on Unter den Linden towards the Brandenburg Gate, even though it would have been the quickest way; instead, she skirted around the small streets at the back of the Reichstag instead. Each of the beautifully ornate buildings now was the headquarters of some aspect of Hitler's Germany. The red and black Nazi flags hung everywhere, and apart from a few elderly people and children, everyone seemed to be in uniform.

She was terrified at the prospect of being stopped and questioned, but everyone seemed preoccupied. Nevertheless, she avoided all eye contact.

She hurried on, towards Leipziger Platz, and passed the famous Wertheim department store. She remembered going in there so often both as a child and as an adult, and it always impressed her with its eighty-three elevators and glass-roofed atrium. The name of the Jewish family was gone from above the door now and had been replaced by AWAG, an acronym for some Nazi commercial entity no doubt. She wondered what had become of the Wertheims. Had they been removed from society too, despite their great wealth?

She skirted rubble and dangerously precarious buildings, street after street, until finally reaching her destination.

The paint was blistered on the big black door of the house beside the shoe shop on Wilhelmstrasse, and it was slightly ajar. Ariella pushed it, and the wood scraped the dirty tiled floor inside. The house, which had been divided into apartments, smelled of old food and unwashed bodies, and she tried not to wrinkle her nose. She had no idea which apartment to try. To her left were pigeonholes. The ground floor apartment had the name Gruber, and several weeks' worth of mail was stuffed in it. Perhaps they were gone; Berlin seemed empty. The second pigeonhole, presumably for the second-floor apartment, had a piece of card stuck over the aperture so no post could be delivered, and the third hole held one key on a ring. *The stuffed one is vacant surely?* she thought. *The other doesn't want post. Would you draw the attention of the post office by doing that if you were trying to keep a low profile? Surely you'd just empty it.* The key on a ring – she had no idea what to make of that. But she thought she would knock on that door and take it from there.

There wasn't anyone about, so she made her way to the stairs. Several of the spindles were missing from the bannister, and the treads were bare. Her legs and arms moved painfully, unused to the exercise, but she gripped the rail and half walked, half pulled herself up to the third floor. She didn't want to look conspicuous if anyone came in behind her or down the stairs, so she tried to keep her gait as normal as possible.

There was only one door that looked in use on the third floor, and it was closed. Two others were locked with padlocks and clearly hadn't been opened for a long time. They looked more like closets anyway. She knocked, her heart in her throat. Sweat pricked her back, and she tried to inhale and exhale normally. What if it was a trap? What if the police were watching the building?

After what seemed like an eternity, the door opened, but the person remained behind it. The room inside was unremarkable.

'Um, I was wondering... I was looking for Herr Olfson?'

'Why?' asked the person behind the door.

She inhaled. She would have to reveal herself, even if it was a trap. It was a gamble she had to take. 'I need papers.'

She heard a muttered oath of frustration, then a hand reached around the door and grabbed her, pulling her inside. The door was kicked closed, and before she knew it, she was up against it with a gun to her temple. She opened her mouth but no sound came out.

Inches away stood a youngish man with receding brown hair, hazel eyes and a thin wiry frame.

'Who sent you here? The truth. Or this bullet goes right in your brain,' he whispered, the vice-like grip of his other arm across her chest never loosening.

'I'm a Jew,' she managed to whisper.

'No, you're not,' he hissed, increasing the pressure on her chest and releasing the safety catch with the other hand. The click sounded so loud so close to her ear.

'I am. I attend the Rykestrasse Synagogue. The rabbi in 1939 was Max Weyl...'

'What happened there in 1934?' he whispered in her ear.

Ariella exhaled and swallowed, then said in as clear a voice as she could, 'The choir at the synagogue, led by Kurt Burchard performed the new Friday liturgy. It was in February and Jakob Dymont composed it based on the melodies of chazzanut following the Nussach.'

The pressure on her chest was removed instantly. The man stood back and stuck the gun in the waistband of his trousers.

Now that she could see him properly, she realised he was no older than his mid-twenties. He had a boyish face and ink-stained hands. He wore a beige pullover and dark-brown trousers, and his dark hair was neatly combed. He looked like the kind of boy any girl would be happy to take home to her father.

'Who hid you?' His eyes never left hers.

'I can't say.' She would not betray Frau Braun.

He gave a snort of derision. 'If you are wandering the streets looking for me, they don't care too much about you.'

'Circumstances changed. There was nothing else to do.'

He shrugged. 'Name?'

'Ariella Bannon.'

'That's not Jewish.' His brow furrowed once more.

'My husband was Christian.'

'And where is he?'

'Dead. He tried to defend a Jewish woman in the street. He was sent to a camp and died there.' The words felt like sawdust in her mouth.

'Kids?'

'They are safe. I put them on one of the last Kindertransports.'

'Lucky them.' He went to the window and stood to one side, observing the street below. Then he turned to her again. 'So Frau Bannon.' He smiled laconically, as if they were meeting in a salon over coffee. 'What can I do for you?'

'I need papers.'

'Have you money?'

She opened her purse and took out the notes, thrusting them at him.

'Is this all you have?'

'Every penny.' She thought quickly and then removed her wedding ring. It was twenty-four carat gold. 'But you can have this?'

He took it and held it up to the light. 'Nice.'

'It was made in Geneva.'

He popped it into his pocket and returned the notes. 'You'll need that for food, and anyway, it's not enough. I'll keep the ring though.'

'Fine,' she said, her voice barely a whisper.

'Right, let's get this done. Stand over there please.' He directed her to the corner where a white sheet hung on the wall.

She did as he bid her, and he picked up a camera. Quickly, he took a shot of her head and shoulders, then gestured that she should sit on the dusty armchair beside the empty fireplace. As he busied himself at a large untidy table piled with papers and stamps and blades, she scanned the room. It had large shuttered windows overlooking the wide boulevard below, and the elaborate cornicing and ceiling rose spoke of a time when none of this misery existed.

There were a blanket and a pillow on the only other piece of furniture in the room, a cheap old battered sofa. She assumed he slept there.

'I'm just taking this to the makeshift darkroom. I won't be long,' he said with a smile, and left the room.

Was he really developing the photo? What if he had gone to call the authorities? In one of the papers Frau Braun had given her, there were several advertisements encouraging citizens to do their duty and report anyone suspicious. Perhaps people were even paid to hand others over.

The urge to flee was tempered by the fact that she had nowhere to go. Assuming this man was genuine and gave her a fake identification card, a certificate of Aryan descent and a food ration book, and assuming the papers would pass an inspection, what then? She took the roll of banknotes Frau Braun had placed in her hand and counted them. Thirty Reichsmarks. As she rolled the notes back up, the man returned.

'It won't be long now. You're lucky to have lasted this long, but if you can stick it out for another little while, you should be fine,' he said, and she noticed his German was accented, though she couldn't determine where he was from.

'Pardon?' She didn't know what he meant.

'This.' He waved in the direction of the windows. 'The Allies are almost ready, the Americans are in England, the end is nigh,' he said dramatically, and grinned once more.

'Do you mean Germany will not win the war?'

He chuckled. 'You have been under a stone. No Frau Bannon, Germany is completely kaput.' He drew his finger across his throat.

'How do you know?' she asked, trying to quell the excitement in her chest. Was he right?

'Everyone knows. But I get my information from the BBC – I have a radio. And in this line of work, you get to know people.' He grinned at the shock on her face. Listening to foreign radio was punishable by death.

'They'll shoot me if they catch me forging papers anyway, so I might as well break all the rules, eh?' He chuckled. He sat down at his desk and began writing, then clipping and stamping. He beckoned her over. 'Sign here, Marta Weiss.'

She did as he told her and handed him the piece of paper. He assembled everything, stamping and sticking with a pot of gum on his desk. Finally, he took the paper he was working on and dipped it in dark liquid. She watched, fascinated.

'Coffee, or at least that disgusting ersatz stuff they make with acorns,' he explained. 'All papers and cards now are battered and damaged, so yours must be too. Pay attention. You are Marta Weiss from Fallersleben. You got bombed out, and you are here in Berlin looking for your aunt and uncle. You came here because you have nowhere else to go. Marta sadly is no longer with us, so she was a real person and her papers are genuine – I just needed to insert your photo. It's better to use real papers, safer, but it's not always possible. Your mother was called Margareta Schmitt and your father was Otto Weiss, both from Fallersleben, both dead. You're an only child now as your older brother in the Luftwaffe was killed in 1940.'

He appraised her critically. 'Now, she is only twenty-seven, so you'll have to act and try to look a bit younger, but everyone looks old and haggard these days, so it shouldn't be too hard.' He handed her a bundle of papers. 'Good luck.' He winked and smiled once more.

She took the bundle and shoved it into her handbag. 'I...I don't have anywhere to go. Do you have any ideas?' She knew she sounded pathetic. He'd done his job and she wasn't his responsibility, but she hated the thought of going back on the street, even with her fake papers.

He stopped his clearing away and turned to her, his face kind.

'Look, you are one of the submerged now. You might feel alone, but you're not. There are lots of Jewish men and women, just like you, hiding in plain sight. It's not easy, but it can be done, but you must be on the lookout, never let your guard down. Some morons are still loyal, and they'll report you for anything suspicious. Stay away from uniforms, all of them, and try to get out of the city – it's too dangerous here for lots of reasons. People are offering information to the Nazis for money, for food, so trust nobody. You know about Stella, right?' His eyes searched her face for a glimmer of recognition.

'I...I don't know who that is,' she said quietly, and he sighed in exasperation.

'Stella Kübler, she's one of you, a Jew, but she's getting three hundred marks a head for each one of you she gives up to the Nazis. She's all over the city, and if she spots you, well, she's like a vulture – she'll get her prey.'

Ariella was shocked. How could someone of her faith do such a thing? For money? It was inconceivable.

The man noted her look of incredulity. 'She's been promised she and her family will be spared. They probably won't, of course, but she thinks they will, so watch out for her. And it goes without saying that if you're caught, you never heard of me, right?' His tone was conversational, but she felt the note of sincerity in his voice.

'She doesn't know me, I don't know her...' Ariella began, as much to reassure herself as him.

'Doesn't matter.' He shrugged. 'She has an uncanny knack for spotting Jews. I don't know how she does it, but she can. So just watch out.' He opened a drawer and extracted a photograph of a good-looking woman. She looked no more Jewish than Ariella did; in fact, she looked like a very glamorous Aryan. 'That's her. If you see her, get yourself the hell away as fast as humanly possible. Her handlers know to act quickly.'

He threw the picture back in the drawer carelessly and rooted around in it with his fingers until he found a small pin for the Nationalsozialistische Frauenschaft. It was a small triangle of black enamel with a white cross, in the centre of which was the omnipresent swastika. He pinned it to her lapel with a grim smile. 'All right, you're ready,' he said.

She had hoped he might have more ideas about what she should do or where she could go.

'Keep your head down. Try to buy some food, but be careful – there is almost nothing to buy except on the black market, so don't betray yourself. And find somewhere to sleep. As I said, it won't be long now, but the bombing will probably get worse before it gets better. And remember, trust nobody.'

'I need to get out of Germany…' she said.

'Don't we all, sweetheart, don't we all?' He placed his hand gently in the small of her back and ushered her towards the door. Their dealings were over.

CHAPTER 8

*A*riella stood in the Tiergarten across the road from Nathaniel and Gretel's house. Though she dreaded implicating or endangering her friends, she had no choice. They lived in a part of the city that had managed, inexplicably, to avoid the worst excesses of the bombing raids. How many times had she and Peter gone to supper there? They'd spent Christmases together, Ariella had taken care of their children whenever Gretel had an appointment, and the other woman had returned the favour too many times to count.

Nathaniel and Peter had worked together at the bank, and both started on the exact same day. They shared a sense of humour and a love of tennis, and it was to the men's relief that their wives formed a firm friendship from the moment they met.

Gretel, like her, was from Berlin, but she said she envied Ariella her education and her ability with languages. Gretel had finished school at sixteen and was clever. However, she met Nathaniel at a church social, and once her parents were satisfied that he was a suitable husband, they courted for a year, were engaged for another year and married when she was eighteen. She became pregnant with Kurt and then the girls, and her family was her life.

Ariella tried to recall the last time she'd seen her friend. Perhaps a week or two before Peter intervened in the altercation between the Brownshirts and that old woman? They had gone for a picnic out to Potsdam – yes, that was it. They hadn't discussed anything in particular. The children had played together happily in the park, and she and Gretel sipped hot coffee from the thermos she'd brought and nibbled gingerbread, fresh from Gretel's oven. Gretel was an expert baker, and her figure was showing the signs of it.

Ariella smiled at the memory of Gretel bemoaning how her skirts were too tight and hoping it was the cakes and not another baby on the way. She'd had a hard time being pregnant with Elke and a long and difficult labour, so she confided in Ariella that she would be happy if Elke were her last baby, though Nathaniel would love enough children for a football team.

Ariella had wondered at the time about a relationship in which a wife couldn't discuss her fears and preferences with her husband, leaving her fate to chance alone. She never said it, but she and Peter had the kind of relationship where they discussed everything. She would have liked to have had another child after Erich, but it wasn't to be. But if she hadn't wanted it, there were ways and means, and she knew that Peter would have supported her completely.

Nathaniel was a lovely man but very much the traditionalist. His wife and children were his responsibility, and he made all of the decisions. He probably had to join the Party; it seemed like everyone did. Nathaniel was a pragmatist, where Peter was an idealist. Even if her husband had survived, she could never imagine him sporting a Nazi pin; he just wouldn't, regardless of the consequences. She looked down at the hateful symbol on her lapel but repeated her mantra: She would see Liesl and Erich again, whatever it took.

She watched for as long as she dared; she was very wary of acting suspiciously. No movement in the house could mean anything. It was coming up on 7 p.m. now, and people were home, eating whatever food they could get, praying they would survive whatever hell would fall from the skies that night. She'd seen, as she walked the streets of her battered city, mothers frantically ushering children along the streets. Everyone looked harassed, hungry, down at heel.

This was not the chic, modern city she remembered. Was Gretel like that?

She forced herself forward. It was no good waiting any longer – she would have to just knock on the door. She had not one other soul she could call upon for help. She was an only child, as was Peter, and her parents were dead – at least they were spared this horror. They died in a house fire when she was pregnant with Liesl, from smoke inhalation in their sleep, so it was painless. She recalled wishing she felt more as they were buried, but she just hadn't.

Her mother would have had no idea how to cope with this situation; her father would have buried himself in his books. They were observant Jews, but their faith was private and they never talked about it. Ariella had loved the synagogue since she was a little girl and chose to bring her children up joyous in their faith. She had two aunts living a couple of hundred kilometres away – her mother's sisters, spinsters. They never approved of her father, thought him too old for their sister, and so relations were never warm. She wondered if they had survived. It was doubtful. Two old Jewish ladies against a well-organised regime determined to destroy them... Well, they wouldn't have stood a chance.

Her father's family were from Dusseldorf, and again, contact was minimal. Her father was an academic linguist at the university and was gentle and kind but far more concerned with the world of books than the world of his little daughter. His wife, Ariella's mother, was a celebrated artist who smelled of linseed and spent most of every day and many nights in her studio. Ariella suspected their marriage was one of convenience: Her father allowed her mother to paint and didn't expect meals to be cooked or his shirts ironed, and she in turn made no demands on him. They were well off and so had staff to see to the running of the household, and to her recollection, her parents rarely communicated. How they conceived her was a total mystery. She spent a lonely childhood in the company of a governess, Mrs Beech, who insisted she spoke several languages fluently. Her father's rare enthusiasm for his daughter was found when he heard her sing in French or recite Homer in the original Greek. To relish these rare moments of his love, she was a studious child. Her mother didn't take any interest in her childish paintings, and when Ariella overheard her explain to Mrs Beech that she didn't want her daughter wasting her time on art when she'd clearly not inherited her mother's talent, it had cut her deeply.

She could not recall one single warm moment with her mother – not one. Sometimes she wondered if that woman had conceived and delivered her at all. They passed in the house occasionally, and if her mother addressed her at all, it was to tell her to tidy her hair or tie it back more. She'd hated her daughter's red hair.

She had vowed to be a better mother to her own children.

It was her inheritance from her parents that they'd used to buy the American shares after the 1929 crash. Over the years, her money grew exponentially. The share certificates were still back in her old apartment, but Peter told her that in the event of ever needing them, the American broker had copies – Hervey and Goodbloom Investments, on 9th Avenue in New York. *Funny,* she thought, *the things you remember.* If she was going to make it out of this mess and reclaim her children, at least she wouldn't be destitute.

Peter's childhood had been the polar opposite. His father was a loving Irishman who adored his son and in turn his grandchildren. He'd worked hard all of his life but had no great fortune. He was lovely, and when his German wife died, leaving him with five-year-old Peter to raise alone, he threw himself wholeheartedly into the task. The only time she'd ever seen her husband cry was the day he buried his father.

Reminiscing wasn't going to get her anywhere, she admonished herself. Now was the time for action. She crossed the road and all too quickly found herself at Nathaniel and Gretel's door. With a trembling hand, she reached up and seized the heavy brass knocker. She rapped twice, her heart pounding.

No answer.

She tried once more; perhaps they hadn't heard her. The kitchen was at the back of the house, and Gretel might be there, preparing an evening meal for the family; with the door closed, there was a chance she'd missed the knock. Ariella reached up and once again rapped the knocker – four times this time – as hard as she could.

She waited. Still nothing. Then, as she was about to turn away, she heard a faint shuffling noise from inside. Had she imagined it? Through the heavy front door, it was hard to hear anything, but she stopped and listened – there was the sound of the latch inside being pulled. The door opened a crack, then a little more, and soon enough, the opening revealed the face of her old friend.

'Gretel.' Ariella felt tears prick at the backs of her eyes. Her dear friend's face was no longer plump and jolly as it had been; the roses were gone from her now-gaunt cheeks.

The other woman made no gesture of recognition, just gazed at her.

'It's me, Ariella. Don't you recognise me?' she whispered. She should use her false name, she knew, but not with an old friend – that would be ridiculous.

'Go... I'm sorry, I can't... Please, just go.'

To Ariella's astonished dismay, Gretel pushed the door closed.

Instinctively, Ariella reached out and stopped it from closing fully. 'Please, Gretel, I don't have anywhere else to go. You and Nathaniel are all I have...'

'Nathaniel isn't here, and I can't... Please, it's not safe! Go...go now...' Ariella heard the panic in her friend's voice.

'But could we just talk...' Ariella begged.

'Come back tomorrow then, in the morning, after ten.' Ariella could feel the desperation to be rid of her. 'And come around the back. But now you must go.' With a shove, Gretel closed the door, and Ariella stood on the pathway, stunned and distraught.

She knew anyone watching would have thought the scene odd and so decided she had no option but to do as Gretel said. She crossed the street and retreated into the Tiergarten once more. The large public park had been the site of so many picnics and walks in her life, it felt familiar and comforting.

She stood in the shadow of a large beech tree, watching Gretel's house, wondering what to do. She mustn't panic. This was her city, her home, and she knew it like the back of her hand. She would think of something if only she could stay calm.

Around the corner came Kurt, Nathaniel and Gretel's son. She would recognise him anywhere. He looked just like Nathaniel, tall and handsome, blonde hair cut in a military style. He was wearing a uniform, and to her horror, it was the shorts, brown shirt and tie of the military, with an armband bearing the ubiquitous swastika of the Hitler Youth. At his waist, attached to his belt, was a scabbard from which poked the handle of a military-issue knife.

He walked with a swagger that she'd never seen in the boy before, and she was horrified to see him almost push an elderly man off the pavement for getting in his way. He let himself into the house and shut the door behind him. She'd escaped with moments to spare.

Could it be that sweet little Kurt, Liesl's playmate and the boy Erich looked up to as a wonderful footballer, was an enthusiastic follower of Hitler? Surely not. Nathaniel and Gretel would not have allowed their son to go down that road!

Though he was gone, she retreated further into the woods. No wonder Gretel had been so anxious to get rid of her. The idea that her dear friends had gone over to Hitler's side hurt her, but she couldn't dwell on it. Survival had to be her only concern. The war was almost over; all she had to do was hold on – the forger's words rung in her ears. She had not survived this long to fall at the last fence.

Her stomach growled painfully, and she wondered where she could go to get something to eat. She could possibly go to a café, but she had so little money that she wanted to keep it for a real emergency. She would hold on until the next morning. A thought struck her – was it safe to go back to Gretel's house now that Kurt was one of them, maybe Nathaniel and Gretel too? Maybe the pressure to join, to be part of Hitler's way of life, had been too much. Would her old friends feel like it was their duty to betray her? She refused to accept that idea. The baker and the bicycle repairman were one thing, but Gretel and Nathaniel were her and Peter's dearest friends. They wouldn't turn on her – they just wouldn't! But the niggling voice in her head urged caution.

She forced herself to go over her options. She could start walking out of the city, towards the west. She could sleep rough, try to get to France. The man with the papers said the invasion by Allied armies would be soon, so maybe she could get across the lines, get to Liesl and Erich that way?

She racked her brain, tired and woolly from aching limbs, hunger and a sudden chill that came in the air now that the sun was going down. She'd never spent a night outdoors before. On and on she walked through the Tiergarten, hands by her sides, deep in thought. Apart from their investments, she and Peter had money in the bank, but she had no way of getting it. She knew from before she went into hiding and through the subsequent newspapers that Jewish bank accounts had been frozen and seized. But Peter wasn't Jewish, so it was most likely their bank account was just sitting there untouched, but it was still useless. She had no identification now – Ariella Bannon no longer existed. She was Marta Weiss, Aryan, in Berlin without a friend.

Perhaps there was a charity she could go to. She remembered there was a place that she and Peter used to donate to, a place for down-and-outs, a hostel of some kind. It was beyond the zoo on the far end of the Tiergarten, on Burggrafenstraße. She would try there, admit she was destitute.

She held her breath as two uniformed men walked past her. Did she imagine it or did they give her a funny look? She strode on purposefully, repeating over and over in her head that her name was Marta Weiss, she was from Fallersleben, the address on her card gave an apartment on Brandenburg Platz, her father was called Otto, her brother Fritz was killed, he was in the Luftwaffe, she was searching for her aunt and uncle. What if someone asked for their address? She panicked – she had no idea about that. She passed the zoo and came out at the other end of the huge public park. There in front of her was a gaping hole where several buildings once stood. She remembered the name of the street – Budapester Straße. Her mother used to frequent a shoemaker there, but he died a few years ago... *What was his name? Hans something.* She forced her brain to remember. *Hans*

Froegel, that's it. Hans and Marine Froegel. They were her aunt and uncle, she decided. Marine was a sister of her mother, Margareta Schmitt, and she was there in Berlin looking for them. If anyone checked, they had been real people and had lived over his little cobbler's shop.

As she walked, she fleshed her story out more. She used to come to Berlin as a child on holidays, and she used to go to the zoo and for ice cream at the café there. Slowly, Marta Weiss became a real person, not just a name on an identity card. She spoke in her mind with the broader vowels of the Fallersleben region. She could do this.

The incessant bombing of the city surely must mean that the authorities had other things on their minds than single women searching for family? The entire city was in chaos.

She passed the Johanneskirche, the Catholic church she'd attended once for a funeral of a friend of Peter's. The square tower of the church had taken a hit, but the building was still standing. As she looked up at the grey façade, she noticed a man in cleric's garb go in the door.

'Excuse me,' she called.

He turned. The man was in his fifties, unshaven, and his dark-brown wavy hair needed cutting. He wore simple black trousers – shiny with wear, and the seam on one of the pockets had burst – a home-knitted cardigan the colour of a puddle and a black shirt without a collar. He walked slightly stooped, something she'd noticed some very tall people did, and his hands were like shovels.

'Yes?' His face was kind and his brown eyes were warm.

'I wonder if you can help me. I came from Fallersleben. I don't have anyone left there, but my aunt and uncle lived around here. Hans and Marine Froegel, do you know them?' She hoped she was convincing enough. Maybe he would take pity on her and offer her some food at least.

'No, I'm afraid I don't,' he said, his brow wrinkling as he tried to place the name.

'They lived at 332 Budapester Straße...' she went on, knowing that was right in the middle of the bombsite.

51

A look of pity crossed his face. 'All of the buildings from 290 to 350 on that street were hit a while back, and they were destroyed. I don't believe there were any survivors.' He delivered the news as kindly as he could, and Ariella tried to look crestfallen.

'Oh, I see...' She managed to let a tear fall, feeling like a complete fraud.

'Come inside. Let me get you a cup of, well, I don't have coffee, but I make a tea from something growing in the garden, so I can offer you that?'

At last. Someone to help. Even if it was just a cup of tea, it was so welcome. 'Thank you,' she said. This time the tears were genuine.

He led her into the sacristy and offered her a seat. The place smelled strange, of sweet incense and dust, but it wasn't unpleasant; in fact, it felt safe.

He made her a cup of tea that tasted of mint and something else, and she sipped the warm drink gratefully.

'So what made you think coming to Berlin was a good idea?' He smiled to take the accusation out of his tone.

'I had nowhere else to go. My parents are dead, my only brother was in the Luftwaffe and has been missing since 1940, and our house no longer stands, so I thought I would come to my Aunt Marine and Uncle Hans. But now, well, I truly have nobody, and nowhere to go.'

'And were your aunt and uncle part of this congregation, to say you looked for them here?'

'Yes, they were Catholics. So am I,' she said, hoping he wouldn't cast one of the faithful out on the side of the street.

He looked at her and nodded. 'And you have nowhere to go? Have you a ration card?'

She nodded and extracted her card, worn on the creases and with several stamps clipped off it. She handed it to him.

'I can get you some bread perhaps, though not much else, and you can sleep in here if you don't mind sleeping on that.' He pointed to a hard wooden bench. 'I can get you a blanket.'

'I'd be so grateful, and if you need anything doing, cleaning or anything, I'm happy to repay you. I have a little money, not much, but...' She reached into the purse and extracted the small bundle of notes.

'Keep your money, you'll need it.' He held his hand up. 'I am Father Dominic, by the way. It's nice to meet you, Marta.'

'It's nice to meet you too.' She smiled.

CHAPTER 9

*J*uly 1944

DANIEL WAS UNUSUALLY SOMBRE. He'd hardly said a word all evening, and even over dinner while the children were brim-full of plans for the upcoming school holidays, he barely spoke. The children were in bed now, and Elizabeth was knitting by the fire. Though it was summertime, there was a chill that evening, so she'd put a match to the fire Daniel had set a few days ago. She glanced over at her husband. He had a book in his hand but had not turned a page for ten minutes. She wondered what was on his mind. He would tell her in his own time; she wouldn't badger him.

Daniel Lieber was the best thing that had ever happened to her, and she loved him deeply. His love was like a strong tree, growing in the centre of the family they had cobbled together. Liesl and Erich loved him too, and in the absence of their own father, Daniel was an excellent substitute.

To break the silence she said, 'The children got a card from Bud today. It was sent weeks ago, but he's doing well and is in Italy apparently. Erich was proud as punch taking it to school this morning. He still sees Bud as his own private Yank.' She smiled.

Bud, a native of Biloxi, Mississippi, had joined the RAF before America entered the war as his mother was British. While stationed at the RAF base up the coast, he'd made friends with Erich and Liesl. He wanted to learn some German, so Erich had ostensibly taught him, but in reality, it was Liesl who had the aptitude for teaching. The result was that he became their friend, and they loved him. He was just a boy really, and brave as a lion despite his tender years. Elizabeth prayed each night for his safe return to Biloxi.

'I'm glad,' was all Daniel said.

'Will I put on the wireless?' she asked, and Daniel started. He was miles away.

They normally turned on the wireless to get the ten o'clock news before going to bed. The progress of the war was all that was talked about. She noticed the reports were more detailed now, knowing that the Germans were on the back foot, she supposed, though undoubtedly they were still not being told everything.

The Allies had landed last month on the beaches of Northern France, and after terrible fighting, it seemed now like they were driving the Germans back. The last German base in Soviet territory had fallen to the Russians, so they were losing on both fronts as the Americans were pushing up through Italy. But it wasn't all plain sailing. The fighting for the cities of Caen and Saint-Lô was fierce, and the Germans seemed to have redoubled their efforts with those horrible flying bombs. London was being evacuated once more, with women and children moving back to their country billets where it was safer. But the war was going to end with an Allied victory for definite now, everyone was saying it, and the sense of optimism and determination was palpable, even in the little village of Ballycreggan.

Like everywhere, the village had had its losses: young people, whose whole lives were ahead of them, snuffed out like a candle and their parents and families left with a lifetime of grief. Elizabeth knew it was probably wrong to pray that someone would have a slow and painful death, but she wished that on the evil Adolf Hitler and his followers. Such misery they had caused, such pain in millions of hearts that would never be eased.

She thought of Liesl and Erich, asleep upstairs. She loved them with all of her heart, and while she wished for nothing more than the safe return of their mother, she couldn't imagine her life without them now.

'Not tonight, if you don't mind. I… There's something I need to talk to you about.'

Daniel looked pained and she felt the panic rise. What had happened? Daniel was not one for dramatics. Whatever he had to say, it wasn't good news.

'What is it?' she asked.

He placed his book on the sofa beside him and gestured that she should join him. Wordlessly, she stood and crossed the room, cuddling up beside him. He put his arm around her and kissed the top of her head.

'Rabbi Frank called me in today. He's just back from London, you know?'

She nodded. He'd been gone for two weeks, and the place wasn't the same without him. The children were so excited that he had returned.

'Well, while he was there, he met up with some people. One man in particular, who had managed to escape from one of the Nazi camps.'

Elizabeth waited.

Daniel exhaled raggedly. 'It seems that it's not just rumours or propaganda. The Nazis really are killing all the Jews. This man, he's Czech I think, somehow escaped and got to London, but he saw, with his own eyes, huge chimneys where they were burning bodies. They were taking people off trains – women, children, everyone – and sending them to be gassed, and then burning the bodies in this big incinerator. He seemed to think this was happening in more than one place too. Like it's a plan of theirs. I…I had heard – of course we did – but part of me just couldn't believe it. But it seems it's true…' He couldn't go on.

'Oh my God.' Elizabeth's thoughts immediately went to Liesl and Erich, and then to the children at the farm. Could this be the fate of their families? It was inconceivable, even with all that was being said about the Germans. Surely they couldn't really be doing that?

'There were articles and things, but I suppose we just...' She had no words.

'The rabbi is so shaken, he doesn't know what to do. Should he tell everyone here what he knows? Or would it make it worse? He wanted my advice, but I had no idea. I said I'd talk to you, that you would know better than us what would be best for the children, and he agreed.'

Elizabeth was glad at least that the rabbi didn't reveal this new horror without consultation. The rabbi was a very good, kind man, but he was so invested in the afterlife, that sometimes he didn't see how important people's feelings were in this life.

Elizabeth recalled how, two years ago, Daniel had been arrested and accused of spying for the Nazis. The punishment for espionage was death, and she remembered how circumspect Rabbi Frank had been as she fought tooth and nail to have Daniel exonerated. As it turned out, the real spy, a young woman called Talia Zimmerman, was arrested before Daniel was charged. She committed suicide in custody, but before she died, she did ensure Daniel was set free. Elizabeth recalled Rabbi Frank's response to her outrage over Daniel's potential execution during that whole nightmare. The rabbi was not sad, because to him, death was going home to God. He was a deeply devout Jew and a kind leader of the community, but he seemed incapable of understanding the loss of a loved one. Love of life was central to Jewish philosophy but the events of the last few years seemed to have made the rabbi less concerned with this world, choosing to focus instead on the next.

'What do you think?' Daniel asked her.

Despite her good relationship with the Jewish community at the farm and their respect for her as the children's teacher, she was surprised the rabbi was consulting her, albeit through Daniel. The Jews were a self-contained group, and while they worked well with the people of Ballycreggan, all pulling together to deal with everything the war brought, the adults on the farm took their responsibility for those children very seriously and tended to deal with things internally. They felt they were in the position of the children's parents and so acted accordingly.

'I suppose they will have to be told something, but the idea of it, trying to explain something that defies explanation, I don't know, Daniel,' she said. 'What do you think?'

'I think let them have as long a childhood as they can. Maybe I'm just too soft to tell them the truth, but Levi agrees with me. He thinks there is no point in telling them before we have to. But then, as Ruth says, they are hearing things on the news, seeing newspapers, sensing the war is ending sometime soon hopefully. And they talk about going home, seeing their families, going back to their schools, and we all know that nothing like that is going to happen. Maybe other Jewish children are more aware, but we kept it from ours inasmuch as we could. They have an idea, of course. They know that the Germans have killed some Jews. But the scale of it, the sheer bloody numbers...'

She heard the catch in his voice and turned her face towards him, laying her hand on his chest. His handsome face was creased in pain. Not for himself, she knew. His parents were dead before the Nazis came to power, and his only brother had been killed in a road accident, so he didn't have anyone of his immediate family sent to the camps. But the pain that would be inflicted on these children, the little boys and girls he had come to see as his responsibility, was very hard on him. He loved them and they loved him.

'Viola even – I mean, she's Liesl's age – told me she was knitting a sweater for her father because she was afraid they might have lost their house. They lived in Warsaw. I couldn't respond, Elizabeth. I just couldn't say anything. How do you tell a lovely young girl, on the brink of life, that her parents were most likely herded into a ghetto, and after that, taken to a camp and killed there? How do you tell a child something that unbelievable?'

'You don't.' Elizabeth was as sure of this as of anything in her life. 'We don't know the scale of this or which countries are worst affected or anything really apart from what this man said. I'm not doubting him, and God knows it's hard to comprehend, but we have no idea what happened to the children's families. So until such time as we do, we just need to reassure them. Liesl said to me that they were all worried they were going to be put back on trains, unceremoniously dumped back onto the railway platforms they left from. So our job is not to explain the unexplainable, but to reassure them that they have a home here and that we'll take care of them for as long as they need us to. And that when the time comes, we'll help them to find their families. Nothing more than that. That is the most important thing, that they know they have a home, forever if need be.'

'But how can we assure them of that?' he interrupted. 'The Jewish communities of Dublin and Belfast have been more than generous – they have opened their wallets and their hearts, as have the people of Ballycreggan – but we can't expect that to go on indefinitely. The land is rented, the rent will have to be paid, and even if we could manage that, what about the running costs – food, clothes, schoolbooks? We can't keep the farm going on fresh air, and we certainly can't expect the Irish Jews to support us forever.'

She thought for a moment. He was right of course, but keeping the farm afloat was not her main concern. They would come up with something – they had to.

'Look, there is absolutely no way on God's green earth I am letting one of those poor little mites out of my sight until it is into the arms of their family. I don't care what anyone, government or anyone else, has to say about it. So that's what they need to know. We can't tell them what we don't know anyway. We have no way of telling what each individual situation is, and maybe it will be a long time before we have any information. The rest of it – who is going to pay for it, or the farm or whatever – are all details, and we'll deal with one thing at a time, shall we?' She placed her hand on his face, feeling the day's stubble there. He should by right have grown a beard by now – adult Jewish men were expected to – but she liked his face clean-shaven so he didn't. He was such a handsome man and turned heads wherever he went, but she was so secure in his love, she never worried.

He smiled, turned his head and kissed her palm.

She smiled back at him. 'We'll go up and talk to the rabbi and the others,' she said, 'explain that we can't terrify the children with half stories. If their families have perished, then we'll deal with it when we know for sure. But for now, we must make them feel secure and loved.'

'I love you, Elizabeth. You are an amazing woman, you know that? I don't know what any of us would do without you.' He held her close.

CHAPTER 10

*A*riella had spent almost three months in the sacristy of the
church at night, and while she might have, in another lifetime, found the experience a little creepy, she had no such feeling
now. She usually got up early every morning and left. The local
primary school had been bombed and was closed, so she sometimes
hid there, and if there was activity around there, she walked, staying
out of the main streets, only returning at nightfall. Father Dominic
had explained that it would be best if people didn't see her. There
were so many destitute, and he and the other priests were doing their
best, but if he were seen to help one over the other, it would be difficult. She understood completely. She was profoundly grateful to
Father Dominic for his hospitality.

One morning she'd slept late, something she'd never done before,
and she only woke as the priest arrived for early Mass. He asked her if
she would like to attend. She had been to Peter's father's funeral Mass
and a few funerals for other friends, and she and Peter went to a
wedding once, a colleague's daughter. However, apart from those few
instances, she had never attended a Catholic ceremony. Peter's father
wasn't practising, but when he died, Peter thought he would like to be

buried in the faith of his childhood. Peter himself was agnostic but had no objections to her raising Liesl and Erich as Jews.

She had lied and said she was Catholic, so it would be odd for her not to attend Mass. A young local boy appeared and donned vestments too, just as Father Dominic did. He knew exactly what items were needed, and man and boy busied themselves with the preparations. She took the mantilla he gave her, a square of lace, and let herself out into the church, vacating the sacristy to allow him to prepare.

She slid into a seat behind a group of middle-aged women, planning on following their every move. It was crucial to her survival that she pass as a Catholic now.

The Mass was a series of movements – stand up, kneel down. Father Dominic spoke in Latin with his back to the congregation. She had been so heartbroken the day her father-in-law was buried that she had taken no notice of what people were doing.

Father Dominic chanted in his deep sonorous voice, and the gathered faithful responded accordingly. She tried to mumble along but didn't know the responses.

Then it came time for everyone to go up to the priest for communion. He placed the host on their tongues, and each took a sip from the chalice. She recalled reading something about transubstantiation, where Catholics believed that a miracle happened at each Mass when the wafer and wine were transformed into the body and blood of Jesus Christ. She thought quickly. It was probably against every rule for her to follow the other people up to receive, but not to do so would attract attention, so she slipped out into the aisle.

She took her place in the line behind a woman in a torn and dirty coat and tried to see what was happening. As they approached the altar, people knelt down at the rail and opened their mouths. The boy held a golden platter under each person's chin as the priest placed the bread on their tongue. When it came to her turn, she did as the others had done. Did she imagine it, or did Father Dominic catch her eye? She closed her mouth, allowing the wafer to dissolve on her tongue, crossed herself as she had seen Catholics do in the past and returned to her seat.

As she slid into the pew, she caught the eye of a woman sitting on the other side of the aisle. Instantly, the woman turned her head and her lace mantilla covered her profile, but Ariella's heart thumped loudly in her chest. Was it Stella Kübler? The woman looked like the picture the forger had shown her, but she couldn't be sure. Had the woman been there all along? She risked another glance. The woman was much better dressed than the rest of the congregation. Ariella fought the urge to flee, as she needed to stay in character. The moment Mass was over, the woman slipped out.

Ariella forced herself to wait until everyone was gone before returning to the sacristy.

Father Dominic was dressed in his black garb once more, and the boy was gone. 'I brought you some bread, and there is some more of my tea if you'd like it?' he said with a smile.

'Yes. Thank you.' She fell on the dry bread gratefully; she was very hungry. He brought her something every day, and when she was out and about, she hoped she'd find some food, but it wasn't to be had. The money Frau Braun gave her was long gone – she'd bought what food she could – so now she was entirely dependent on the priest. The tea was still like drinking weed water, but it was warm and helped her swallow the bread.

He said kindly, 'It's not the most comfortable sleeping here, I'd imagine, but it's better than being on the streets.'

'Thank you.' She smiled, wondering what, if anything, she should say about her suspicions. To say she even knew who Stella Kübler was would be to admit she wasn't who she said she was.

'Look, I know you stay out of sight during the day, but I wanted to tell you that Frau Groenig comes in at eleven each day to clean the church. You want to avoid running into her for your own sake.' He pointed to an ornately carved oak box. 'Frau and Herr Groenig are dedicated to the führer.'

Though there was nothing treasonous in his words, his tone

63

revealed just what he thought about that. Why was he warning her? If she was a destitute Catholic, why wouldn't a priest give her sanctuary?

They exchanged a look, then the priest pulled up a chair and sat opposite her. 'What's your name?' he asked quietly.

'I told you, Marta Weiss…' she began.

'Yes, I know whose papers you have, but who are you?'

Ariella swallowed. Despite sleeping in the sacristy all this time, she'd only had minimal contact with him. He left food, but she took care to be gone early and back late. Could he be trusted?

The words of the forger rang in her ears – 'trust nobody'. But the priest had been so kind. Was it a trap? Surely a man of God, even if he was of a different faith, would not betray her.

'It's all right, you can trust me. On my honour as a priest, I swear to you I won't betray you. But you'll have to confide in me. You're in danger, but I can't help if I don't know who you really are.'

Father Dominic's bulk dominated the small room. Even if she wanted to escape, she couldn't – he was between her and the door.

He was large and scruffy and reminded her of a big dog she'd had as a child. Bruno was a mongrel. Her father found him abandoned as a puppy, and he grew to almost the size of a small pony, but he was adorable and loved not just by her but by all the children on her street.

She made her decision. 'My name is Ariella Bannon. I'm a Jew. My husband was a Christian, but he was taken in 1939 and killed. I got my two children on the Kindertransport, and they are safe in Northern Ireland, but I need to get to them,' she whispered, sweat prickling her back as she spoke.

'All right, and how did you survive until now?' he asked.

'I was hidden by a neighbour, but that house is no longer safe.' She still wasn't sure she was doing the right thing. If he asked her who protected her, then she would know that he was on the side of the Nazis. But he didn't; he just nodded.

'I knew you'd not been out in society, something about you.' He smiled gently. 'And the idea that a Catholic would have no idea when to stand, sit or kneel at Mass was a giveaway as well.'

'I'm sorry, I…' Ariella began.

'Nothing to be sorry for. Your country has betrayed you, your fellow Germans allowed you to be persecuted. It is a crime I think history will judge us *all* harshly for, not just the Nazis, and with good reason. But now we need to deal with your immediate safety. I've seen a woman at Mass on and off for the past few weeks, and I didn't recognise her. She was there again today, unfortunately, the one day you go to Mass. I know there is a woman, a Jewish woman, who is working for the Gestapo. She's seeking out submerged Jews and handing them over to the police.'

Ariella recalled the forger's warning. 'Her name is Stella Kübler. I've seen a photo of her, and when I glanced over, I was sure it was her.'

He nodded. 'Well, she's often here, but that doesn't mean she has spotted you, though you'll have to be careful. I think Frau Groenig is an informer as well. She knows that from time to time I allow people to sleep here or in the church if they are destitute, and she watches everything. I am connected to a group, people who are trying hard to undermine the regime, so she's been planted to watch me, I'm sure of it. She's heard me speak out in sermons about the regime, about what's happening in this city, all over Europe, and she's more or less warned me to stop it or things will go badly for me. Already they've rounded up many of my brother priests – there's a clergy wing at Dachau concentration camp, I believe.' He gave a rueful smile. 'I have no doubt that I will see it for myself someday, but I want to stay free for as long as I can, to do as much as I can.

'Now, there were people who were operating escape lines out of the city, but they can no longer do that. Most of them have been caught anyway, so that's not an option at the moment at least. You'll have to stay here in Berlin for now, whatever the outcome, but we'll need to submerge you further. I'm fearful that this Stella woman knows you're here, so you're in deep trouble and so am I. We need to think.'

She knew he was right.

'So the neighbour who helped you before, you cannot go back there? Perhaps the threat has passed?' he asked.

She thought of the horrible dingy attic, and it seemed like the safest, most comfortable place on earth at that moment. However lonely and uncomfortable it was, she had been safe there and Frau Braun made sure she didn't starve.

'No, I can't go back. That house has been allocated as somewhere for bombed-out families or servicemen to get lodging. They had spare bedrooms, so someone from the housing authority came and inspected. I had to leave that day.'

He looked worried. 'Right. Don't worry. I'll do my best.' He moved towards the door. He noted her confusion. 'It's fine.' He smiled. 'You'll be fine. Just stay out of sight, but not here – it's not safe any more. If she sends anyone, I don't want any trace of you. Is there somewhere you can go?'

She nodded. 'I think so.'

'Good. I'll make enquiries, and I'll see you back here this evening. Be very careful.'

'I will. Thank you again. I am trying to get to Northern Ireland, as I said, to my children, but I don't know if that would be possible... Maybe I could walk...'

She thought he might have an idea. All those weeks just holding on, sleeping in the church, walking by day, mile after pointless mile, sitting in churches for hours, air-raid shelters, anywhere people gathered. And everyone was so concerned with their own futures, they took no notice of her. She felt like a ghost, invisible, just wandering aimlessly. She was amazed she'd never been challenged by anyone in authority, but it all felt so pointless. If she was going to have to move on anyway, then maybe trying to get out was as good an idea as any.

The look he gave her made her instantly realise that wasn't an option. 'There is no way that can happen. All transport for civilians is forbidden, so you wouldn't get out of the city, and even if by some miracle you did make it across the border and into France, for example, the Allies are advancing rapidly – you would find yourself in the middle of a war zone. It's dangerous enough here, but to try to get out of Germany at this point would be nothing less than a suicide mission.' His tone brooked no argument.

He turned to face her and placed his hands on her shoulders, looking into her eyes. 'Just try to keep yourself alive for now, that's my advice. I know you're trying to be patient and you want to get to your children, of course you do, but you've lasted this long – it would be such a waste to die now. This is going to be over – not tomorrow or next week, but soon – and then we can all see what's what. Until then, it's simply a matter of survival as best we can.'

'Is it definite the Allies will win?' she asked, not caring if she sounded silly or naïve.

He looked furtive and lowered his voice even though there was nobody about. 'There are lots of people who are deluded into thinking Germany can still prevail. That's nonsense, of course. If the Nazis had any defences left, don't you think the air force would be up there, repelling the Allied bombers out of the skies? No, it's over, but a dying wasp is a dangerous thing as it has nothing to lose. But if we can just stay alive, then this city will soon be liberated, either by the Russians or the Americans. The Russians most likely, unfortunately.'

'Why unfortunately?' she asked. 'Surely anyone who can defeat the Nazis is good at this stage?'

Father Dominic paused, weighing up what he was going to say next. 'What our troops did over there, the way they treated the Russians, well, they won't want a nice diplomatic peace agreement. If the British or the Americans get here first, then they'll sit down, extract a surrender from whoever is left of the regime and set about restoring some kind of civilised life. But the Russians, they will want revenge.' His voice sounded tired.

'Then will be the time to get out of the city, I would suggest, but until that time, staying hidden is probably the best option. Now' – he ran his hand through his mop of hair, which was flopping into his eyes – 'I'll see you later.' He let himself out of the church.

Ariella decided to go to Gretel despite the reception she'd received when she called and the sight of Kurt in that uniform. She hadn't gone back the following day as Gretel suggested. Ariella knew her friend had only said it to get rid of her, and the look of sheer terror on her friend's face made her realise that she could not rely on her. But now,

things were different, and something made her want to see her friend
one last time. She felt like the net was closing in, that every moment
was precious, and Gretel was, apart from Father Dominic, her only
friend. She would make sure not to endanger her, but she wanted to
ask if there was somewhere she could hide. Not at their house probably, but maybe Nathaniel could think of somewhere at the bank or
something? She was desperate, and she had to try.

She scanned the entire street outside the church; there was no sign
of anyone.

Maybe that hadn't been Stella after all, or maybe it had been but
she was just trying her luck, searching for anyone who looked Jewish,
not her specifically. She had papers saying she was Marta Weiss, she
had red hair, and she should be fine, she told herself, so long as she
was careful.

She walked through the Tiergarten, something she never did
because it was too busy. She tended to stick to more suburban areas
where there were fewer uniforms, but if she wanted to go to Gretel's,
it was the only way. She entered via one of the many city gates and
strolled on, trying to look as weary and resigned as her fellow citizens. The bright summer sunshine warmed her face. It was a lovely
day. It felt so good to have that sensation, that simple pleasure of
turning her face to the sun and feeling the glow. She hoped that Liesl
and Erich were enjoying the summer sun wherever they were. She
knew from their letter that they lived by the sea. She thought it must
be lovely for them, swimming and playing on the beach.

As she came to the gate that led out of the Tiergarten and onto
Gretel and Nathaniel's street, it struck her how no matter what
carnage and destruction abounded, the sun rose and set every single
day. Flowers bloomed in the park – not the beautifully manicured
beds of the life before Hitler, but still some remained and popped
their brightly coloured heads up. Nature didn't care what stupid
messes humans got themselves into; it just carried on regardless.

She went over everything. Father Dominic knew who she was –
he probably knew all along, she realised – and there was a real
possibility that Stella Kübler was looking for her, but she was opti-

mistic. Things were still dire, but she was free, the war was almost over, the Nazis had been all but defeated and seeing her children again was a real possibility. She just needed to hold on and not get caught.

'Halt, Fräulein.' A voice interrupted her reverie. A uniformed policeman stood before her. He wore the green uniform of the Orpo, which everyone called the Grüne Polizei – the green police.

'Where are you going?' he asked politely.

She smiled and broadened her vowels to sound more like Marta from Fallersleben. 'I've come to Berlin from Fallersleben. We were bombed out. I'm trying to find my aunt and uncle.' She tried to keep her voice neutral, though her mouth was dry and she was sure he could hear her heart thumping in her chest.

'Papers, please.' He held his hand out.

She opened the clasp of her handbag and extracted her identity card, her certificate of Aryan descent and her battered ration card. It was the first time they'd been checked.

He said nothing but examined the cards, and several times, he glanced up at her face. After what felt like an eternity, he returned the papers to her.

'And your husband?' he asked slowly.

Her papers said she was Fräulein Marta Weiss, not Frau Weiss.

'I'm not married,' she said, forcing a smile on her face.

'But you have an indent on your ring finger where a wedding ring would go,' he said, taking her right hand in his. She'd taken her ring off to give to the forger, and he was right, the white indented skin did indeed show a mark.

'I wore my grandmother's ring. She gave it to me before she died, but I had to pawn it to get some money. My parents and I were bombed out, and there was just me – my brother was a gunner in the Luftwaffe, and he was lost.' She cast her eyes downward, hoping he would not make direct eye contact with her again.

'So you are not married?' he asked again.

'No...' she said, terrified she would give herself away. Why was he sticking on that point? Did he know she was lying?

'No sweetheart?' he asked, this time bending his head slightly to look into her face. He was smiling.

'No...nobody. I am just trying to find my aunt...' She desperately clung to the cover story she'd invented.

'Please, Fräulein, don't be so nervous. You have nothing to fear from me. My mother brought me up to be respectful to ladies, especially very pretty ones.' He grinned and she returned a weak smile.

She looked at him properly for the first time. He was young, perhaps late twenties, thirty at the most, and he was a perfect Aryan – blonde hair, athletic build, blue eyes. She wondered who he was connected to that allowed him to stay in Berlin as a policeman and not slaving away on the Eastern Front.

'I'm sure she did a good job,' she replied, since he seemed to expect a response.

'She likes to think so.' He winked and chuckled. 'I am her pride and joy, you see. She worries, but if she thought I had a nice girlfriend, then she would relax a little.'

Ariella's mind raced. What was happening here? Was he actually flirting with her? She forced herself to respond appropriately and reflect his jokey manner.

'And do you have a nice girlfriend?' she asked, a smile playing around her lips. This was ridiculous but necessary.

'Alas, no, I don't. I have been too busy with my duties. But I am a lonely boy these days, and I know my mother would appreciate it if I had some nice girl to keep me company.' Again he chuckled, clearly enjoying the morning dalliance. Incredulous as it was in this insanity all around them, he seemed in high spirits and wanted her to join in his banter.

'That would be a lovely prospect, I'm sure.' She smiled. 'Good luck in finding her.' She started to move away, desperate to end the exchange but equally anxious that it end on a friendly note.

As she turned, he placed his gloved hand on her sleeve. She swallowed but managed to giggle coquettishly.

'Perhaps I already have, Fräulein Weiss.' He put his head to one side and grinned. There was a kind of vulnerability to him beneath all the swagger and bravado, and she found herself feeling sorry for him.

'Can we have lunch? I know a place where, well, they are generous with the portions if you know the right people.' He smiled, and the implication clearly was that he was just such a person.

She racked her brain for a response that would simultaneously put him off but not anger or humiliate him.

'I would love that.' No plausible excuse came to her mind, so she decided to make the date and just not show up. She produced what she hoped was a radiant smile of delight.

'Great.' He looked like a child on Christmas morning. 'Tomorrow?' he asked.

'Wonderful. Where should we meet?'

'Where are you staying?' he asked.

Her mouth went dry again. She said the first address that came to her mind – her and Peter's old apartment. She had no idea who was living there now, but their beautiful sunny home was no doubt in the hands of some loyal servant of Hitler.

'I don't know that part of the city well, but I could find it and come and pick you up?' He smiled again, and in another lifetime, she might have just seen him as a boy chancing his luck.

'Well, I could meet you on the corner of that street and Leopold-platz. There is a church there, Saint Anthony's? I could meet you outside that?' She prayed it sounded like she was looking forward to it.

'That's perfect, Fräulein Weiss. My name is Herman Glos, by the way.'

'Herr Glos.' She shook his proffered hand.

'Please, call me Herman.' He smiled.

'Marta,' she replied, noting the pressure of the handshake.

'Until tomorrow, Marta. Take care now, those bombers are on the run, but old Winston is trying one last attempt to break the Reich. It won't work, of course, but I would hate for someone as pretty as you to be hurt.'

Ariella blushed. Was this really happening? In the midst of the

71

chaos and destruction, did men ask women out to lunch? Perhaps they did if they thought that the war was being won in their favour. Who knew?

'See you tomorrow, Herman.' Ariella waved and walked on, her heart rate slowly returning to normal.

CHAPTER 11

$\mathcal{R}$abbi Frank walked around the classroom, admiring the art projects the children were working on. He always called on Wednesday afternoons, and that was when they did art. Elizabeth was anxious at first that he would realise she taught mathematics and English as well as the other subjects, but he was quick to reassure her that he thought she was an excellent teacher and that the children from the farm were in great hands.

'So, Mrs Lieber,' he began after she finished up the lesson and allowed the children outside for lunch. 'I wanted to talk to you about something.'

The rabbi was distinctive-looking. He was small and wiry and wore peyot, ringlets that hung from his temples. He habitually dressed in black but wore a white shirt when he was ministering to his flock. He was seen in the village of Ballycreggan often and greeted everyone warmly. He was a Chassidic Jew, from a very traditional and conservative branch of Judaism, but he had mellowed a little in what he thought was acceptable given the expediency of the situation. He could also be full of fun, and when he danced, he did so with enthusiasm. Daniel explained that in his tradition dancing was a way to purify the soul and to promote spiritual joy. Unlike the Catholic priests, he seemed much more concerned with this life than the next, and the care of his flock was his reason for living.

He had never, for example, expressed disappointment that she wasn't a Jew, though in his eyes, a Jewish man marrying a Gentile would not be acceptable. He never suggested she convert or even follow Jewish teachings in her classroom. Instead, he called occasionally and taught the children a little of the ways of their faith, and she always felt some of the tuition was directed at her. At the farm, he did more in-depth study with the children, and Liesl and Erich attended too.

'Of course, Rabbi, how can I help?' Elizabeth knew what was coming.

He began, his low resonant voice never changing tone. 'Daniel told me what you said.'

She nodded, then waited as he paused. Did he want her to answer? Since having heard the harrowing stories of those who got out of Germany, he'd been even more fatalistic than normal.

He fixed her with a look, and she suppressed the urge to smile. The rabbi never asked for anyone's advice – he was the undisputed leader of his group and was completely sure of his divine right to rule.

She knew from Daniel that the others got frustrated when he didn't seem to share their horror and outrage about what was happening. He would merely shrug as the latest atrocity was discussed and say something enigmatic, such as, 'It was always thus.'

Death, to him, no matter the circumstances, was to be welcomed. It was how one returned to God, and that was the ultimate aim of all Jews. He was circumspect about the war, explaining that Jews had always been persecuted and always would be. He explained to his flock how they were the chosen people and God chose them to suffer in return for eternal salvation. His seeming acceptance of the behaviour of the Nazis as part of God's plan drove the others mad, but it was how he saw it.

He was traditional in his views on other matters as well. The roles of men and women were, in his book, very clearly defined and should not be tampered with. That he was asking the opinion of a woman, and a Gentile on top of that, would certainly cause some eyebrows to raise at the farm.

'Please elucidate your thoughts.'

For a man who didn't speak English when he arrived, he had mastered the language wonderfully.

'Well,' Elizabeth began, 'I know what you found out, unbelievable as it is. But I think, as I said to Daniel, the most important thing is that the children feel they are secure and loved and that, no matter what, they will be cared for.' She tried to gauge his reaction.

As usual, he remained impassive but was listening intently. 'I am glad you have been thinking about this too. It has been on my mind, on all of our minds, what should be said. Please, go on.'

'Very well. I've been thinking. We need to explain that once the war is over, it won't happen right away that anyone will go anywhere. That the entire continent is in chaos and communications will be basic if they exist for civilians at all, so they shouldn't expect their parents to make contact immediately. I know it is likely that for many of them, there will not be a family reunion, but that is something we cannot say for sure nor do we know anything about individuals, so I think our focus should be on making them feel secure and happy and allay any concerns that they will be put back on a train.'

The rabbi nodded slowly, and Elizabeth knew she would have to say the difficult bit next.

'And while, of course, the fact that many Jews are in heaven will certainly give them comfort in time, I think children are more immediate and think only in the now. It is the way of the young, so I think it would be important to acknowledge their worries for the future, and to make sure they feel that Ballycreggan and the farm are home for as long as they want them to be.'

She hoped he would not take offence. She was essentially suggesting he would need to tone down the divine plan line of preaching and try to see them as frightened little boys and girls worried about their families.

Rabbi Frank waited a long time before responding. She had grown used to this trait of his over the years – he had no concept of an awkward silence.

'Faith is important at all junctures of life, Mrs Lieber, a knowledge that this, no matter how sad now, is all part of God's plan. Surely that is comforting?' His intelligent eyes bore into hers.

'It is,' she agreed, but she was determined for the children's sake that he understand her point. 'But it is also important to understand that this life, the one we are living here and now, is valuable, and that we are the adults in charge and that everything is going to be all right, whatever the outcome. It seems inevitable that some of these children at least will face a dark realisation in the future, but for now, we just need them to know they are safe. If they have to face loss in the future, then we will help them through that as well, but let's not preempt what we don't know.' She was sailing close to the wind, she knew. Nobody ever contradicted him.

'You have known loss yourself?' he asked.

'Yes. My first husband was killed on the last day of the Great War. The armistice had been signed, but they wanted to have a symmetry to the peace accord, have it signed on the eleventh hour of the eleventh day of the eleventh month. I'm sure they thought it would look better in the history books, but my husband, a Jew from the North of England, was shot and killed at nine thirty. The deal had been struck for Germany to surrender at 5 a.m. that morning, it seems, but he died four hours later. For nothing. So some generals could make an historic statement. I was so angry for so long. I lost the child I was carrying. So I lost him and our baby, and it almost killed me too.' Her words were barely a whisper now. Even after all these years, and after finding love again with Daniel, she still felt that loss.

'Could anyone have helped you? Given you comfort in those dark days?' he asked, and she felt a rush of admiration and love for the old rabbi. He wanted to help them when they faced the inevitable truth, but he didn't know how.

'No. Not really. But the best way to support someone who is grieving is just to be there. To not try to make it better or explain it away, but just to be there and let them cry, let them endure the pain. Just be beside them so they know they are not alone.'

He nodded slowly once more. 'You are a good woman, Mrs Lieber. God knew what he was doing when he sent you to us.'

'I'm glad you feel like that. I certainly feel very blessed at how my life has turned out. I don't have the answers, and I'm just trying to do the right thing, as you are. We worry – we have come to love these children as our own. For many of the little ones who came here as toddlers, this is the only home they've ever known, and so what is said will have to be tempered to be appropriate for them. But the older ones, they have heads full of memories and hearts full of longing to be reunited with their families. They read the news and they're worried. We need to try our best to make them feel secure.'

'My wife died young, we had no children, I should have remarried I suppose but, I couldn't bring myself to replace her, and now I lack that – I don't know what is the word – empathy, I think, that comes from having a family of your own.' the old rabbi said sadly.

'I disagree.' Elizabeth smiled. 'You have led and held that place together through all of this. You were the one to bring the people from the farm to patch the village up when it was bombed, you reached out to the priest and the vicar, and now you're friends. You share the produce from the farm with the village, and they in turn share with you all. You're the reason that happens. Those children see you as an anchor in a life that has been cast adrift, and they know you love them. When you were in London, they were counting the days until you got back. They love you too.' She hesitated to use that word as he'd never said it to the best of her knowledge, but his actions showed how much he cared for each one of them. 'You have a strong sense of connection to them, and you want what's best –'

'But sometimes,' he interrupted, holding his hands up to stop her speaking, 'I don't let them feel what they feel. I try to explain that this is temporary.' He waved his hand about. 'All of this, it is nothing when compared with the world to come! But yes...now that I have spoken to you, I can see how that might not be helpful.' His shoulders fell. 'My job as a rabbi is to ensure my people keep the commandments, their afterlife is for them and God to deal with, but when this life is so...I don't know...so difficult to rationalise, to explain, I fear I am failing them.'

'You are not. I just think we need to deal with their immediate worries first, but when the time comes to talk to them, afterwards, if they get bad news, then they will need your comfort. Knowing for sure that their loved ones are somewhere beautiful and safe and free from pain will reassure them, of course it will. But yes, the initial conversation has to be a reassuring one. You are a human being, trying your best under such incomprehensible conditions, like us all, you can't explain this. Nobody can, it's insane. We'll do this together, all of us, and hopefully they will feel our love and support.'

CHAPTER 12

*A*riella waited until ten thirty to be sure. The meeting with the policeman had rattled her – and she had no intention of keeping the date – but at least she knew her papers would pass inspection. She would need to lie low because if that was his beat, then he would presumably look for her in the days after her non-appearance at the rendezvous. She'd tried to think of another way out of it, but even half an hour after the event, she couldn't see what she could have done differently. She had taken the only course available to her and accepted his invitation.

Quickly, she crossed the street, skirting around a tangle of metal that once was a tram. A group of children stood on the corner eyeing her, and she tried not to glance in their direction. She went down a narrow alleyway that led to the back of the houses where Nathaniel and Gretel lived. She and Peter had been down that way once before, when they lent Liesl's crib to their friends for Kurt... It was hard to equate the swaggering Hitler Youth with that sweet little baby. They'd brought it in round the back way as that door was wider. Ariella tried not to think about Kurt.

She let herself into the backyard. There was a nice patio area that caught the afternoon sun there. How often had she and Gretel sat there sipping coffee while the children played in the sandpit?

Before she could raise her hand to knock, the door opened and a terrified-looking Gretel pulled her into the back hall behind the kitchen.

'Ariella, I thought you'd... Look, never mind, did anyone see you?' Gretel hissed.

'No...no, I don't think so, but –'

'Nobody would recognise you anyway, even if they did.'

Ariella noted that the same was true of Gretel. She now was thin and drawn. Hard lines had worn into her face and deep grooves ran between her nose and mouth. She had a few-days-old dark-purple bruise on her cheek.

'Gretel, I need your help. I'm sorry to impose again, but...' Ariella began, but the other woman stared incredulously.

'Ariella, I can't help you. Of course I can't! If Kurt knew, if he said anything...' A look of sheer terror crossed her face.

'Well, perhaps Nathaniel?' Ariella was desperate.

'Nathaniel?' Gretel sounded bewildered.

Ariella wondered if she'd gone a bit soft in the head. Some people's nerves couldn't take the bombing.

'Gretel,' Ariella spoke slowly and gently. 'Is Nathaniel here?'

To her horror, she saw Gretel blink back tears as she shook her head.

'Where is he?' Ariella asked, afraid of the answer.

'Gone. They came for him. He had a radio. I begged him to get rid of it, but he wanted to hear the BBC. He was reported and arrested and sent somewhere, I don't know where, and I can't ask because Kurt... Oh, Ariella...' The final words were lost in a sob.

Without thinking, Ariella took a step towards her old friend and put her arms around her. 'Oh, Gretel, my dear...' She had no other words of consolation.

'It was Kurt – he reported his own father. He's one of them, our own son. I'm afraid, Ariella. I can't believe I gave birth to him. He's a monster, and the girls are terrified of him too. He hits them, and me too sometimes.' She touched her cheek. 'And he taunts me, saying that Nathaniel is dead, that he was a traitor, an enemy of the Reich.' The words tumbled from her in a torrent of fear and emotion.

How could this have happened? A beautiful sunny boy, one of them, denouncing his father, a man who loved him so much?

'If Kurt thought for a moment you survived, that you were still here, Ariella... You must get away from here, get out of Berlin!'

'But what about you? Isn't there something you can do?' Ariella, despite her own dire situation, wanted to help her old friend. 'Couldn't you go to Lena and Martin's in Dresden?' She and Peter had met Nathaniel's sister and her husband several times over the years.

'Martin was sent to the Eastern Front – he's gone. And Lena caught typhus and died last winter. I wanted to take their boys in, but Kurt refused. I don't know where they are now. I wish he'd have allowed it – they are his little cousins – but Kurt only has one family now and it is not us. It's like they've possessed him.'

It was clear that all Gretel felt was loss and pain. No matter what he had done, she still loved her boy, or at least the boy he had been.

'Oh, Gretel, I'm so sorry.' Ariella released her.

'So you see, Ariella, you must go, and don't come back here – it's too dangerous. Everyone spies now, everyone. Nobody trusts anyone else... That is what they have turned us into.' Gretel pulled her thin cardigan around herself. 'If it weren't for the girls, I would end my life. For me, there is no life without Nathaniel, and he isn't coming back...'

'You don't know that...' Ariella protested.

Gretel smiled, the saddest smile Ariella had ever seen. She shook her head. 'No, Nathaniel isn't coming back, nor is Peter, and the chances are one of those bombs will get us too. I hope you don't get killed – Liesl and Erich might still be out there somewhere. But there is nothing for me. My girls either. What will be left when all of this is over? Nothing. Nothing at all.' She sighed, and it sounded like it came from the depths of her soul. Ariella could see her exhaustion; she looked like she was to the point of collapse. 'They say the Russians will get here first, and what to do with two pretty young girls then, eh? How will I protect them?'

Ariella had no answer. And Gretel didn't expect one.

'So go, my friend, and good luck. I hope you see your children again, and I hope that for mine, the end is at least quick.' Gretel went to an almost empty cupboard and took out a can. She gave it to Ariella. 'It's not much, but it might keep you alive that one extra day you need. It's all we have.'

'I can't take your last food. The girls might –'

Gretel shook her head and pushed the can at her. 'My children work for the führer now and eat at the barracks. Even the girls. They are in the girls' brigade, and all day, they stay with those people, believing their lies, and I cannot say a word. Kurt has got to them too, so they would denounce me just like he did with their father.'

Ariella was shocked.

'I don't recognise my own children any more. I'm afraid of them. They have been so indoctrinated...' She pointed to her temple and whispered, 'They get inside their heads, the teachers, the youth leaders. Parents don't matter, nobody matters but the führer and the Fatherland. Thank God you got Liesl and Erich out, Ariella. It was such a lucky day.' Gretel shook her head. 'I wish we'd sent ours too, but they have been trapped. They might be perfect Aryans, but believe me, they are every bit as enslaved as yours would have been if they'd stayed.'

Ariella knew that this was goodbye. Gretel couldn't hide her, and there was no point in asking. She couldn't put Gretel in danger by coming again, and she wondered if she would ever see her friend again in this lifetime. It seemed unlikely. Peter and Nathaniel were gone, and now they were alone and facing a future impossible to predict.

'Now, take the food and go. Good luck, Ariella. I really hope you are reunited with Liesl and Erich. Remember us to them if you are. Nathaniel was determined to get them on that train, so at least if you find them again, he will have achieved something.'

Another sad smile passed over Gretel's face, and for a moment, Ariella glimpsed her pretty, funny friend once more.

'We had a good life, didn't we?' Gretel asked, as if she needed confirmation that her whole life wasn't this hell. 'Friendship and laughter… We thought it would always be like that.'

The pain of loss and sadness on her face hurt Ariella to her core. Though she was a Jew living with false papers and Gretel a perfect Aryan and mother to three loyal little Nazis, Ariella knew she would rather be herself. Regardless of what happened next, her friend had no happy future.

Ariella hugged her tightly. 'Goodbye, Gretel, and thank you for everything. I'll pray that we'll meet again when all of this is over –'

But before she could continue, Gretel shook her head. 'No, that won't happen. Not in this life anyway. Good luck.' Gretel kissed Ariella's cheek and gently nudged her out the back once more. The door closed behind her, and she took one last look around the courtyard, the scene of so many summer barbeques, Peter and Nathaniel playing with the children while she and Gretel prepared the food. It felt like another lifetime ago.

She let herself out and walked into the street, taking care not to be seen, and headed back towards the church. The nosey cleaner Frau Groenig would still be there, so she had some hours to kill. She didn't want to run into Herman again, so she avoided the Tiergarten.

She walked, on and on, street after battered street. The hideous red and black flags were everywhere, though many were worse for wear. People pulled trolleys and prams with their meagre belongings – bombed out presumably – and everyone looked hungry, miserable and hunted.

CHAPTER 13

*E*lizabeth let herself into the parish hall through the back entrance. Daniel was already in the little room behind the stage, and he looked up as she entered.

'A full house.' He smiled. All day he and the boys from the farm had been setting up rows of seats, and she'd arranged teas and buns for after the meeting.

'This is the right thing, isn't it?' she asked, suddenly unsure. It had been her idea, but now that she was to address the entire community, she was nervous.

Daniel took her hand. 'I think you are completely right. The farm feels temporary, the dormitories, the refectory – it's more like a boarding school or a barracks than a home. If we can get some help, we could turn the refectory into a big common room with a wireless and some couches and tables. We can get rid of the long trestle table and the benches and instead make tables and chairs, so they eat like a family. And upstairs, we could change the austere look of the dorms. I could make dressing tables and proper wardrobes – they only have a communal rail at the moment. But especially for the girls, if they had a little place of their own to put their things, that would make it feel more like home, wouldn't it?'

'It really would.'

'Well, then, do what you do best. Explain to the good people of Ballycreggan what our plan is.' He kissed her cheek. 'I'll be right beside you.'

They walked out, and the hubbub of chatter died down. Elizabeth strode to the centre of the little stage, and all nerves disappeared. The entire town was gathered. These were her people, and those children were her responsibility. She could do this.

'Thank you, everybody, for coming. I…well, all of us really, appreciate it.'

The front row was made up of the rabbi, Levi, Ruth, some of the Irish volunteers at the farm, the parish priest and the local vicar.

'We invited you all here tonight to discuss – well, to ask for help really, for a project we think is going to become necessary in the coming months and possibly years.'

Every eye was on her, and one could hear a pin drop.

'As you no doubt know, the situation in Europe is horrific, and though the end is in sight after such a long time, the children at the farm came alone. Many of them are very worried they will be sent back and just left to fend for themselves. Of course that won't happen, but the reality is that for many of them, reuniting with their families will be a very difficult thing to do. And in the case of some, it will prove to be an impossibility.'

Heads shook, and the compassion in the room was palpable.

'So we, all of us adults who work with these children, were thinking that the main thing is that our boys and girls feel safe and that Ballycreggan is their home for as long as they need it. I've seen how you all have taken them to your hearts, and I thought you might like the opportunity to do something practical to help them.'

'Hear, hear!' called Mr Morris, the school principal, and several people nodded.

'The kindness and compassion you have all shown to the refugees is an example of how decent people behave, and so knowing you as I do, I'm coming to ask you again.' She smiled. This was going to be fine.

'The farm was a ramshackle old place at the start, and the staff there did a wonderful job making it warm and dry and habitable, but I think it's time to make it all feel more permanent. Who knows when the children will get to go home, but whatever happens, it will be a long time. So I think we could pull together to make it a little more homely for them. Nothing too elaborate. Rationing and everything is still in place. But maybe if you had some wool or old material lying around, the ladies of the Women's Institute might be able to work their magic? Make some quilts, curtains and that sort of thing? And maybe some of the men could give a hand turning the dormitories into more individual rooms, with little lockers and wardrobes? We have some wood – we may need more – but if that was an option?

'Reverend Parkes and Father O'Toole had offered some of the bigger pieces of furniture out of the vicarage and the parochial house. We couldn't take them at the start because we hadn't space at the time, but now that so much has been done up there, we can. Still, we'll need much more. We'd like to create a common room too, a place they could relax and feel at home, but again, we have nothing...'

Everyone was smiling and nodding enthusiastically and murmuring to each other. The atmosphere was positive, and Daniel gave her a wink.

'The people of Ballycreggan have been so kind already that we hate to ask again –' Elizabeth went on, but Father O'Toole stood up and interrupted her.

'I'm sorry to cut across you, Mrs Lieber, but I feel I can speak for the village on this matter?' He raised an eyebrow at Reverend Parkes, who nodded.

'When our village was bombed and we were in a bad way, it was the community at the farm that came to our aid. Not just on the day after, but in the weeks and months that followed. They gave of their time and their skill to put our village back together. They share what they grow with us, and their children are educated alongside the locals.

'The future those children face is uncertain, God love them, and our hearts are going out to them, so I can say with a hundred percent certainty that we will do whatever we can to help.'

He sat down to thunderous applause that went on and on.

The rabbi then stood, holding his hand up for order. 'Mrs Lieber, Father O'Toole, Reverend Parkes, people of Ballycreggan, I have no words, except to thank you all.' The normally stoic rabbi wiped a tear from his eye. 'The kindness and love we have found here is so special. Looking out at so many faces... Doctor Crossley, who never once charged to tend to the children when they were sick and who has come out to look after us at all times of the day and night. Bridie, who always has a toffee or a humbug even when the children have no money and no ration coupon. Mr and Mrs O'Farrell, who allow the children from the farm into the Saturday matinee at the Palace and never charge a penny. The Doherty brothers, who deliver bags of turf to keep our fires going. The ladies of the Women's Institute, who mend and knit and sew so our little ones have clothes. Major Kilroy, who turns a blind eye to the encroachers in his orchard every September.'

This caused a ripple of laughter. The old major chuckled, and even the dour Mrs Dawkins, his housekeeper, managed a small smile.

'Tim Holland, who lends us his prize bull to do the necessary, and Alfie from the creamery, who collects our milk and makes sure we are always paid well for it. You parents, who encourage your children not to just be kind to our boys and girls but also offer the hand of friendship. I think the Ballycreggan versus Europe football match tally is in the thousands now, but it must go on.'

'And we're winning!' Charlie Fenton joked from the back, causing another ripple of laughter.

'Indeed, but the Europeans are hoping for a late surge.' The rabbi chuckled. 'But seriously, they don't go unnoticed, all the little gestures. We see it, and it soothes our troubled hearts. When one of our children comes home with a new sweater or a pair of shoes that someone else has outgrown, delighted with their new-to-them item, or when they bounce in the door, beaming with joy, saying they have been invited for tea at their friend's home, we notice every single thing and it gives us hope. Hope for a future where people are kind and people are judged not by their religion or their nationality but by the way they treat their fellow man. I have not forgotten anyone, but there are some of you who would rather keep your kindness between us, so I will not name you. But know this, every single person in this hall, you have our gratitude and our love, from the bottom of our hearts. And in a time of incomprehensible hatred, surely these children, whom God has entrusted to all, have seen through each of you that there is also great good in this world.'

The thunderous applause as the rabbi sat down caused Daniel to lean over and squeeze Elizabeth's hand. She wiped a tear herself. The rabbi was right – these were remarkable people, doing all they could with so little themselves. Her heart burst with pride for her home-place and its people.

The rest of the evening was spent in organisation, and by the time she and Daniel were home, there had been committees set up and lists of what was needed made. Not only was there to be extensive upgrading of the farmhouse itself, but there was going to be swings and a slide put in the garden and a piece of waste ground was going to be turned into a football pitch. It felt good to be doing something proactive.

They stood in the sitting room, their arms around each other, and she leaned against him, suddenly exhausted.

'You did an amazing thing, Elizabeth, once again,' he murmured into the top of her head.

Elizabeth's eyes rested on her parents' wedding photo on the mantelpiece. She picked it up and looked at it. 'I wonder what my mother would make of me now?' she mused.

'They'd both be so proud of you. I'm sure of it.'

She replaced the photo, running her thumb over the kind face of her father. She rarely spoke of them, and Daniel didn't pry. It was a difficult subject for her.

'When my father died, I was ten. He had a heart attack in the street on the way back from the forge. He'd stopped off to buy me sweets and then collapsed. Someone ran for my mother, and by the time she got there, he was dead. That evening, I don't remember who, but one of the neighbours came and took me to her house, and nobody told me what was happening. I knew something was wrong, but nobody felt they should be the one to tell me. I slept at that house that night, or at least I lay awake, imagining all sorts, until the next morning.' Elizabeth was shocked at how painful it was to tell the story, even now.

'My mother arrived and just told me, matter-of-fact, that my beloved daddy was dead. I adored him, and you know how difficult my relationship was with my mother, so this was the worst thing I could ever have imagined. But do you know something? This village held us up. They cooked dinners for us, they were kind to me when I met them in the street, always saying nice things about my daddy, what a good man he was. The teachers at school didn't get cross if I didn't do my lessons. Everyone was gentle and looked after us because we were one of their own. They see the children on the farm the same way.'

Daniel crossed the room to close the curtains, his broad muscular back stretching as he pulled the heavy velvet drapes. He closed them and then just stood, his hands in his pockets. She wondered what he was about to say. Long moments passed.

'Elizabeth.' He turned to look at her. 'To the Jewish children, you are not just their teacher, but in lots of ways, you are their mother. The women volunteers on the farm are young and undoubtedly kind, but you are the one they go to when they need to talk or are worried. Being Erich and Liesl's mother means they see you as one.'

She knew he was right. She had felt very maternal towards the children in her class for these past four years.

His eyes bored into hers. 'I think you should be the one to explain the changes and tell them about how this is their home for as long as they want it. You'd be best at it.'

Elizabeth found that she wasn't shocked. She'd assumed the rabbi would be the one to explain things, and the idea that it would be her hadn't occurred to her up to this point, but Daniel was right. She was the one who interacted personally with each child every day, and they did see her as a mother figure. All of the men on the farm were kind and did all they could for the children, but they lacked that sensitive touch.

'Would they allow me to do it?' She was referring to the executive council led by Rabbi Frank.

'Of course we would. We'd be grateful. You'd find the right words.'

He placed his hand on her cheek, and she could feel the calloused pads of his fingers. He gazed deeply into her eyes and leaned forward to kiss her gently. 'You're amazing,' he said in a whisper.

'I'm not, but I'm a woman and a mother figure as you say, and in this instance, that's what's called for, I think.'

He nodded and then opened the door to the hallway, his hand extended. 'Let's go to bed.'

She took it, and together they climbed the stairs.

As they undressed, he said quietly, 'She loved you.'

She knew he was talking about her mother. Their relationship had been playing on her mind a lot lately, and he sensed it.

They got into bed, and she rested her head on his chest, his arms around her.

'You know that now from all the letters and cards you found in the attic, but imagine what it was like for her telling you that your papa was dead? It must have been so hard, especially knowing you loved him more.'

'I know.' She sighed. 'I never understood her really, but then I don't think she ever understood herself. That suitcase of letters and cards that she wrote but never posted showed a totally opposite woman to the one I knew. It's like she was two totally different people. I can't imagine holding a grudge against Liesl or Erich, and I'm not even their real mother, but she never said one word to me for twenty years. She died having not spoken to me, all because I married a Jew.'

He chuckled. 'And to put the tin hat on it, you went and married another one after that.'

'Indeed.' She smiled. 'I think she might like you if she met you. We'll never know now though.'

'You are a very good woman, Elizabeth Lieber, and I am a very, very lucky man.'

'We're both lucky, and so are our darling boy and girl. I pray every night that Ariella comes back, but in the meantime, at least they have us and a home and the knowledge that they're loved and wanted. We have to try, inasmuch as we can, to reassure the others that they won't be abandoned, that we'll still take care of them even if they eventually get the worst news.'

'Which I fear many of them will,' he said with a deep sigh.

'Maybe, and that will be awful, and that's why knowing they are safe here is so important.'

'God planned this for you,' he said with certainty. 'You know that, don't you?' Her childlessness was a subject that for many years nobody would dare broach, but he knew her as well as she knew herself and so went on. 'The sadness that you had no child of your own, that a baby was so cruelly taken from your womb, it was so hard for you, I am sure. I cannot imagine. But God's plan was for you to be a mother to these lost babies, all of them, not just Liesl and Erich. And perhaps if you'd had your own family, you would not have been here, in the right place at the right time, to be the mother they so badly need.'

From anyone else, that statement might have sounded heartless, but she knew Daniel loved her and was speaking the truth. If Rudi had survived, if she'd not had a miscarriage and lost their only child twenty-six years ago, her life would have taken a very different direction. She'd never for a moment imagined, all those years as a spinster schoolteacher in Liverpool, that she would ever come back to Ireland, let alone with two little children in tow, and then to inherit another twenty-five. She had closed her heart off to feeling anything. It was hard to imagine now that she was capable of it, but she had. When Rudi died and then she miscarried, she wasn't speaking to her mother – or more accurately, her mother wasn't speaking to her – and her father was dead. The nuns in the school and the other teachers were kind. They saw her pain, but then she learned to hide it under a mask of efficiency. After she snapped at a few people who enquired after her, they soon learned not to pry.

She felt awful being rude as she knew people meant well, but their sympathy made the situation worse. Nothing could be done. Rudi was gone, so was her baby, and there was nothing for it but to get on with things. People constantly asking if she was all right was so hard. She'd wanted to scream, 'No, of course I'm not all right, you stupid woman! My heart is broken, and I feel so bereft and alone in this horrible cruel world that I think about ending my life very often.' Either that or she wanted to collapse in a fit of sobbing in their arms. But that would shock them and possibly precipitate the loss of her job, so a curt one-word response and a rapid change of subject was how she coped. It took a while, but she persevered, and finally, people knew not to ask.

Meeting Daniel, falling in love with him, she felt like a girl again, like the entire world had changed from sepia to bright technicolour once more. The war and all the horror and loss and destruction were not irrelevant – it impacted everyone – but in many ways, the war had given her her life back. She had Liesl and Erich, she had moved back to Ballycreggan, she married her soulmate…all because of Hitler. She hated him, of course, but if he hadn't done what he did, then she would probably still be a lonely spinster, living half a life.

'I feel like their mother – I genuinely love them, I worry for them, I fear for their futures. The trust, their innocence, breaks my heart sometimes, and if it's all right with the others, I will talk to them about the future, and I think I actually am the best person to do it.'

CHAPTER 14

'May I use the bathroom?' Ariella asked.

She had gone back to the sacristy once the sun set, but Father Dominic had intercepted her at the door and led her to the parochial house. She stood in his office now for the first time. It was a large house with a lot of people coming and going, and she could feel the tension in the air. Her being there was dangerous, not just for her and the priest but for everyone in the building. But the church was probably more so. Father Dominic wanted to help her, but it was so risky.

'Er…yes. Yes, of course. Let me check that the landing is clear first.' He went out, and she heard him exchange a few words with someone. Then he returned.

'Quickly, second door on the right. Stay in there until I knock three times on the door to let you know it's clear again.'

She nodded and scurried past him, rushing to the lavatory. She finished, washed her hands and gazed at her reflection in a cracked mirror over the sink. She looked so different. For a moment, she'd forgotten that her hair was cut. The wave arranged by Frau Braun was gone, and her curls hung loose, though her hair was cut just below her ears. She wished she had some pins or something. She splashed some cold water on her face and dried with a clean but frayed and greying towel hanging on a nail. Then she waited until she heard his knock before emerging into the corridor once more.

He held his office door open, and she rushed inside to the sanctuary. He turned the key, locking them both in, and pulled out a spindle chair for her to sit on. The large room was sparse, just a desk and two chairs, a cupboard and a dresser full of what she assumed was liturgical paraphernalia. On one wall were shelves containing hundreds of books, mostly with dark spines, and in the corner was an old armchair covered in a dark-green cloth.

'Right, I've spoken to some people, but getting you out at this stage is as I suspected – impossible. I would say to just stay in hiding in the sacristy, but between Frau Groenig and Stella Kübler, it's too dangerous. She was seen again this afternoon, by the way, while you were out. One of the other priests spotted her.' Father Dominic spoke quickly and quietly.

This last piece of information solidified her decision.

'She may have been watching the forger's place, or maybe Frau Groenig spotted something was amiss and alerted someone who put her on the case. It doesn't matter anyway. The point is they are looking for you.'

Compassion and kindness spread across his careworn face. 'I wish I could do more, but you can't stay here – it's too dangerous. And, well, if they found you, they might find others, and I can't risk that. But I don't want to abandon you. So I was thinking. There is a tiny room, not much more than a broom cupboard really, up in the gallery, behind the organ. Nobody goes there, and I've used it from time to time. Maybe we could put you there until I think of something else?'

He ran his hands through his grey hair, and she felt a wave of affection for him. He was trying his best, but it wasn't fair – he had enough to worry about. She knew he wouldn't let her go, but that was exactly what she was going to do. If Stella Kübler found her, she would surely lead the authorities to Father Dominic and whoever else he was hiding as well. She couldn't have his death on her conscience. She'd have to go it alone. As she'd walked all day, she'd formulated a plan, and while it wasn't ideal by any standard, she was going to have to give it a go. In the meantime, she would pretend she was going to stay.

'Thank you, and hopefully it won't be for long. It's almost over. We just have to hold on.' She smiled.

'Oh, it's over all right. Paris was liberated last week. The Allied armies are meeting the Germans head on and winning, though progress is slow. They have the might of the USA behind them now. The panzers are down south – they weren't expecting the Normandy attack – and the maquisards are doing a great job of disrupting the Germans getting troops up through France. The Russians are powering through what's left of German defences on the Eastern Front, but they are still deadly dangerous.'

She had a moment's doubt. This man was offering her a lifeline. Maybe she should take it and hope for the best... But she couldn't put him in that much danger. She thought of Liesl and Erich and the feeling of them running into her arms. She longed to hide in that cupboard, but it wouldn't be right.

Her eyes burning with intensity, she spoke. 'Thank you, Father Dominic. I really appreciate what you are doing for me. My children are Liesl and Erich Bannon. They are living with my husband's cousin, a lady called Elizabeth Klein, in a village called Ballycreggan in County Down, Northern Ireland. If anything happens to me, can you try to get a message to them, tell them that I love them so very much and that I tried my hardest to get back to them? Tell them I wish long and happy lives for them and that their papa and I will be watching over them every day of their lives with love. And please thank Elizabeth for me. There are no words to convey my gratitude and love for her and all she has done.'

He took a sheet of paper from his desk. 'Write to them. I'll see they get it,' he said. 'If I survive.'

'Thank you.' The gesture meant so much.

Ariella moved her chair towards the desk and took the sheet of paper and pen he offered. She wrote her note quickly, sealing the envelope he gave her, writing her children's names on the outside. She handed it to the priest, who placed it inside a book on his shelf.

'Can I write one more?' she asked.

'Of course, but we must be quick.' He handed her a second sheet.

She wrote once more, folding the letter and handing it to him. He placed it in the same book.

'I'll see they get them, but I hope I won't need to.' He went to the door, but before opening it, he turned to her. 'All right, go over to the church, make sure nobody sees you and go up the stairs to the gallery. To the right of the organ pipes is a small door. It is unlocked, but I'll have to lock you in for safety. I'll come over in a while, in time for Benediction, so it won't look odd.'

'Thank you, Father Dominic, for everything.' She stood.

'Hold on.' He dug in his black jacket pocket, producing a worn headscarf. 'Use this to cover your hair as the red hair might give you away. Also these.' He took a pair of horn-rimmed spectacles from his other pocket. 'Put them on as well. It's not a great disguise, but it's better than nothing.'

Ariella did as he instructed and looked down at the dress she'd been wearing since she left the Brauns'. It was bright and would be memorable. She pointed to the dark-green fabric covering on the armchair. 'Could I borrow that?'

'The chair?' he asked, confused.

'No.' She smiled. 'Just the cover. This dress is easily recognisable. I can wrap that fabric to make it look like a dress, and I'll be less identifiable. I'll give it back.'

'Of course, take it.' He crossed the room in three long strides and pulled the fabric off to reveal a particularly horrible brown cabbage-rose pattern on the chair, the arms frayed to almost threadbare.

Ariella winced. 'I can see why you covered it.' She laughed although she felt bad about taking the covering.

'Hmm,' he said, glad of a moment's levity to ease the tension. 'I'll try to find something else. No doubt one of the ladies of the parish will find something.' He shrugged and gave a chuckle, a lovely gurgling sound from deep in his chest, and it reminded her of her father-in-law's laugh. How she missed him.

She wrapped the material into a skirt over her dress, tucking it in at the waist, and put the blazer on over it. With the headscarf covering her hair, the heavy glasses and the more dowdy colours, she did look different. She just hoped it was enough.

'Well, I'd better go,' she said, trying not to betray the terror she felt at leaving the protection of his office.

'One moment.' He opened the door and checked the corridor and staircase. 'All right, it's clear.' He held the door open for her. 'Good luck, Ariella. I'll check on you after Benediction.'

'Thanks.'

She passed him and ran out the way she had come in.

CHAPTER 15

The plan was that the children would gather in the refectory after prayers. The long, low building was where most things happened – homework, eating, playing – so it felt like the right place. It had been constructed from scratch by the men of the farm in the early months of 1940, and while it did the job, it was very utilitarian looking. Elizabeth couldn't wait to get started on the refurbishment to soften it all up and make it more welcoming. Daniel had been the supervisor of the original project, as he was with all construction since, and even he agreed it was less than ideal.

The only really lovely place on the whole farm was the synagogue. The community were justifiably proud of their place of worship. It wasn't as ornate or beautifully decorated as the ones they had worshipped in at home, but there was a simplistic beauty to it. Elizabeth enjoyed being there. It felt restful and serene, and in the endless hustle and bustle of the farm, it was an oasis of calm.

Despite the functional nature of everything, the entire farm was a miracle really, she thought as she walked up from the village. They grew or produced almost all their own food, reused everything and were frugal with everything so as not to be any more of a burden on their benefactors than need be.

Daniel had offered to drive her, but she'd sent Liesl and Erich up earlier with him in the car for prayers and opted to walk. She wanted the time before the meeting to clear her head and try to find the right words.

As Daniel predicted, the committee were happy for her to address the children on the possible future they faced. Rabbi Frank had thanked her sincerely for offering and blessed her courage and love for those little ones in their care. He said he was sure she would find the right words. Right then, she wished she shared his confidence.

As she approached the farm, it struck her how quiet it was. Usually it was a hive of activity – people working, children playing, food being cooked, laundry being done – but everyone was at prayer. It was the only time the place was quiet.

She sat outside the synagogue, enjoying the late summer sunshine and going over her speech in her head. She had no notes. These were the children she explained things to all day every day in school, and she would use the words she always used, the tone they were familiar with.

She said a quick prayer to her parents, and to Rudi. She wasn't religious in the sense of belonging to any church. She was raised Catholic but had not been involved in the church in any way for decades. Daniel, Liesl and Erich were Jews, but she didn't feel a strong pull in that direction either. However, she did believe that this wasn't all there was. She felt a strong sense of spirituality, that those who went before were not gone, that there was some master plan. If not, well, then the last six years, or indeed the Great War before that, were just answering some egomaniac's need for power, and she couldn't countenance that.

She composed her prayer and said the words in her head as she waited outside. She could hear the murmur of voices inside.

Mammy and Daddy and Rudi, I need you all now. I have to do perhaps one of the most difficult things of my life, so please be by my side as I try to find a way to reassure these little children. I don't feel like I have the right words. I know there are no right words, but help them to understand that we'll look after them no matter what. Thank you.

She inhaled and exhaled slowly and deliberately, the breaths bringing calm.

She heard the doors of the synagogue open, and she crossed to meet Daniel, who stood there as children and adults alike poured out. Three white feathers floated before her on the light summer breeze. She smiled. Her daddy used to say that whenever you saw a white feather, it was the souls of the dead reminding you that they were watching over you. The chicken coop was nearby, so a sceptic might dismiss such a fanciful notion, but that evening she chose to believe her parents and Rudi were with her.

'How are you?' Daniel murmured as she stood beside him.

'Fine, I think.' She exhaled raggedly.

The children were doing as Levi instructed and stacking chairs and then gathering in the refectory. There was a bit of moaning, as they wanted to go outside and play in the late evening warmth, but Levi and Ruth shepherded them inside. Elizabeth noticed Ben, the boy from Dublin who took up so much of her darling Liesl's daydreams, help Liesl and Viola with their chairs. Several other young Irish Jewish volunteers had joined the community and were in varying degrees helpful around the house and farm. They all meant well, and the European Jews were unfailingly welcoming and friendly, but Daniel confided that some of them were as useful as a chocolate teapot.

There were lots of people always coming and going. Daniel, Ruth, Levi and Rabbi Frank were the only adults who had been there since the beginning. Ruth and Levi had eventually got married, much to everyone's relief. Both could be taciturn and difficult, but undoubtedly they made each other happy. Nobody ever mentioned Talia Zimmerman.

'Right, I'm as ready as I'll ever be,' Elizabeth replied, giving his hand a quick squeeze. Rabbi Frank had had to make many concessions to a less orthodox way of life since coming to the farm, but public displays of affection would still be very much frowned upon.

The rabbi approached and invited Elizabeth into the farmhouse. The refectory was to the left as she entered, and behind it was a large industrial kitchen with a large serving hatch out into the dining hall. All of the children sat on the benches, with a few of the older ones, like Liesl and Viola and Viola's sister Anika, sitting on the tables along the walls. Erich sat with Simon, his best friend, a boy from Bavaria. She smiled as Abraham Schultz, a heartbreakingly handsome nine-year-old gave her a wave.

Ruth helped the really little ones up onto the bench. The babies, as they were called, were aged between eighteen months and three when they arrived and had been cared for mainly by Ruth and some of the Irish volunteers. But as time passed, they too came to school, and so now Elizabeth knew every child on the farm.

Rabbi Frank stood at the top of the room, and everyone fell silent. 'Now, boys and girls.' His tone was kind. 'Mrs Lieber has joined us tonight because we all need to tell you about something exciting that is going to happen here over the coming months.' He saw the smiles on their little faces and quickly said, 'We all know how Mrs Lieber is wonderful at explaining things, so I've asked her to talk to you this evening.'

Ruth and the other adults went in the kitchen and began making hot chocolate and taking some freshly baked buns out of the oven, another of Elizabeth's suggestions. Let them feel the refurbishment of their home was a cause for celebration. The aroma of baking and warm chocolate was working its magic already.

They all nodded in enthusiastic agreement. So many children had stories of teachers in the past who used sticks and shouting to get them to behave. But everyone wanted to please Mrs Lieber, and if anyone misbehaved, all it took was one look from her and the child rethought their actions.

All eyes were on her, and she clenched and unclenched her fists, a gesture she'd carried through from childhood and used when she was worried.

She moved into the centre of the room, though there had been a chair set up for her at the top. She sat on the table, beckoning them to come closer. That is what she'd done each Friday afternoon in school for story time, and even though the older children didn't have to participate and could do their homework if they wished, she often smiled to find them just as enraptured with her tales as the little ones.

'So today I need to tell you something.' She smiled. 'As you all know, the war is almost over and Germany will be defeated. So that is wonderful news, isn't it? Hitler and the Nazis will have to surrender, and things can start getting back to how they were.'

They all nodded; it was great news. Their trusting eyes pulled at her heart.

'But some of you might be worrying about what is going to happen next, or thinking maybe that because you came here by train that you will be put back on trains.' She knew by their faces that was exactly their fear.

'Well, the first thing I must tell you is that is definitely not going to happen. When the end of the war is announced, hopefully soon, we must expect that it will take a very long time for things to get sorted out. Lots of people – soldiers, children, everyone really – have been moved all over the place, and a lot of the roads and train lines have been damaged, so getting people back to where they once lived will be very hard. And it will take a long time.'

She paused. 'Do you all understand that? Why it is going to take a long time?'

Several children nodded, and she went on. 'So what we want is for each of you to understand that this is your home. This farm, and all of us, are your home for as long as you want it or need it. Nobody is going to send you anywhere alone.' She looked around, making eye contact with each of them in turn. 'Do you have any questions?'

'But didn't the government say when we came that at the end of the war, we would have to go back?' It was Simon, Erich's friend.

'They did, Simon, that's true, but that was at the start of the war when we thought it was going to be over quickly. Now everything is all up in the air, and the rules will have to change to suit the circumstances. But listen to me – I want every single one of you to hear this. Nobody – not me, not Daniel, not Rabbi Frank, not Ruth, not Levi – will ever let you out of our sights until it is back to your family, and only then if you want to go. I give you my word.'

She waited for the words to sink in. The other adults stood around, and Daniel backed her up.

'She's right. Nobody will take you from us. It doesn't matter what anyone says, all right?' He glanced at the rabbi, who took the cue.

'God put you in our care, children, and we will take care of you, I promise you. You are safe now, and you will always be safe with us.'

Hearing it from all three of them seemed to have the desired effect. Elizabeth went on. 'And so, because we are all staying here for the foreseeable future, we thought we might do a bit of a job on the place and make it more like a home. So we were thinking we could put some sofas in here, maybe even get a carpet and a wireless, and you can bring some of the board games from school, and it would be a place you could all relax and be together.'

This news was met with mixed reactions. The little ones seemed delighted, but the older ones looked worried. She would have to address their concerns at least a little bit – this was going to be the hardest part. She prayed she could strike the right balance.

Ruth seemed to sense it was a good time to split the group into younger and older, so she appeared with buns and cocoa. The smaller children descended on them, unused to such treats, as Elizabeth stood and addressed a group of the older children.

'We don't know what has gone on in your home countries, and we have no way of knowing for a long time yet. So how about we just take one day at a time? For now, just know that you are all loved by all of us. We are not your parents, we know that, but we feel like we are and we intend to take care of you, all right?'

'Can we ask you something, Mrs Lieber?' Viola, Liesl's friend, asked.

'Of course,' she said, sitting down again. 'Anything.'

Viola spoke again, but Elizabeth could feel ten or twelve pairs of eyes on her. She guessed what was coming. They would not have said anything in front of the younger ones.

'At the cinema, the news said about the camps, and how the Jews were sent there, and how cities like Warsaw were destroyed.' Viola was Polish and her family lived in the capital. 'And so we are wondering how we can find our families if they have been sent away, and what we should do.'

'They are saying in the newspaper,' Haim Bonhoffer, a quiet sixteen-year-old from Bremen, said, 'that Hitler killed a lot of Jews. Sean's father was reading about it, and Sean asked him what it was and he told me.'

'They are saying the Jews are all gone.' This time it was Dieter Schultz, Abraham's older brother. He was a rogue, and if there was ever mischief going on, you could be sure Dieter or Abe was at the centre of it, but they had kind hearts.

Her eyes rested on each one in turn. Viola and her sister, Anika, Simon, Yuri, Rachel from Munich, Michael from Leipzig, Konrad and Piotr Mann from Salzburg… She needed to tell them some version of the truth.

'My darlings,' she said, forcing her voice to stay steady. 'It's true that some terrible things have happened, and it may be a very long time before we can find out exactly where your families went. And yes, hard as it is to imagine, some Jews have died.'

The realisation that it must be true if Mrs Lieber said it was like a physical blow, and she hated being the one to deliver it.

'But we don't know anything more, and so we must not assume the worst. I wish I had answers for you, I really do, but I just don't. None of us do. And it will, as I said, be a long time, so all we can do is wait and see. Your families put you on those trains to keep you safe, and they would want you to stay here, safe and loved, until they can come for you or we know more. Once peace is declared, we'll do all we can, but all I can guarantee is that nobody will be sent anywhere until they have someplace to go.'

They stood close to each other, not moving. She had their undivided attention. At the other end of the room, the happy chatter of the little ones filled the air.

'I know you want to go home.' She sighed and smiled. 'You worry about your families, and you want to see them as soon as possible. But until such time as that can be arranged, you have a home with us. For as long as you need it, forever if you like. Rabbi Frank, Daniel, and

Levi are in the same position as you all. They've lost touch with people they loved too, and they've lost their homes and everything. Just as much as they've made a home for you, you all have made a home for them as well. Families can come in all shapes and sizes, and we are a family now, all of us, and we'll stick together. So while I know you are feeling so confused and worried now, and that's totally understandable, you do have this family, and we're not going anywhere.'

To see them comfort each other made her realise that her words were true. They were a family.

She knew she had said enough. The gruesomeness of the mass killings would be something they would learn about in due course. They would find out eventually, she supposed, what happened to their specific families, or maybe they never would, but for now, this was enough.

CHAPTER 16

*A*riella forced herself to walk at a normal pace, not rushing but not dawdling either. Her false papers were buried deep in her bag. It was only a thirty-minute walk. She could do it; she had no other choice.

She knew exactly where to go, which streets to take to get to Frau Braun's house once more, but nothing looked as it once had. The beautiful wide boulevards of her city were reduced to a crumbling, smoking mess, and she wondered what the Nazis thought when they saw the carnage they had brought down on their beloved city. Did they think it was worth it, this destruction? It was hard to imagine how, if ever, it could be restored to its former glory.

As she walked, she tried to envisage the scene that would await her. It wasn't ideal, but it was her only option. She'd seen the droves of people fleeing the city, and so perhaps the need to take in boarders was gone; there appeared to be hardly anyone left. Now that she had papers, maybe she could pose as a bona fide boarder.

The urge to join the throngs of those trying to get out was strong, but Father Dominic had warned her. There was no food or water for travellers, and huge numbers of those who left were either dying on the roads or returning in a worse state than they'd been in when they left.

Frau Braun took her in once; perhaps she would again, especially now as she had papers and a ration book. She could pose as a genuine boarder, a bombed-out victim. Over and over, she planned her speech, praying she'd find the right words.

Frau Braun's main opposition would surely be her husband, but Herr Braun wouldn't recognise her. She'd only seen him once or twice in the years before the war, and they had never spoken. Besides, she looked nothing like her old self.

He'd worked before the war in some low-grade clerical job in the city, and since joining the Party, he'd been elevated. That was the case with so many of them, Peter had remarked. Men who'd not achieved much suddenly found a way to rise up through the ranks of society quickly on account of their devotion to National Socialism. Even at Peter's bank, he'd seen men promoted, who up to then had shown no promise or talent, just because they were connected to the Party. The governors of the bank had no choice – it seemed they were told who to promote and that was that. It drove Peter mad, and once or twice he'd objected as a director of the bank but was told to keep his opinions to himself for his own good.

Those men who had no merit or talent suddenly swaggering about like they were someone important, issuing commands and barking orders at their former superiors – it was hard to take. That's possibly why they were all clinging to what surely must be a lost cause at this stage, because without the Nazi Party and their affiliations to cling to, they went back to being nobodies.

Nobody from her former neighbourhood would recognise her either. She looked so different and could play the part of Marta well by now. Over the months, she'd encountered a few people when she was out and about and had casual conversations, and in each one, she expanded the character of Marta. She knew her now, wore her like a second skin. She could convince anyone she was, in fact, Marta Weiss. All she needed was for Frau Braun to agree. She had a ration book, so they could get food legitimately, and she wouldn't have to hide her.

Whatever had made her take her in the first time might still be there. It was a long shot, but it was all she had. Stella Kübler would not look for her there, Frau Groenig either. It was her only hope.

A group of Hitler-Jugend passed her, and she got off the footpath to allow them to walk three abreast. One of them smirked at her, delighted that his uniform wielded such power, though he couldn't have been more than twelve or thirteen years old. She thought of Kurt, of Erich. They were only children, but nobody was spared in this horror. Every home in Germany would be forever altered by these years. That was all that was in the future of a once learned, cultured nation: grief, loss, shame.

She passed a few groups of people, all down at heel, all hungry and tired looking.

So few men remained in the city now; those who did were only the young and the old and the hopelessly injured. It was a city of women and children, but the bombing was nonetheless relentless. Germany would pay dearly for what they'd done – the Allies would make sure of it.

Eventually, she rounded onto the street where the Brauns lived. She paused for a moment outside, but however nervous she was, she didn't want to draw any attention to herself by loitering. She opened the little wrought-iron gate and knocked on the big oak door with the spaces for six yellow glass panels on top, two gone altogether, the apertures filled with pieces of cardboard, the other four shattered in bomb blasts but held in place by tape.

She heard footsteps, and then the door opened. Ariella felt the colour drain from her face. A slight pause, a moment of recognition and then…

'Good afternoon, Mrs Bannon,' said Gefreiter Willi Braun, who was wearing the full uniform of the Wehrmacht.

CHAPTER 17

*L*iesl chose her dress carefully, brushed her dark hair until it shone and wondered if she would get away with a tiny bit of lipstick. It was the fair day in Ballycreggan, and Daniel and Elizabeth had said they could have some money for the hook a duck and to get a toffee apple. Bridie in the sweetshop had been making them all week with sugar she made from sugar beets, and the aroma was tantalising. Rumour had it she'd managed to make one for every child in the village, including the gang from the farm, and the excitement was at an all-time high. Major Kilroy, a doddery old retired army officer who had an estate on the outskirts of the village and who turned a blind eye every year to the children who scaled his orchard wall and went slogging apples, had delivered two boxes of apples himself apparently. However, his housekeeper, the sour Mrs Dawkins, showed no such kindness to children desperate for a treat. There had been so little sugar available – sweets were a rarity, even with ration coupons – so the delicious Cox's Orange Pippins from the major's orchard were in much demand.

Mothers who might previously have admonished their offspring for stealing now quietly took their booty and turned it into jelly, or if there was a birthday or a special occasion, they might even use up the flour ration to make an apple tart.

Their family managed well enough, though Liesl dreamed of German chocolate, because Elizabeth's father had planted a vegetable and fruit garden and the old bushes and trees gave abundant fruit each autumn.

Erich's job was taking the apples and pears and wrapping them in newspaper to store them for winter. Liesl picked blackberries, raspberries, gooseberries and strawberries, which she and Elizabeth made into jam. The jam was runny as they had no sugar to set it, but they added stewed apple, and the pectin in the apples thickened it enough so it was a spreadable consistency. They also had hens, so they had a plentiful supply of eggs, and Daniel brought milk and cream home from the farm. They grew potatoes, carrots, cabbages and peas, so their tummies were never empty, but Liesl did miss treats.

She hoped Ben would come to the fair. It was always fun. The adults were in good humour, and all the farmers came in from the countryside with cattle and horses to buy and sell. The tinkers came too, offering their services to fix anything broken about the house, and Elizabeth said she wanted the handle put back on her large saucepan and a lid made for an oval cast-iron pot she found in the shed. Daniel could have done it easily – he was able to do almost everything – but Elizabeth explained that she wanted to give the tinker the work.

Last week, they'd taken all the clothes that were too small for Liesl and Erich and divided them up. Some went up to the farm where they would be distributed among the smaller children, and some were given to the tinker's wife who came to the back door with her paper flowers and prayers for the family. The travellers always seemed to have lots of children, and the woman was expecting another baby, so Elizabeth tried to give her all she could spare.

Liesl examined herself in the full-length bevelled mirror standing in the corner of her bright sunny bedroom. She and Erich were so lucky, she knew. The people up at the farm were in dormitories with no privacy – though plans were underway to change that. At least they were safe and well fed. The stories from Europe were horrible, and Liesl wouldn't admit it to anyone, but she tried to tune out whenever people spoke of it. It was just all too sad and miserable. She'd had nightmares, picturing her mother in those camps, but during the day, she pushed all thoughts of her to the back of her mind. It was hard, but she couldn't deal with it. The fair was the first nice thing to happen in ages.

She forced herself back to the present.

Her body was changing now, and she liked it. Her breasts were filling out her dresses, and her hips were getting more rounded. She looked a bit less awful and not like the beanpole that she'd felt like for years now.

Elizabeth was always saying how pretty she was, but she had to say that. Liesl thought of herself as looking like a big black crow most of the time. Elizabeth's hair was that lovely chestnut colour, brown but with tinges of copper, but Liesl's was just plain dark brown, not even black. Black at least would be dramatic. She had her father's hair, not her mother's beautiful copper curls.

She thought about her papa and *mutti*, and she felt ashamed of how distant their memory was. It felt like such a long time since she'd seen either of them. Elizabeth and Daniel felt like their parents now, and while neither of them ever tried to undermine the position of their real parents, the truth was that when she and her brother thought of parents, they pictured Elizabeth and Daniel. Peter and Ariella were just ghosts.

She tried to visualise them in heaven. Were they together? She hoped so. She had longed for so long to see her mother again, but now it seemed so unlikely and she had come to terms with the possibility that she would never see her again.

Though nobody discussed the news in any great detail, there were newspapers and BBC radio in their house, so they were more informed than the others who were kept in the dark. It was a relief in lots of ways for them to know that everybody wouldn't be going home the day after the war ended. Her best friend, Viola, had talked all the time about going home to Poland, seeing her parents and grandparents again, even her dog Kacper, and Liesl had never said anything. They'd even had a falling out over it, with Viola accusing her of not caring about her family and going silent every time she told a story about her papa or her darling Labrador. Now that Viola knew that going home was unlikely, at least in the short term, she had become silent herself.

Liesl had hoped she'd come to the fair, but her friend had declined. She didn't want to pretend like everything was all right. When Liesl had begged her to come, Viola said she only wanted her there so she could see Ben without anyone raising eyebrows. It was so unlike Viola to be so catty, and Liesl did admit that it was a bit true, but she wanted her friend to smile again too.

'It's all right for you, Liesl,' Viola had said bitterly. 'You're fine. You have your brother and a new mother and father and a lovely home and everything, but me and Anika don't have anyone. We are alone in the world, and I can't just pretend everything is all right and go to fairs and talk about stupid boys, so just leave me alone!' She'd slammed the door on Liesl and left her standing there alone.

That had happened after Shabbat last week, and she'd not seen her friend since. She longed to go up there, to see her and try to talk it out, but she didn't want to risk it. What if all of the others felt the same way, that she and Erich didn't understand, that it was all right for them?

Elizabeth put her head round Liesl's door. 'You look lovely. Are you ready to go?'

Liesl looked up. Elizabeth looked lovely too in a cornflower-blue dress that had belonged to her when she was a girl and had lived in this house.

'You do too.' Liesl stood up.

'Do you want to come with us or wait for Viola?' Elizabeth asked, and the shadow that crossed Liesl's face caused her to sit on the bed and pat the space beside her. 'What's up?' she asked, putting her arm around Liesl's shoulders.

One of the many things Liesl loved about Elizabeth was how easy she was to talk to. Ever since that first day when she'd picked her and

Erich up from Liverpool Street station in London, during all the time they lived in Liverpool, even enduring the bombing there and the destruction of their house and school, Elizabeth had been open and honest with her and her brother. They knew that whatever she said was the truth, and she didn't believe, like so many adults did, that children should be seen and not heard. She talked to them like they were important, and she listened too. She didn't just dismiss childish worries as being silly but took their concerns seriously.

'Viola is cross with me, so she's not coming to the fair,' Liesl said.

'Why is she cross with you?' Elizabeth asked. 'Do you know?'

Liesl sighed. 'Well, she says it's because I only want her to go so I can talk to Ben, but that's not true. I wanted to cheer her up. She's been so sad since you told them the truth about not being able to go home to their families. And she said I don't understand, that everything is so much better for me and Erich than the others.'

Elizabeth pulled Liesl's head onto her shoulder and gave her a squeeze. 'She's hurting, pet. You know the reason we are going to make the farm much more welcoming, don't you?' Elizabeth's eyes locked with hers.

She nodded and said the words out loud for the first time. 'Because some of them won't be going home ever.'

'Exactly. I couldn't say it as bluntly as that, but yes, that's probably the truth. We'll do all we can to find their families, but in some cases, I fear it won't be possible.'

'We read about Warsaw in the paper, so I think she kind of dreads hearing any more news.' Liesl's heart broke for her friend.

'It's impossible to say, and even harder to imagine, but yes, Warsaw seems to have been particularly badly affected, so she has every reason to worry. I know it's hard, but maybe we need to just be patient with her.'

'Yes. But she says it's all right for Erich and me because we've got you and Daniel and this lovely home. That so even though we're sad about our parents, it's not as bad for us. And she's right.' Liesl struggled to give her friend the benefit of the truth.

Elizabeth took Liesl's hand and looked into her eyes. 'Sometimes when we are hurt, we hurt others just… Well, I don't know why, but we just do. Trying to make other people feel as bad as we do or something, I don't know. My mother loved me, I know that now, but I spent all my adult life thinking she didn't because she was so hurtful to me when I married Rudi.'

Liesl listened carefully.

'But now I realise she was lonely. She didn't want me to marry someone English and never come home, and because she was so hurt and so sad, she drove me away instead of holding me close. She was the same with my daddy. He loved her, and she seemed like she was always mean to him, but in those letters I found, the ones that she'd written for years to me but never posted, she talked of how her heart broke the day he died, how she never really got over it. How losing me too was the hardest thing, but that she knew I loved my father more and that if I had found happiness with Rudi, I wouldn't want to come back anyway. It was all so wrong, Liesl. She got it all wrong, but by the time I realised it, it was much too late.'

'But what does that have to do with Viola?' Liesl asked.

'Viola is hurt. Her little heart is broken because the chances of anyone surviving in Warsaw are slim. After she read that article, she asked Levi to tell her the truth about all of it, and he did, so that's why she's lashing out. She's angry and confused and so deeply sad, and those are all normal reactions. She loves you, Liesl, but she'll need some time to come to terms with this, and all you can do is be there for her when she needs you. Let's invite her for lunch on Saturday – I'll make something nice. Remind her that you do understand, that you lost your home and family too. And yes, you do have Daniel and me, but it's not the same as your own parents…'

'It kind of is though…' Liesl said quietly.

The words hung between them.

'What do you mean, sweetheart?' Elizabeth asked.

'Well, I know I shouldn't say this, and I feel really guilty about it, but honestly I think even if I could go back now, to Berlin I mean, I wouldn't want to. I feel like our home is with you and Daniel. I know

Papa is dead, and we don't know about *Mutti*, but even if they weren't...'

'Oh, my lovely Liesl.' Elizabeth rubbed her hair and kissed her forehead. 'I'm so glad that you feel like Daniel and I are your parents. It feels like that for us too, and we love you both very much and feel so privileged to have been blessed with you and Erich. And of course you are bound to feel a little detached from your life before. It's how we cope, you know?'

She didn't want Liesl to feel guilty about being happy, but it was inevitable, she supposed.

'I thought for years that I had no feelings about my mother, but then I came back here and realised I had lots of feelings. I had just bottled them up because it was too hard to deal with them every day. Your *mutti* and papa are in here' – she laid a finger on Liesl's temple – 'and in here' – she pointed to the girl's heart – 'and they will be there forever. The love you have for them and they for you, nothing can erase that – not time, not distance and certainly not that evil man Hitler. But in order to function on a day-to-day basis, we put things away.'

She tucked a strand of Liesl's hair behind her ear. 'So don't worry, darling. You are not forgetting them in favour of Daniel and me. We all love you – Ariella and Peter and us – and you never have to choose, ever. I pray to my parents and to Rudi all the time, though I'm not much of a churchgoer as you know, that one day you will be reunited with Ariella. And when that day comes, my wish will come true and I'll have to let you go. And that will be the best day of my life and also the worst, but it's what I wish for with all my heart.'

'I love you, Elizabeth,' Liesl said.

'And I love you, my darling girl.' Elizabeth squeezed her hand. 'And don't worry about Viola – she'll be fine. You all will. You won't ever forget, of course not, but hearts are like legs or arms that break – even if you don't want them to, or could never imagine them healing, somehow they do. Viola needs time and lots of love and support, and you are a great friend, so I know you can do this for her.'

'I'll try anyway,' Liesl agreed, feeling better.

'And on the matter of Ben...' Elizabeth went on.

Liesl coloured. She didn't want anyone to know how much she thought about him.

'He seems like a very nice boy.' Elizabeth smiled.

'He is,' Liesl agreed, flushing a darker red.

'And we don't mind you being friends, so it's not like you need to have a chaperone to pass the time of day with him. We don't want you to feel like you're doing something wrong. But you are young and he's a bit older, so we're trusting you not to get yourself into any situations that wouldn't be right for someone your age, all right?'

'All right.' Liesl smiled. 'But we can spend some time together, on our own?'

'Hmm.' Elizabeth raised an eyebrow. 'Alone but in company, is that fair enough? So you can chat with him when we visit the farm, and you can even invite him here for his tea one evening if you like, but no sneaking off anywhere, just the two of you.'

'He's a nice boy. Even if we were alone, he wouldn't...' Liesl was anxious that Elizabeth like him.

'I know that, and believe me, if we thought he was otherwise, he wouldn't be coming within a donkey's roar of you, our precious girl. But hard as it is to imagine, I was once a young girl, and more to the point, Daniel Lieber was once a boy and knows what goes through the minds of young men when it comes to pretty girls.'

'Something similar to what goes through the minds of old men, I'd imagine,' Liesl responded, and Elizabeth pealed with laughter.

'You are one hundred percent correct, my love. That's exactly what they think about, so as the nuns would say, it is up to us much more sensible female creatures to curb the worst of their carnal desires!'

'But not too much,' Liesl said with a mischievous wink.

Elizabeth chuckled as she rose and pulled Liesl up with her. 'Don't let Daniel hear that, or he'll have poor Ben thinning turnips until he's so exhausted all he'll think about is sleep!'

CHAPTER 18

*a*riella was rooted to the spot. Every fibre of her being told her
to run, but she couldn't.

Willi's strong arm pulled her inside, and she noticed that he
walked with crutches – one leg was gone from the knee down.

She struggled to take in the scene. Frau Braun was in the kitchen,
nursing a wound on her face – the door from the hall was open so
Ariella could see her. Willi went to her, examined the cut and held a
blood-soaked cloth to it, but that was not what was most shocking.

On the floor, in the middle of the narrow hall, was Herr Braun,
blood congealing on his head. He'd been shot and was clearly dead.

'What...' Ariella asked, unable to formulate additional words.

Willi looked at her while still tending to his mother. 'I came back
to find him attacking her. I just...'

She could tell he was going into shock. He was deathly pale, and
his hands were trembling as he dabbed his mother's wound.

'Frau Braun.' Ariella skirted around the body and the blood oozing
onto the tiles. 'Are you all right?'

The woman who had kept her safe for four long years seemed
strangely calm. 'He found your letters and the bed in the attic. He
knew I was hiding someone. He demanded that I tell him where you

117

were. I didn't know...' She spoke as though she were in a trance. 'He attacked me, and then Willi...'

Ariella thought quickly. 'He's a Nazi official. Someone will come looking for him. We should get rid of the body.'

'No.' Willi seemed calmer now. 'Mrs Bannon, my mother told me what she did.'

Was he going to hand Ariella over, even after killing his father? He must have noted her look of terror.

'I'm so proud of her, and I'm so glad she was able to help you. Please, don't worry.' He pointed at his uniform. 'I hate this, I hate them, everything they've done. You have nothing to fear from me.'

Relief flooded through her. There was something about him; she trusted him.

'Now, let's see what we can do. I'm not sorry – he was a terrible person and the world is better off without him – but you're right, they will come looking for him. We could drag him out into the street, as there are so many dead bodies these days, but we might be seen. I have a plan.'

As Willi outlined his idea, both Ariella and his mother listened incredulously. When he'd finished, Ariella was the first to recover. 'And you're sure this friend's house is empty?' she asked.

'A hundred percent. He and his family have fled the city. He gave me the key in case I needed it. We are both involved with the White Star, a resistance movement, so he knew an empty apartment might come in useful.' Despite the gravity of the situation, Willi grinned. He was as she remembered him, a cheerful boy, now a man.

'And we just go and set up there, leaving your father's body here?' Ariella was trying to figure everything out.

'Look, people are being killed every day. There is no possibility of them knowing who did it, and I'm sure a man like Hubert Braun has plenty of enemies. We leave him here and say nothing. People will just assume we've fled the city. Nobody round here will care anyway – they have enough to worry about, and he wasn't exactly popular.

'My friend's place is on the other side of the city. We move in, you and me as a married couple and my mother. Nobody will bat an eyelid. If anyone asks, we were sent there by the housing authority after we were bombed out – me being a wounded veteran fighting for the glorious Reich meant we got a nice place. We'll let on we are well connected, and nobody will dare question it.'

She agreed, and together they cleaned up the still traumatised Frau Braun as best they could. Her husband had punched her full in the face and had been wearing a ring, so he'd cut her badly. Ariella went upstairs, got her some clean clothes and discarded the blood-spattered ones. She helped her dress while Willi packed a bag of anything he could put his hands on. They would not be coming back.

As they went to leave, Frau Braun pointed to a framed photograph of a little boy on a tricycle; it was of Willi aged around five. 'Bring that, and the one of you with the football cup upstairs beside the bed.'

With a mock groan, Willi gathered the photos and dropped them into the bag. 'I was a good-looking kid, wasn't I?' He grinned.

Ariella was astounded he could be jovial, but she smiled – his grin was infectious. 'You were,' she agreed. He was as incorrigible as she remembered him.

Luckily, injured people no longer drew any attention. They let themselves out the back, neither Willi nor his mother casting even a backwards glance at Hubert's body.

The walk across the battered city felt less terrifying for Ariella now that she was with the Brauns. Her situation was only slightly less precarious, but at least she was no longer alone. They walked for over an hour. When they arrived at the apartment, it was late, and the streets were in darkness. The hallway smelled musty and of cooked cabbage, but they climbed the stairs to the second floor gratefully.

The small two-bedroom apartment was comfortable, and the family must have taken nothing with them when they left as it was fully furnished; they had just locked the door and told nobody but Willi of their plans. Ariella and Willi put Frau Braun to sleep in one room that had a single bed and warm blankets. The older woman was exhausted, and the wound on her face looked sore.

They stood in the parents' bedroom.

'Best we both sleep in here in case anyone bursts in – at least we can stick to the story. I'll sleep on the floor, and you take the bed,' Willi offered, and she agreed. She was shattered. She had no night-clothes, so she just crept under the covers as she was.

She was tired but couldn't sleep. Willi was on the rug beside her. She'd given him the quilt and had kept a sheet and a thin blanket, but she could hear him struggling to get comfortable.

'Please, this is your friend's place. You should have the bed,' she whispered, throwing back the covers.

'No, I'm fine. Go to sleep,' he whispered back.

She stood over him and saw him wince in pain. 'Is it your leg?' she asked.

He nodded. 'It got me home, though, so I'm actually grateful. Otherwise I'd be preserved in Russian snow for all eternity.' He struggled to laugh.

'Do you have anything for the pain?'

He shook his head, his teeth clenched.

She crept to the bathroom and looked in the cupboard under the sink. Nothing. The family had left, taking almost nothing – surely they had a medicine chest?

She went to the kitchen, quietly so as not to wake Frau Braun, and opened each of the doors. There was very little in the way of food, but to her relief, over the Bakelite oven was a white tin with a red cross painted on it. She opened it and found some sachets of meperidine. She remembered the dentist giving some to Peter for a savagely painful toothache. She took one and mixed the powder with a little water from the tap – the mains were thankfully still connected – and returned to Willi.

'Drink this,' she said, and he willingly swallowed it down, wincing at its bitter taste. 'It will work in a while. In the meantime, please get into the bed.'

'No.' Then he reconsidered. 'Look, this is not an untoward advance, but it's a big bed. We could share it?'

'Fine.' She got back in her side, and Willi lay on the other, fully clothed. She felt him twist and turn for a while, trying to get comfortable, but eventually he was still and snoring gently. She turned and looked at him in profile. The meperidine was working. His dark hair was longer now than was military regulation, and he looked more like the boy she remembered. With his dark curls, brown laughing eyes and olive skin, he looked more Mediterranean than German. He had been a handsome boy, and despite everything, he had retained his good looks. She drifted off to sleep herself.

Days slipped into weeks as they managed in the new apartment. As Willi predicted, nobody questioned them, and he went out and came home with a little food most days.

Willi had false papers and new ration cards made for himself and his mother, and he'd had Ariella's papers changed to indicate she was a married woman. They were now Frau and Herr Weiss, and his mother was Katrina Weiss. He even found a piece of copper that he polished and made into a ring for her. It slipped easily into the indent left by her beautiful Swiss gold band.

Once Willi's mother went to bed, he and Ariella would talk long into the night, and she found him such an easy companion. She wept for Peter and her children; he told her how much he hated his father and how he'd vowed as a boy to one day kill him for all the abuse he meted out to his mother.

He described the events of the day before she knocked on the door. He'd come back to find Hubert laying into his mother, demanding she tell him who was hiding in the attic, and something had snapped in him. Willi had endured his father's brutish behaviour for so long, and now that he was back and so proud of his Nazi connections, Willi could take no more. He took his father's pistol and shot him with it. He felt no remorse.

He told her about his involvement with the White Star since before the war, his horror at being conscripted. That a teenage group of resisters to Nazi Germany even existed was news to Ariella, and that Willi Braun was a member since the start was at such odds with the image his parents had presented to the world.

Willi explained that he refused to join the Hitler Youth, even though his father had beat him mercilessly. He hated what the Nazis stood for and so sought out the company of other young girls and boys who refused to conform. They wore their hair longer – Ariella remembered Willi's long dark hair before the war – and rejected the military look so much admired by their peers, opting instead to wear lederhosen and loose jerseys.

At night as they lay beside each other, he explained how their resistance started small – letting the tyres down of the bicycles of the Hitler Youth and things like that – but it escalated to stealing their supplies, putting water in the petrol tanks of Nazi officials and generally trying to disrupt life for the regime they so despised. As the war escalated, so did their actions.

The reason Willi's friend Walther and his family fled the apartment the Weisses now inhabited was Walther had been caught storing Allied leaflets urging people to resist the Nazis and had been arrested. He was tortured by the Gestapo, but his father got him released with a huge bribe. His parents realised the only way to save their child's life was to get out of Germany. They used the escape lines that had been set up to get out of the city, accompanied by people who knew the forests and countryside. It was incredibly dangerous and eyes were everywhere, but Ariella was heartened to hear that they'd managed to get several people out of Germany and to safety that way.

And so time slid by. The autumn came and went and the hard winter set in, making life even more unbearable. Willi did his best to keep their spirits up, even dragging a tree up the stairs at Christmas. Though it wasn't the holiday of her faith, she'd always loved the smells and sights of Germany at Christmastime. They would go tobogganing up to Teufelsseechaussee, and then she and Peter would take the children to the markets, where they had cinnamon cookies. They'd wrap their little hands around mugs of warm chocolate while she and Peter sipped cups of hot *glühwein* with schnapps.

All of that felt a million years ago. And still the war ground on ceaselessly, the promises that it was nearly over ringing hollow now. People had been saying that since last June when the Allies landed in France. The plan to hide out in the apartment as a family that had seemed ludicrous at first had been working for the last five months.

As 1944 rolled into 1945, she and Willi toasted the new year with a cup of ersatz coffee as Frau Braun slept. There were no bells to ring in the new year, but she stood and proposed a toast. 'To 1945. To peace.'

He clinked her mug and echoed her toast.

They stood there, in front of a smouldering fire – any wood he could find was wet, but it was better than nothing. He put his arms around her, and she allowed herself to lean into his embrace. He held her. Her ear was to his heart, she heard the rhythmic beat, and she relaxed against him.

'Not too much longer,' he whispered, and she nodded. 'You'll ring in 1946 with Liesl and Erich, and there'll be champagne and cake.'

The idea made her smile. 'And you, where will you ring in 1946?' she asked.

'Oh, I'll be tripping the light fantastic in one of the ballrooms of Monte Carlo,' he joked, 'a gorgeous blonde on each arm.'

'Blondes are your weakness, are they?' she teased.

'Actually no.' He paused. 'Blondes don't attract me at all. Much too Aryan for my liking.'

She chuckled. He was a tonic; even in the worst of times, he could make them smile.

Willi easily reconnected with those who remained in the White Star and was active in their efforts to sabotage the Nazis. Occasionally, people stayed overnight, Jews who were submerged, and once an Allied airman who was passing through having survived being downed by the Luftwaffe – the resistance were trying to return him to his regiment.

As winter wore on, all around them the Allies were closing in. The Soviets had one decisive victory after another on the Eastern Front, the British and Americans on the west had reached the Rhine apparently, and yet the wheels of the Reich seemed to keep turning. The Nazi radio had just the other day announced the appointment of Wilhelm Mohnke as commander of the Reich Chancellery, and Willi had laughed.

'The Americans are bombing the living daylights out of them, the Russians are on the way, the Allies are cleaning the Nazis out of

Western Europe – they reckon they dropped two thousand tonnes of bombs three days ago – and still they keep up this charade.'

His mother urged him to keep his voice down. She was a bag of nerves these days, and the nights in the air-raid shelter at the corner of the street while the city was pounded hour after hour did nothing to improve the situation. She was waif thin, and even what little food they had she refused. Ariella begged her to eat, to nourish herself somehow, but it was a struggle.

'Oh, thank God you're back! We were so worried.' Both Ariella and his mother rushed to Willi as he came home after being gone all day and helped him off with his soaking coat. It was snowing lightly outside, the February cold chilling them all to the bone, and he was wet through.

Frau Braun went to get him a dry shirt and trousers as he stripped, and Ariella arranged his wet things in front of the meagre fire. Willi had managed to find some more wood and dragged it home a few days ago. It was as wet as the previous lot, smouldering rather than burning, and it had been painted with tar or something so it gave off horrible fumes, but it took the freezing sting out of the room. In desperation for some heat, they had moved both beds out into the living room as they could only heat one room. They had a paraffin ring for cooking.

Willi winced when taking off his trousers; his amputation scar looked raw and painful. They had long since used all the medicine left in the house, and Willi hadn't managed to find any more anywhere. At night it was the worst. She could feel him grinding his teeth in pain but knew he hated to be fussed over, and anyway, she had nothing to give him, so she pretended to be asleep, though her heart went out to him. He never complained.

Ariella handed him a bowl of the stew, and he took it gratefully, shovelling it into his mouth. He was so thin – everyone was, she supposed – but he was strong and had learned to navigate life on his crutches with remarkable dexterity. He wore his army uniform every day, though he despised all it stood for, because it meant he didn't come under suspicion. His army issue greatcoat was steaming as the snow melted off the shoulders in front of the fire. He was unusually silent.

'What's wrong?' Ariella asked quietly as his mother went to get him another bowl of stew. That would mean she wouldn't eat today, but there was no point in talking to her.

Willi looked at her, his face unreadable. 'The Americans are coming, but the Russians are only sixty kilometres from Berlin. The talk is that Eisenhower and Churchill will hold back and allow the Soviets to take us, and if they do, well, there will be carnage.'

'More bombing?' she asked.

'I don't know. Probably. Though they may not want to waste the bombs. The city is more or less flattened now anyway, and there's nobody left here but cripples and kids, a few old people and women, but I suppose they'll pound us again. But that's not the biggest threat.' He sounded exhausted.

'They won't need much to end it, but I'm worried for you and for my mother. What was done over there... I was there, Ariella. I saw it with my own eyes. It was horrendous. The slaughter, the viciousness of it, I...I can't describe it. What we did to them... And now their moment is here. They will exact their revenge.'

He ran his hand over his stubbled chin. 'I think you and *Mutti* should hide when the time comes. I'll try to bring you food, but it is vital you are not seen.'

Ariella didn't understand. 'But I'm a Jew,' she whispered. 'I can surely just say that. They are liberating us, not trying to hurt us...'

He smiled, the saddest smile, and her heart melted for this boy with so much goodness in him.

'You are a pretty woman, and what these Reds are promising to do to the women of Berlin... Ariella, they won't care. You are for all intents and purposes a German woman, married to a German soldier. That's all they'll see. They used to taunt us in the night out there – when they got to Berlin, our mothers, our sisters, our sweethearts, our wives, nobody would be safe from them, and their commanding officers would do nothing to stop them. They see it as a reward, revenge, I don't know...' He ran his fingers through his hair. 'What this war has made us, all of us... Ariella, the reports of what is being done in East Prussia, to the women there... They are raping all females, regardless of age, and their officers are standing by, participating even. It's not scaremongering, I promise you. It's true.'

She could see Willi wanted to spare her the gory details but needed her to understand the depth of the danger they faced.

'Despite the horror propaganda about the base nature of the Russians from that liar Goebbels, he was right about this. They will spare nobody when they get here – not you, not *Mutti*, nobody.'

She dug deep. She would survive. She had to – Liesl and Erich were waiting for her. 'Will the Reds get much resistance from the Germans?' she asked as Frau Braun returned and handed him another bowl.

He nodded, smiling his thanks to his mother for the food. 'They will, more than they expect actually, I think. Only the most faithful are still here, which makes them the most dangerous. There are various ragtag divisions of Waffen-SS, Hitler Youth, bits of army, all assembled on the Seelow Heights – a hundred thousand they are saying, but who knows if that's true or not. Over a thousand tanks too. It won't be enough, nothing like it, but it will be a bump in the road for the Russians all right.'

The idea of huge regiments of Russians invading the city both excited and terrified her. The Americans would have been much better. Were they really standing back, letting the Russians take Berlin as a prize in return for their invaluable contribution? Surely the British and Americans wouldn't be so callous? The city needed to be liberated from the evil grip of the Third Reich, not made to pay more. They had nothing left. Their home was in ruins, their families torn apart, people on the brink of starvation... And surely none of the Nazi ringleaders were even in the city any more – they wouldn't endure this torture the way the ordinary people had to.

'So now we wait?' Ariella asked, fearful of the answer.

'I suppose so. Try to stay alive and hope for the best.' He shrugged. 'How's Mutti today?' He jerked his head in the direction of his mother.

Frau Braun was so quiet these days that it startled both of them when she spoke.

'The same. Today the only thing she said was, "I don't care. I'm old, and there is nothing for us after this anyway. Russians, Americans, British, who cares? And they'll kill us. They don't care that we have suffered. We are Germans, my husband was a Party official, my son a soldier. It is over now anyway."'

'Still cheery and optimistic then?' He chuckled. Ariella laughed despite the situation.

Ariella and Willi had spoken about his mother's ever-darkening mood, and Willi did his best to make her smile. But when he was out, she hardly ate and barely spoke, convinced he wasn't coming back, though he always did.

She appeared with a cup of the tea they were making using leaves. It was fairly tasteless but it was warm. As she handed him the cup, Willi put his hand out for her to take, which she did, and he spoke sincerely to her. 'Mutti, please, just hold on. We'll get out of here, go back to the Black Forest, get a little house, and we can live there in peace, just the two of us.'

Ariella knew Willi had been selling her this idea since they'd moved to Walther's apartment. Every time she panicked, fearful that the next bomb would get them or that he had been picked up, he would reassure her with this dream. A little house in the country, just mother and son, living happily ever after. It soothed her nerves. She jumped at the slightest thing, but his plans for the future gave her a little hope.

Willi caught Ariella's eye; he needed her to back him up. His bond with his mother was lovely to see. Though she was hard and bitter, she softened around her boy, and he loved her deeply. They never spoke about his father; it was as if he'd never existed.

'Willi's right, Frau Braun. It will be over soon, and the liberating armies are civilised people. They won't want to hurt anyone except those responsible for this horror, and that's not us, not ordinary people. We will be liberated, and you and Willi can leave for the south and I'll begin the trek to Ireland to see Liesl and Erich. We'll have survived.'

She was conscious that her tone was wheedling. It reminded her of the voice she used to use to get the children to eat their vegetables or wear a coat when they were little and didn't want to. She owed both Willi and his mother so much as they'd taken an inconceivably huge risk in taking her in. She would make sure they made it too if she could.

Willi shot her a glance of gratitude.

'But my son is a German soldier. Are you stupid? They'll know who we are, they'll know who Hubert was... I don't care about me, but they will kill my boy...'

Ariella heard the note of hysteria in her voice and knew what to do. She crossed the room and knelt before the older woman. Though physical contact between the two was rare, Ariella took Frau Braun's hand in hers. 'I know how it feels to worry about your children. I know the sick feeling thinking that something has happened to them, that they are in danger. And though mine were little when I saw them last, I'm sure that doesn't change as they get older. But Frau Braun, I have an idea.'

Willi looked at her questioningly. There was some truth to his mother's concerns. He was living openly as a veteran. If an Allied soldier saw him, or someone said who he was, it could go horribly wrong. He would have no time to explain his resistance connections.

'There is a prayer, a Jewish prayer, that all Jews know. I'll teach it to you both so that when the liberators come, whoever they are, we can identify as Jews. They will know of the Nazis' treatment of our people, so they will help us. People won't have documentation – Jewish identity cards were a death sentence – so this is how we will prove we are Jews. There are lots of submerged Jews living here in Berlin alone, not to mention all over Europe, and they will want to help us. And if you can say this prayer and you know a bit about Judaism, then I think we can get out of this.'

'But we're not, and people here, they've seen Willi in a German uniform –' Frau Braun started.

'When the time comes, we will dress him as a civilian. We'll walk away from here towards the liberating army and tell them we are Jews,' Ariella explained gently.

'But will they believe that? I mean, I don't look... And anyway, I don't know, it feels wrong...' Willi said. It seemed his mind was racing.

'I don't look Jewish either. Contrary to what the Nazi propaganda machine had to say, not all Jews look the same. Trust me, I think knowing this prayer will be enough. I'll teach you about Judaism so you can answer some basic questions. And as for it being wrong, well, you helped a lot of Jews through the White Star and you helped me. There is a phrase from the Talmud that says, "He that saves one life saves the world entire." That's you, Willi, and your mother. You are righteous in the eyes of the Jews. They would want you both to survive.'

'You were circumcised when you were born,' his mother interjected.

Willi coloured at discussing such things in front of Ariella. He smiled and shrugged, looking embarrassed.

'That's good,' Ariella said, ignoring his discomfort. 'I doubt they would check, but still...'

Frau Braun exhaled raggedly, and both Ariella and Willi looked at her. The words came out slowly, painfully, as if each one was agony. 'Your mother had you circumcised, before you were mine.'

Willi's face registered confusion. 'What are you talking about? *Mutti*, maybe you –' He clearly thought she was raving, but Frau Braun raised her hand to stop him.

'It's time you knew the truth, Willi.' Her voice was strong now, more like her old self. 'You are a Jew.'

'What?' he said, confused.

Frau Braun inhaled, gathering what remaining strength she had. 'Your mother was a servant in our house. Her name was Rachel, and she was a Jew. Hubert is your father.'

'What? I don't understand... What are you talking about?'

Frau Braun rubbed her son's hair, such love in her eyes. 'I'll tell you the whole story. It is time you knew, and it might just save your precious life.' Her voice sounded stronger now.

Ariella sat beside Willi on the couch. He reached for her hand and she took it.

'I grew up in Ludwigsstadt, in the Black Forest. My father was the mayor, and my mother the daughter of a local merchant – we were the wealthiest family in the town. That was why Hubert was interested in me. I was plain, but believe it or not, as a young man, he was handsome.' There was no self-pity in her tone.

'He came from Freiburg, on the other side of the Schwarzwald.' Her voice sounded wistful, like she was losing herself in the mists of time. 'His family were nobodies, his father a drunk, his mother went with men for money. He came to Ludwigsstadt, got a job and realised I was his ticket into society. So he courted me. I couldn't believe my luck. My sisters were so jealous. He was athletic and very charming. My parents loved him too – he could turn it on when he needed to. So when he asked for my hand in marriage, he didn't just get the daughter of the wealthiest man in town, he also got a plum job running one of my father's mills and a lovely house into the bargain.'

Willi's hand tightened on Ariella's, and she wanted to reassure this brave young man, to spare him whatever he was about to hear.

'I knew he didn't love me, of course I did, though he did a good job pretending in front of my family in the early days. My papa thought I was wonderful and believed every word that came out of that lying toad's mouth. We had the big wedding, paid for by my family of course. I don't think anyone came from his side, not one person. Can you imagine it?' The question was directed at Ariella.

Ariella thought back to her own wedding day, such a happy occasion. Her parents had looked awkwardly out of place at the start, but Peter's father being his usual welcoming, open, smiling self soon melted their *froideur*. It had been a day of friends and food and music.

'No, I can't,' she said quietly, and it seemed that was enough of a response for Frau Braun to go on.

'He hit me on our wedding night. Got blood on the new dress my mother had made for me. I was so shocked. Nobody had ever hit me before. He said that I would do as I was told and that I was his wife now. All because I mentioned how kind my family was to us. He went mad, saying that he didn't owe anyone anything and that if I thought he was going to snivel and be grateful all his life, then I could forget that.'

'Why did you stay?' Willi asked, his voice sounding choked.

'I don't know. Pride? Ashamed to admit he'd used me? Worried everyone would see me as foolish for falling for his lies, as if someone like him would look at someone like me?'

Ariella longed to comfort her, even now, after all these years.

'So he carried on like that. Violent, abusive. He had affairs. People gossiped, so I knew. But when my father heard the rumours and confronted him, he wormed his way out of it. He said he was sorry, he just wanted a son so badly and I couldn't give him that.'

Willi listened intently, the lines of his face hardening.

'I thought if I could just get pregnant, have a child, then he would be happy, but... Well, he had more interest in the women he found in the bars and on the streets than in me.'

Ariella heard the pain still there.

'Then he moved one of them into our house. A housekeeper, he said. He was obsessed with her and wanted to rub my nose in it, I suppose. I'd threatened to leave him just before she arrived, told him he would lose everything, but he just laughed at me. Told me I'd never have the guts to go back, to face my father and mother with my tail between my legs, have everyone pity me to my face and laugh at me behind my back. And he was right. As if to prove the point, he moved this woman in – she was a girl, really, not a woman – and he put her in the room downstairs.'

'That is horrific. Did you not, even then, want to go?' Ariella was appalled.

'I was going to. I was going to tell my father what was going on and ask him for the money to leave, to go to another city, start fresh. But then I heard her, the girl, throwing up every morning and knew she was pregnant.'

'So what did you do?' Ariella asked, too involved now in the story to worry if she was overstepping any boundaries. Willi was silent.

Frau Braun laughed, a strange hissing sound. 'I did what I should have done from the start but for my stupid pride. I went to my father at the mill and went into the office. I told him everything, how Hubert beat me, how he and I could never have a child because we were never together in that way and how now this woman, Rachel, was pregnant.'

'And what did he say?' Ariella was intrigued.

'He offered to fire him, take everything back – the house, the job, all of it – but I told my papa that wasn't what I wanted. I wanted him to love me. It was stupid, I know, I can see that now. But I was young then and naïve, so I thought if we had a child, things would be different. My father felt so bad that he'd allowed such a man into our family, he was willing to do what I wanted, so he paid Rachel off, sent her to a nice Jewish nursing home – there was one near Freiburg – and when the baby was born, he was circumcised. A few days later, Hubert and I collected him and we moved to Berlin.'

'And that baby was me,' Willi said.

'Yes, my darling boy.'

'And my mother? What happened to her?' His voice was a dull monotone.

'She moved away, I'm not sure where. I should have asked, but I didn't want to know, and that's the truth. I had a baby, and I loved you so much. I didn't want any contact with her. I'm sorry, Willi. She was just a girl.' Her voice was pleading now, begging him not to hate her.

'Go on,' Willi said.

Frau Braun swallowed nervously. 'Having you made me braver. Hubert knew he was only enjoying the life he had because of me. My father had a stern word with him before we left, putting him on notice that if he ever touched a hair on my head again, he would use his influence to make sure Hubert Braun would suffer. My father had connections even in Berlin, you see. It worked, and when we arrived here, everyone assumed you were ours of course. My father sent us money, but only in drops, no big sums any more. He didn't trust Hubert. He got him a job with a friend of our family and warned the owner to keep a close eye on him. Hubert hated it and felt trapped. But in a way, so was I. He knew that Willi wasn't mine, so he would hold that over me, threatening to tell my son the truth, tell everyone that I'd stolen another woman's child. Of course it would have been the end for him too if he'd done it, but nonetheless, he and I were stuck together in a marriage of hatred, both afraid of how the other could destroy us.

'He knew he couldn't beat me any more. He tried, of course, but when he gave me a black eye, I called the police. As a result, Hubert was demoted at work to an even more menial job, just as my father promised. He was furious but could do nothing. We were living on money from my family. My father bought the house but kept it in his name. My husband only became a man in his own right when he joined the Party.'

'So nobody ever knew?' Willi asked.

'No. Nobody. When my father died, he took the secret with him. Even my mother and sisters didn't know – I'd begged my father not to tell anyone. I just wrote to say I'd had a baby, and they were happy. It was all fine.'

'And your husband was happy to accept this as well?' Ariella asked.

'By then he had no choice.'

'So I am a Jew,' Willi said.

Frau Braun nodded. 'Yes, you are. So let Ariella teach you her prayers because it might just be the thing that saves you.'

Willi turned to his mother, released Ariella's hand and stood painfully. He hobbled on his crutches to where she sat, dry-eyed but heartbroken.

She stood, and he towered over her. Awkwardly, still leaning on a crutch, he extended his arm, and she took a step forward and rested her head on his chest. He kissed the top of her head. 'You're my *mutti*, you always have been and you always will be. I don't know how I feel. I had no idea, but now that I know, at least I did a little bit to help. Ariella will teach us both. I'll learn it only if you will too, because whatever we do, us three will stick together, all right?'

'All right,' she muttered. 'All right, Willi. If that's what you want, then that's what we'll do.'

Shortly after that, Frau Braun got into bed, exhausted by the events of the day. Willi and Ariella sat side by side on the sofa, discussing it all. She let him talk, quietly so as not to wake his mother, as he made sense of it all in his head. Eventually, bone-tired and in pain, he lay back, staring at the ceiling. 'So we are both Jews, you and I?'

'It seems so.' She smiled, and he returned the grin.

He said nothing, but his eyes searched her face. Eventually, he put his arm around her, drawing her head onto his shoulder. He'd never done that before, but she didn't mind.

'Thank you, Ariella.' He held her close to him.

'It's I who should be thanking you and your mother. Without you –'

'Will you take care of her if anything happens?' he asked, interrupting her.

'Of course. We are bonded now, and wherever one goes, we all go, at least until we are living in some kind of normality again.'

'Thank you. She deserves some happiness, a bit of peace. She's had a hard time for so long, and I just want her to have a nice life at the end, you know?'

'I do. And I know it won't, but if anything does happen to you, I give you my word that I'll take care of her.'

He exhaled and reached over to the side table where he kept his cigarettes. Each one was precious, but he lit one now, the match illuminating his boyish face in the pitch-darkness. He inhaled and then blew out a long plume of smoke.

'And how do you feel about it, now that you know?' Ariella asked.

'I don't know. I'm all right.'

'Would you like to know more about your birth mother?' She had grown so close to him in recent months, she didn't feel like she was prying.

He sighed. 'No. I don't think I do. *Mutti* is my mother. She cared for me with all of her heart, and she even stayed with that monster because she was afraid that he would take me from her, knowing how much she loved me.'

He smoked silently for a few minutes, and a companionable silence settled over them.

'Will you stay in Germany after the war?' she asked.

'*Mutti* is too old to go anywhere now, so I'll stay with her. But after that, I don't know, America maybe?' He finished his cigarette and crushed it out on a saucer. 'How about you? I know you want to go to Ireland, get your children back, but then?'

'I've not thought that far ahead, to be honest. I just want to see them, to hug them. They are being cared for. They're happy. Maybe they'll want to stay in Ireland. I don't know.'

'They'll want to be with you,' he said quietly. 'You're their mother.'

'Maybe, but as you know, the person who raises you is your mother, not the person who gave birth to you. Maybe they'll see Elizabeth as their mother now, and who could blame them? She has been.'

'They'll want to be with you,' he repeated with such certainty that she longed for him to be right.

CHAPTER 19

*A*riella took her task seriously, drilling both Willi and his mother on aspects of Judaism each day until they could pass as reasonably devout Jews.

Willi continued to see people from the White Star and foraged around the city for food, but he insisted Ariella and his mother stay indoors. It was warming up a little and spring had sprung, but the city was entirely lawless now. It was safer if they stayed inside.

The reality of most people's existence meant they only had concern for their own problems – getting food, not getting blown to bits. The uniformity, the regimented control of society of just a few short years earlier was gone completely.

Willi said all anyone could talk about was how near the Russians were. What would they do when they got there? How would life be? People were terrified of them. News from the areas already in their control was chilling. The roads out of the city were clogged with people trying to escape the Red Army.

Ariella spoke English, so they were able to listen to the BBC on a DKE 38 radio, called a Goebbels-Schnauze by everyone. It had taken some tinkering with the frequencies, as it was only supposed to be tuned to the Nazi stations, but Willi managed to pick up the BBC faintly on it. The progress was heartening, and she was glad to hear good news about Allied advances.

They watched the evenings lengthen, and they moved the beds back into the bedrooms, so she and Willi were alone once more at night. She found herself looking forward to the evenings, when they would talk quietly in the dark. Food, while still in pitifully short supply, at least was growing again now, so what remained of the market gardens would surely produce some food soon. Someone in the resistance had given Willi a bag of oats, so they were making porridge with water. It bore no resemblance to the creamy morning bowl of goodness she used to make for the children, with cream and cinnamon and brown sugar, but at least the thin gruel filled their empty stomachs.

Willi kept them abreast of developments: the Allies were ever advancing, the Germans were decimated, the top brass were trying to broker a deal but Hitler wasn't having it. He was still in the city, a fact Ariella found incredible, and was apparently still convinced the war was winnable.

The only time a shadow crossed Willi's face was on the subject of the Russians. He didn't go into details, but he warned them time and again not to leave the apartment. They could come any day.

When his mother slept, he told Ariella of the rumours coming from the east. The stories of the tortures the Red Army were exacting on the civilian population chilled her blood.

When she wasn't drilling the Brauns on their prayers or aspects of the Jewish faith, Ariella went back to her old habits of spending the hours when she couldn't sleep quietly reciting poems in German, translating them to English, then to French, Italian and Spanish.

'What are you saying?' Willi asked one night.

'Nothing, just a poem. When I can't sleep, I translate poems from different languages in my head,' Ariella answered.

'How did you learn all those languages?' He sat up; he couldn't sleep either.

'My parents hired a governess to teach me – I didn't go to regular school – and she was fluent in many languages. My parents thought that a useful skill, so she taught me multilingually.'

'You came from money then?' he asked with a smile.

'Well, not really, but I suppose my parents were reasonably well off. My father was an academic, and my mother was an artist who didn't have much interest in children to be honest, so it was a lonely childhood. I tried to be different with my own children.'

'I think you were. I remember them, sweet little kids. I used to see you all having picnics at the park. I remember your husband too – he and I used to talk about football when I delivered your paper. I supported Hertha and he was a Union fan.'

'That's right, I remember.' She smiled at the memory. 'It's hard to imagine that life was ever normal, isn't it? That we cared about such things as football or picnics?'

'I know. It does.' He sighed.

'I wish it was over. Whatever is to come, let it come. Let's just get on with it, you know? This waiting, it feels so long.'

'Yes…' He paused. 'And no.' The words hung between them in the night air.

'Why no?' she asked.

'Because when it's over, you'll go to Ireland and we'll stay here, and this life we have made together will be over.'

'You'll miss the watery porridge and the cold?' She chuckled.

There was a long silence and then he said, 'No, but I'll miss you.'

CHAPTER 20

*B*allycreggan, 2 May 1945

Elizabeth was midway through explaining how to make a fraction into a percentage to her class, who were all looking longingly at the school football pitch as the emerald grass was buffed gently by the warm spring breeze. Their minds were on freedom, ice cream and trips to the beach. Daniel and the rabbi appeared at the door of her classroom. She threw Daniel a questioning look. School had just begun for the day, and she'd seen him at breakfast.

Her husband tapped on the glass and entered the room, beaming. The rabbi wore not his usual working clothes of black trousers and white shirt but his black jacket and overcoat as well as his hat; the warm weather was irrelevant to him today it would seem. The children knew when he dressed like that that something important was happening. His long beard had been salt-and-pepper-coloured when he arrived in 1939 but now was totally white, matching his hair. He looked every inch a Chassidic rabbi.

'Mrs Lieber, please forgive the intrusion, but I felt it was warranted today,' he said, and she suppressed a smile. She and Daniel joked about how he had learned to speak English in precisely the same archaic way he spoke German. His accent was as strong as ever, but some words had a definite Ballycreggan lilt, no doubt picked up from his two friends, Father O'Toole and Reverend Parkes.

The news about what Hitler was doing to the Jews had special resonance in Ballycreggan, the community at the farm putting a human face on the atrocities, and the locals had become increasingly protective of the group they now saw as 'their refugees'. The work on the farm was almost complete, and the entire place was practically unrecognisable. The hard functional rooms had been transformed into cosy, warm, colourful places. So many pieces of furniture were found, and quilts and cushions appeared from all quarters. Each of the twenty-five children now had their own little room, with a bed and a quilt, each child's name done in embroidery by the Women's Institute. They each had a wardrobe and a locker where their things could be kept private, and each child got to pick the colour of the paint for his or her room. The garden too had undergone a makeover. There were swings and a slide and a seesaw, and farmer Jeremy O'Rourke had donated his goats to graze an empty, fairly flat meadow. When the goats had the grass down, the boys rolled it with the heavy roller, and Daniel oversaw the manufacture of a set of goalposts. The children had helped enthusiastically after school every day, and the locals pitched in whenever they could, so the transformation was much quicker than anyone had anticipated. Even the little ones were allowed to paint the walls of the common room, so while the images were a little abstract, they added great colour. All of the children were as proud as punch.

Father O'Toole donated the parish gramophone, and some records were found in Dublin. Mrs Thomas, the village librarian, donated two boxes of books from the children's section. The project was such a success, nobody knew why it hadn't been done earlier. It had also strengthened the ties between the village and the farm.

It was quite common now to see the priest's housekeeper, Mrs Forde, giving Daniel a pot of her special marmalade to be delivered to the farm because 'the rabbi loves a bit on his soda bread' (it was special because everyone knew it contained a generous glug of poitín, the illegal spirit made with potatoes), or to see Levi delivering extra vegetables grown on the farm to the church to be distributed among the village's most needy families.

All of the children played together, and birthday celebrations were grouped in these straitened times – Elizabeth's idea – so there were four birthday parties a year held in the village hall. The year was divided into three-month sections, so if a birthday fell in the first three months, that child shared a party with all others in that time-frame. Bridie in the sweetshop did her best to provide some treats, and it was common to hear 'Happy Birthday' being sung to 'Katie and Haim and Seamus and Abraham'. Everyone pitched in what they could spare for the occasion, knowing their child would benefit when his or her time came. It was always a really jolly affair despite the depriva-tions of the seemingly endless war.

'Of course, Rabbi. Close your maths copies, children, please.'

They did as she asked, delighted with the distraction. They gazed expectantly at both the rabbi and Daniel.

'Today, my little ones, I have some very good news.' The rabbi smiled, a rare enough occurrence to pique their interest even more. 'It is not the Jewish way to delight in the demise of another, but in this one case only, I think it is justified.'

Twenty-seven pairs of eyes focused wordlessly.

'Today we have heard on the news from the BBC in London that Adolf Hitler is dead.'

The spontaneous cheering, the tears, the hugging of each other was both heart-warming and so sad. They'd lost so much. For the vast majority, that man and his horrific ideology had destroyed all they held dear.

Daniel walked to Elizabeth and put his arm around her. 'It's true, he's dead. The Germans announced it on the radio. Sombre music, fallen fighting Bolshevism or some rubbish like that. Who cares? The most important thing is he is dead.'

Relief. The war was surely over now. They would not keep going. The Russians were in Berlin, the news full of how the Germans were making one last pitched effort but that Berlin was falling to the Soviets. And now that malicious beast was dead. Surely it was just a matter of announcing it was all over?

The news over the last few days said that several high-ranking German officers were anxious to make a deal but the Allies were adamant that no such deal would be made. Unconditional surrender, with no provisos, was the only acceptable outcome. But the death of Hitler must mean that.

Liesl and Erich rose from their seats and walked into her and Daniel's embrace, tears running down both of their faces. The children had gathered around the rabbi, and now Ruth and Levi appeared too. The sounds of whooping and applause brought Mr and Mrs Morris, the principal and his wife, to the room, followed by their charges. Elizabeth and Daniel welcomed them in, and soon the room was packed to capacity. Voices of children and adults melded together in a cacophony of sound and emotion. Locals and refugees alike comforted each other and cried. The Jews were not the only ones who had suffered; so many of the young men of Ballycreggan would never come home again. After a while, the rabbi called for silence and everyone did as he asked.

'Now, little ones, this is the end. Welcome to our friends.' He held his hand up in a gesture of welcome to the Morrises and the other children. 'That terrible man is dead, he will be dealt with by Almighty God, and he will have to answer for his crimes. Soon the war will be over. Now let us pray for all those who did not live to see this day.'

He stood before them and intoned El Maleh Rachamim, the prayer for the dead. It was less well known than the Kaddish, but Elizabeth found the words deeply moving. The rabbi said it first in Hebrew and then in English, and his congregation either stood silently or allowed the tears to fall.

'God, filled with mercy, dwelling in the heaven's heights, bring proper rest beneath the wings of your Shechinah, amid the ranks of the holy and the pure, illuminating like the brilliance of the skies the souls of our beloved and our blameless who went to their eternal place of rest. May You, who are the source of mercy, shelter them beneath your wings eternally, and bind their souls among the living, that they may rest in peace, and let us say...'

The crowd responded, 'Amen,' in unison.

Elizabeth squeezed Daniel's hand, thinking of her parents, Rudi, Peter, his parents, his brother and so many more. She liked the imagery of their souls illuminating the skies.

Mr Morris then spoke up. 'Now then, boys and girls, this is such a happy day. There has been much sadness, but for now let's celebrate. The dark days of war are almost over, and we survived. And what better way to do that than by taking the rest of the day off!'

He beamed as the children whooped with delight. The solemnity wasn't gone and the reality of their uncertain futures was never far from their minds, but for today, they wanted just to be children in a world where good had won over evil in the end.

Within seconds, the classroom was vacated and only the adults remained. Father O'Toole and Reverend Parkes had driven up to the school upon hearing the news. Just last month, they'd had news that Reverend Parkes's son had been killed. He had been a captain in the Royal Navy, serving aboard the *HMS Royal Beech*. The vicar's wife had not been seen in public since.

Mrs Morris managed to produce a fruit cake she'd been saving for her niece's wedding. They moved out into the sunshine, sitting on the benches the children normally used to have their lunch, and watched the endless Europeans versus Ballycreggan football game that had begun in 1939 and was currently standing at 3,015 goals to 3,075 to the locals. The five-year score was a matter of continuous contention and argument that any sensible person would steer well clear of. With the late spring sun on their faces, the Catholics and Protestants, and Jews and Irish, English, Germans and Austrians, sat together, discussing the future, drinking tea and eating cake.

'Let's have a party tonight,' Elizabeth suggested. 'The farm looks so lovely now, and I know the children would love to show it off to everyone who donated things. What do you think, Ruth? Can we cobble together a bit of a spread?'

'Of course we can.' Ruth smiled, resting her head on her husband's shoulder. 'I'll put the word out that it's a bring-whatever-you-have, and we'll manage something.'

'Mr Morris, you'll bring your fiddle, I hope,' Elizabeth suggested. 'And would you believe Major Kilroy donated a piano to the farm? I don't know how in tune it is, but Mrs Morris might lead us in a sing-song?'

'We'd love to.' The Morrises grinned.

The day was spent in industry in Ballycreggan as word of the party spread. Baking was done, sandwiches made, and everyone was in high spirits. The death of Hitler was the first real reason to celebrate in years, and they were embracing the opportunity as a community.

Later that evening, as Mrs Morris was leading a rousing version of 'It's a Long Way to Tipperary' on the only slightly out-of-tune Brins-mead piano and the boys were playing football on the new pitch in the last of the late spring daylight, Elizabeth found Daniel on the porch, sipping a cup of coffee.

'Hiding out here so you don't have to share your secret coffee stash, are you?' she teased as she sat beside him.

'You caught me.' He grinned. Daniel was the world's most generous man – he would give anyone the shirt off his back – but he'd managed to keep a small trickle of real coffee coming throughout the war. He did regular work in Belfast for a man who was an importer, and while for almost everyone coffee was impossible to get, he kept Daniel in a small supply in return for maintenance work. It was his secret, and he only drank it alone.

'Imagine – soon we'll be able to buy it in the shops! And sugar and flour and all sorts. I'll get fat and I can't wait.' She laughed.

'I'd love you anyway. Maybe we'll both get fat and lazy when this is all over.'

'Oh no,' she joked. 'You better stay fit and handsome or I might run off with a Yank.'

He chuckled. The local girls were very much enamoured with the American soldiers stationed in Northern Ireland. The soldiers had made a headquarters at an old stately home called Langford Lodge, and the comings and goings of the Yanks were a source of tremendous interest to everyone. The local lads' noses were well out of joint when the girls seemed much more enamoured of the exotic Americans with their supplies of nylon stockings and chocolates than the home-grown variety of boyfriend.

'I'd better lay off the cake so. Mrs Forde's fruit cake was so good,' he said, patting his flat belly.

She cuddled up to him, not caring if some of the children or even the rabbi saw them. It was a special day, and they listened to the sound of happy voices all around them. 'That's because every single thing Mrs Forde makes is laced with poitín, including her cakes, and including herself if I'm honest.'

'Really?' Daniel was surprised. 'But isn't she the priest's housekeeper?'

'She is, with unlimited access to altar wine.' Elizabeth winked and Daniel laughed.

'Ballycreggan never ceases to surprise me.'

CHAPTER 21

*W*illi and Ariella knew they would have to convince his mother of the plan, but it wasn't going to be easy.

'*Mutti*, please listen. The Russians are here, and it's not safe. You and Ariella must go into hiding, just until this is all sorted out. They are running amok, and women are the targets. Their officers aren't stopping them.' Willi was pleading now.

'Her maybe.' Frau Braun nodded in Ariella's direction. 'But I have nothing to fear. They won't have any interest in a dried-up old woman.'

'I wish that were true, *Mutti*, but it's not. There are stories all over the city of rapes, attacks, on all women. Old, young, they don't care. It's about hurting the German men, paying us back. We need to get you both out of sight, just for now.'

'But where can we go? Even if I agreed to go, there is nowhere.' Frau Braun sighed. She was so fatalistic anyway, and this news would just drive her further into her dark depression.

Ariella and Willi shared a covert glance; she gave him an encouraging nod.

'Look, I know you won't want to, but I went back to our old place.

Hubert's body is gone, and we could use the attic again, where you hid Ariella all that time.'

Frau Braun snorted in derision. 'Absolutely not, that's insane. How would we get there, for a start, and there isn't room up there for one person, let alone two. No. Let her go up there if she wants, but I'm not going.'

Willi placed his hands on his mother's shoulders and looked deeply into her eyes. 'I've never asked you for anything, have I?'

She averted her eyes from his, but he gently took her chin, moving her head so their eyes met again.

'Have I?'

She sighed and shook her head.

'So I'm asking you now. Will you do this for me?'

It was his trump card, he knew. She could refuse him nothing.

'Fine,' she huffed, and he winked at Ariella over her head.

The journey across the city was terrifying. There was even more carnage now, and the Russians were everywhere. They kept to the back streets and ducked into doorways and down alleyways when they saw soldiers. Eventually, they reached the Brauns' old house. The back door was no longer hanging, having been kicked in, probably by looters, and there was a large brown stain on the tiles in the hallway where Hubert had lain. But they had no time to dwell on that. Willi helped as best he could, but it was Ariella who managed to manoeuvre Frau Braun and herself into the attic's small space.

The sight of the makeshift bed, her home for four long years, made her shudder. Not long now, she told herself. She would be free, but they had to wait for the Americans.

Willi would sleep in his old room, and he'd managed to clean it up a bit. Someone, or possibly several someones, had used it. The sheets and blankets were gone, and there were empty bottles and cigarette butts all over the floor. Luckily, they'd brought a little bedding from Walther's place, and Willi said he would go back and get more now that they were safely in the attic.

Once she and Frau Braun had managed to scramble up, in lots of ways it was as if she'd never left. Ariella felt so sad about her letters that Herman Braun had found. She'd kept them, her last physical link to Liesl and Erich, under the pillow for so long.

Each day, Willi gave them whatever food he'd managed to find – usually not much – and they drank the water from the tank. It would have been nice to keep the trapdoor open, as they could feel close to him that way, but it was too risky.

Frau Braun lay beside her, day and night, getting ever more listless. Ariella tried to encourage her to exercise, but she refused. The noise outside was never-ending. The bombing had stopped thankfully, but there were gunshots, tanks rolling by, loudspeakers with rough Russian voices, screaming...constant screaming. Willi told them what he saw when he went out, and it was blood-chilling. Apparently, the rumours were true; Russian soldiers were raping all women and girls, dragging them from their homes, attacking them right in the street. It was hard to comprehend, but it was happening. Ariella wept for her city. How much more could it endure? Surely it had been through enough?

Willi made them promise to stay where they were. He would take care of them, but they must not come out under any circumstances. She wasn't sure he was right. She wanted to approach them, tell them she was a Jew, that they all were, but he said she was being stupid and naïve. It was the only argument she and Willi ever had. He'd been unusually cranky, but she knew his leg was extremely painful and thought she smelled something putrid around him. She'd asked him if the wound looked different or if it was any worse, but he'd snapped that he was fine and hobbled downstairs. She had no choice but to close the trapdoor.

* * *

FATHER DOMINIC STOOD across the street from the church, his heart sinking. His fellow priest, Father Alphonse, was being manhandled into the back of a Russian army truck. He knew enough Russian to know they suspected him of being a Nazi collaborator. They were wrong actually. There were some of his brother priests who had not been as vocal as they should have been, but Alphonse wasn't one of them. He was a soft-spoken man, but he'd stood up to the Nazi bullies more than once. He was a pious man from Frankfurt, but that wouldn't matter now.

Father Dominic wanted to intervene but knew it would be pointless. He would just get himself thrown in the back of that truck too. Communists hadn't much sympathy for clerics anyway, and now that the city was in their grasp, he wasn't hopeful for his future.

He was bone-weary. Maybe his life coming to an end now would be a blessing. He could go home to God and leave this hell. Every day, he'd faced a new horror, and he was so very tired.

One of his parishioners, a man called Gerhardt Richter, had been shot by the Russians two days ago. The Reds had come into his house and attacked his youngest daughter, Hilde. His older girl, Anya, had been killed in a raid two months ago. Dominic had given both girls their first communions and confirmations.

Once several of the soldiers had had their way with her, the poor girl dragged her wounded father to the church, both of them bleeding, but it was too late for Gerhardt.

The loss of her father, the only one of her family left, proved too much. Poor Hilde had walked outside and approached a very drunk Russian in the street. He went to grab her, thinking his luck was in presumably, but in the melee, she took his pistol from his holster, calmly put it in her mouth and pulled the trigger. She was only nineteen.

Dominic found himself envying her, her father, her sister – all those who were gone.

The war was over. There had been an unconditional surrender. Germany was beaten. The sense of relief, or even happiness that it was all over, was notably absent because those who remained in Berlin were so terrified.

Of the purveyors of the lies, those who boasted of the glorious 1,000-year Reich, there was no sign, and all that remained of Adolf Hitler's dream was a broken people, being further brutalised by those who saw themselves as having the right to exact revenge. It was impossible to ever imagine normal life again. Perhaps if it had been the Americans or the British who'd marched on Berlin, then there might have been some chance, but now, the damage that was being done, it was beyond endurance.

His leg ached. He'd been hit repeatedly with an iron bar the last time he was taken in for questioning, and he doubted he'd ever walk again without a limp, but that was nothing compared to the others.

The priest let himself into the parochial house, and for once, it was deserted. He went to his room and then to his bookshelf and extracted the letters Ariella had written.

He felt nothing but gratitude for her bravery, and he thought of her daily. She knew he was helping others and that Stella Kübler was aware of her presence. She could have availed of his offer to hide her but took her chances instead. He prayed nightly that she survived, though he had to admit it was unlikely. He could be picked up any day himself, anything could happen, so he decided what he should do.

He grabbed a notepad and began to write. Once he was finished, he took her letters, put them all in an envelope and went to meet the British agent operating deep undercover in the city. He and the priest had exchanged information, money and even Allied servicemen over the years, so Dominic knew he could trust him to get the letters out and posted. At least he could do that much for her.

CHAPTER 22

*E*lizabeth looked at the sincere young man who'd called to see her and Daniel in such a formal way. Daniel saw Ben every day at the farm, but tonight he was dressed in smart trousers and an ironed shirt. Elizabeth knew he'd asked Ruth to show him how to iron it properly in honour of the occasion.

He cleared his throat and his cheeks flushed. 'So, Mrs Lieber and Daniel, I wanted to call to ask you both formally if I could take Liesl to the dance in the village hall to celebrate the end of the war? I promise you I would behave like a perfect gentleman, and we would be chaperoned at all times, and I –'

Daniel raised his hand to stop him. His face was stern, an emotion Elizabeth knew he didn't really feel, but he was very protective of Liesl and would have to be completely sure that this young man had no dishonourable intentions. She knew her husband liked Ben actually, but he explained to Elizabeth that he didn't want the young man to feel anything but complete terror for Liesl's surrogate father.

She thought he was being a little hard on Ben. He was a sweet boy and really smitten with Liesl, who had grown up to be a beautiful girl with an equally lovely temperament. She was serene and gentle and highly intelligent. Elizabeth thought Daniel should give her more credit, and told him so. She'd met Rudi when she was sixteen and had fallen in love, so she knew how Liesl felt.

'You're forgetting, my darling wife, that I was once a boy like Ben, and however it looked on the outside, I can assure you that when it came to pretty girls, my intentions were far from pure,' he'd said wryly as she cuddled up to him in bed.

'Well, maybe you shouldn't judge others by your lecherous standards.' She'd giggled as he caressed her. 'Not everyone is as lustful as you are, Mr Lieber.'

He chuckled and kissed her. 'Oh, we're all like this, I can assure you. Some of us just hide it better.'

He'd arranged for Ben to call and ask formally if he could court Liesl.

'And if we allow this dance – and it's a big if – you give us your word that you will collect her here at the appointed time and return her to this door within fifteen minutes of the dance ending?' Daniel asked.

'I will, Daniel, I promise.' Ben swallowed.

Elizabeth smiled at the boy. He was good-looking and she could see why Liesl was enamoured with him, but there was also a kindness to him that she liked.

'Ben,' she said, 'Liesl, like all of the children on the farm, has been through an awful lot, and as you know, her and her brother's care was entrusted to me by their mother, and now to Daniel as well, so we are very protective of them both. You seem like a nice lad, and I'm sure Liesl would love to go to the dance with you, so we'll trust you to behave properly. It's a wonderful thing that this awful war is over and that the right side won, and of course you young people should celebrate – it's a time for joy after such sorrow.' She placed her hand on Daniel's arm as he was about to speak. 'We'll call it a trial run, but let me assure you that the eyes of the village will be on you, and anything untoward will be reported to me and Daniel quicker than you can imagine. The jungle drums work very well in Ballycreggan.' She smiled to take the severity out of the warning, but it was a warning nonetheless.

'I understand, Mrs Lieber, but I swear, no matter if I was being watched or not, I would never do anything to hurt or embarrass Liesl. She's…' He blushed again. 'She's a very special girl.'

'Indeed she is, Ben. So I think…' – she looked at her husband, giving him the signal that it was time to put the poor lad out of his misery – 'we think' – and Daniel nodded – 'that it will be all right. The dance starts at seven, so pick her up here at quarter to?'

'Thank you.' Relief flooded his face and he seemed to relax before their eyes. 'That's great.' His eyes shone, and even Daniel couldn't help smiling. The boy left, presumably to inform Liesl how it all went, and Elisabeth kissed Daniel on the cheek.

'What was that for?' he asked, unused to her publicly displaying affection.

'Just for being a wonderful father.'

'Well, I'm learning as I go along, but I'm doing my best.'

'You are doing very well. I had no idea when they came to me how to be a mother, but I figured it out some kind of way. I always hope, though, that we are bringing them up the way their parents would have wanted. It is so hard to know having never met them. I mean, this is a good example. Would Ariella and Peter be appalled that their daughter was going to a dance with a boy?'

Daniel followed her out to the kitchen, where she put the kettle on to boil. It was a Saturday morning, so they had no work to go to. The children were usually busy with their friends on Saturdays, so it was their morning to have breakfast together, just the two of them.

They'd fallen so easily into the rhythm of domestic life, and they prepared breakfast together, both knowing what to do. She made tea and toasted some soda bread, while Daniel fried two eggs and put a precious piece of bacon on the pan for her. Neither he nor the children ate pork, but she loved a crispy rasher on the weekends, so Daniel insisted she have it, even cooking it for her. Some Jews would frown on that, but he didn't worry about it. His faith was deep and meaningful, but he didn't necessarily follow all the rules. He and Rabbi Frank had many discussions about it, but Daniel was his own man, and though he embraced the faith of his birth wholeheartedly, he could not subscribe to some of what he saw as the more archaic demands.

Just as they sat down, there was a knock on the door.

Erich was up at the farm since dawn – he and Simon were making a go-cart apparently – and Liesl was with Viola, though in reality the two girls were probably waiting to hear the outcome of Ben's meeting with her and Daniel. Things with Viola had settled down, and the girls were best friends again. Liesl had taken Elizabeth's advice and explained that she did in fact understand, and while yes, she and Erich had a home with Elizabeth and Daniel, they missed their family and worried about their mother. Viola had apologised and explained she was so distraught at the news of her home city that she'd lashed out and didn't mean it. The new surroundings at the farm really helped the children feel more secure, and a kind of peace had been restored. Nobody expected to hear from their families, and so it was as if the immediacy of the ending of hostilities on the 7th of May was a day for rejoicing but not necessarily anything else. They all knew that there was going to be a very long wait, and that for them, life would go on as normal.

Daniel wiped his mouth with a napkin and went to answer the door. He went out into the hall and returned moments later with an envelope addressed to Elizabeth. It had a British stamp on it, but when he handed it to her, she didn't recognise the writing. It was addressed to Elizabeth Klein.

Funnily enough, she didn't keep in contact with anyone in Liverpool despite living there for almost twenty years. She was so devastated by Rudi's death and the loss of her baby that she realised now she'd closed herself off, keeping everyone at arm's length. It was only when she came back to Ballycreggan with Liesl and Erich and met Daniel that she actually began to live again.

Elizabeth turned the envelope over; there was no return address. Brow furrowed, she took a clean knife and slit the thin envelope. Inside, there were two sheets of paper and another envelope, folded in two. That one simply said, 'To my darling children, Liesl and Erich'.

Elizabeth's hands trembled, and she found it hard to focus on the words. 'Read it for me.' She thrust the sheet of paper at Daniel, her heart pounding. Was Ariella coming for them?

Daniel extracted the two pieces of paper, laying the envelope addressed to Liesl and Erich to one side. The first one was dated the 29th of August, 1944. He read it aloud in a sombre voice.

Dear Elizabeth,

I do not have much time. I just want to thank you. Those words look so tiny, so insignificant written down, and they cannot possibly convey the depth of my and Peter's gratitude for what you have done for our family. You're an angel, and I pray that you will be rewarded in this life and the next for your unending kindness. My children love you. I give you now, to keep forever, my precious babies. Thank you, dear Elizabeth.

Ariella

Elizabeth was incapable of speech. A lump lodged in her throat, and hot stinging tears slid down her cheeks.

'Will I read the other one?' Daniel asked, and she just nodded.

He unfolded the other sheet. The address was a church on Budapester Straße in Berlin.

Dear Mrs Klein,

My name is Father Dominic Hoffer, and I am a priest in Berlin. I knew Ariella Bannon, and she wrote these letters and asked that if she did not survive this terrible war, that I would see these delivered to you and her children.

The last time I saw her, she was alive and well, and that was in August of last year, 1944. She'd spent most of the war in hiding – a kind person here hid her – but when that became impossible, she and I met and I tried to help her. She had good friends here. I cannot name names for fear of this letter falling into the wrong hands even at this late stage, but rest assured that people made enormous sacrifices to keep her safe. She left the sanctuary of my church because she did not want to endanger anyone, including me. From what I knew of her, she was a brave and strong woman, determined to be reunited with her beloved children. As I said, I have not seen her since, and I pray she survived, but as I do not know what fate awaits any of us in these dark and dangerous days, I felt I should post these letters. I will pray they are superfluous and she gets to tell the children and you in person all she wants to say.

Should her children wish it in the future – I do not know where I will be, but if I survive – I would be happy to meet with them and tell them what I knew of their mother and these years. Perhaps I can be contacted through this church. Please explain to them that she endured tremendous hardships but none of it mattered to her because she so badly wanted to be reunited with Liesl and Erich. She loved them very much and was so grateful to you, Mrs Klein, for all you did.

God bless,

Fr Dominic

Only as Daniel finished did Elizabeth allow the tears to come. He pulled her to her feet, holding her tightly as she wept.

CHAPTER 23

*E*lizabeth trembled as she held the letter addressed to the children. Liesl and Erich were in the kitchen eating their lunch, jabbering away happily. The mood since the German surrender had been jubilant; it was all anyone could talk about.

She and Daniel were in the sitting room, and Elizabeth had composed herself after the shock of the letters that morning.

'Will I bring them in here?' Daniel asked, and she nodded.

She looked around her mother's sitting room. The décor had changed since she moved in. The dark browns and greens had been replaced with lighter pastel colours and bright rugs. It was in this room that she had told the children that their father was dead. They were so young then – it was four years ago – and they had been devastated but had suspected it. He'd been missing for months before Ariella put them on the Kindertransport. Elizabeth had encouraged them to continue to write to their mother, to send her their news. She didn't think for a moment Ariella received the letters. Writing them was for the children's benefit really, to keep their spirits up and their hopes alive.

'Do.' She swallowed.

Before he left the room, he squeezed her hand. 'You can do this.'

His eyes blazed with intensity and conviction. 'This is potentially good news.'

'I know. I just don't want them to raise their hopes only to have them dashed. I...I don't know what to think, Daniel.'

'We'll tell them the truth like we always do and take it from there, all right?' He smiled and gave her shoulder a squeeze.

She nodded and returned his smile.

'Can you two come into the sitting room for a minute? We need to talk to you both.'

She heard the scraping of chairs, and within seconds, their two precious faces appeared. Liesl, just on the cusp of womanhood, and Erich looked just like a bigger version of the adorable little boy she'd collected from Liverpool Street station in 1939. Where he'd been small and stocky when she met him, he was stretching up at a phenomenal rate, his arms and legs gangly now, but his silky brown hair and dark eyes still melted her heart.

They knew something had happened.

'What is it?' Liesl asked, her voice betraying her panic.

'Sit down, darling.' Elizabeth patted the sofa either side of her, and they sat. She took one of each of their hands in hers and swallowed once more. How could she do this?

'What's wrong, Elizabeth?' Erich asked.

She inhaled and caught Daniel's eye. He was standing by the fireplace and gave her a small nod of encouragement.

'My darlings, we got a letter today from a priest in Berlin.'

'Is it about *Mutti*?' The excitement in Erich's voice tore at her heart. 'Is she safe?'

'We don't know.' Their faces, a mixture of dread and grief already, almost took her breath away. 'The letter from the priest said that he knew your *mutti* and that she was hidden for almost all of the war by somebody kind. But something happened – he didn't say what – so she couldn't stay at that hiding place. She met this priest, and he was trying to help her, but she left before he could because she didn't want to put him in danger.' Elizabeth wished she didn't sound so vague, but it was all she had.

'She might be hiding again, or coming to find us... The war is over now, so she might be on her way. She wouldn't stay a moment longer than was necessary, I know she wouldn't...' Liesl didn't sound like her usual mature self; she was the little girl Elizabeth first met again.

'Well, exactly. We just don't know, so we'll have to wait and see. But Berlin is in Russian hands now, so...' Daniel said.

'The Russians are on our side. Maybe they've brought her to somewhere safe.' Erich's eyes danced with hope. He had no inkling of the reports of the brutal treatment of the Berliners by the advancing Red Army.

'Perhaps.' Elizabeth caught Daniel's eye. 'As Daniel says, we just have to wait. But the priest was holding some letters – one to me and another to you – that he was to post if she didn't survive. He doesn't know where she is, but he felt he should post them now. He wrote one himself explaining things a little bit.' Elizabeth was wary of fanning the embers of the little glimmer of hope they had. What if it was a false hope?

'What did your letter say?' Liesl asked.

'Wouldn't you rather read your own letter?' Elizabeth asked.

'Tell me what your letter said first,' the girl insisted.

So Elizabeth stood and took the note from the mantlepiece, unfolded it and read it aloud. They sat and listened in horrified silence.

'And what did the priest's say?' Liesl managed, her arm around her brother now.

Daniel read it aloud.

'So *Mutti* wrote those letters in case she died, but she didn't and he sent them anyway? Why would he do that?' Erich's voice cracked with the strain of trying to understand it all.

Elizabeth looked at Daniel.

'I think he was worried that maybe if he didn't survive, the letters would never be sent, and then if your *mutti* did die, you would never hear from her how much she loved you both and how brave she was,' Daniel explained calmly.

'Well, yes. And wasn't she brave to not put the priest at risk like that? I've never met her, but your mother sounds like a very special woman.'

'She is,' Liesl said quietly, trying to process it all. 'But I don't understand – where is she now? The war is over. Can't she just make contact with us herself?'

Elizabeth silently begged Rudi, her parents and Peter to help her give them enough information that they understood but not too much.

'Well, like we've been explaining' – Daniel sat beside Liesl – 'the entire continent is in total disarray, so many people, millions of people, are all in the wrong place. Telephones and all that will be needed by the military, so if she survived, then it might take her some time to get in touch.'

'She might be gone to find the Americans. Bud said if he got to Berlin, he was going to try to find her, and when I wrote, I told her about Bud, so maybe she's gone to find him. I told her his regiment and everything, so maybe she asked someone where he was and is looking for him because she knows he's our friend and can help her get to us...' Erich was babbling now, clinging to the hope that his American soldier friend was helping his beloved mother. Liesl pulled him closer to her, and he clung to her as she stared silently into the middle distance.

Finally she spoke. 'Can we have our letter, please?'

Elizabeth handed it to her, and Liesl released her brother from her embrace to read it.

'Would you rather we left you alone?' Elizabeth asked, uncertain what to do.

'No.' Liesl looked at her. 'Please stay.'

Daniel remained beside Liesl and placed his hand on Erich's shoulder. The girl's hands were trembling as she opened the envelope, and Elizabeth felt her inhale before she started reading.

My darling children,

I am sitting here in Berlin, and it is the 29th of August, 1944. I have survived so far due to the kindness of Gentiles. Never forget, darlings, that people are good. I know it must seem a dark and frightening world we live in, but there is light and hope too, and I have seen that never so much as in these darkest of days. So do not despair, my lovely little ones, there is good in this beautiful world.

If you are reading this, then I did not make it through. The monstrous beast that has destroyed our people is not finished yet; in fact, he is at his most dangerous now that the end is in sight. But it is only a matter of time until he is gone for good.

Your papa and I love you more than words can ever say. I died a little the day I put you both on that train, but it saved your precious lives, and for that I am eternally grateful. I cannot imagine if you'd stayed, and knowing you were with the wonderful Elizabeth all these years has made my life so much better. I got a letter telling me you had moved to Ireland – thank you, my darlings, that meant so much. I couldn't reply for safety reasons, but getting it and hearing all about your lives in Ballycreggan... Well, it kept me alive and that's the truth.

I wish the best of everything for you both. I know you will always love and care for each other, just as you always did. I wish more than anything that I could be there to see you, to hold you in my arms, to hear your joyous voices. I want to see you so beautiful in your wedding dress, Liesl, and I want to see how my handsome little boy has grown to be just like the fine man his father was. I believe I will see those things, either in this world or from heaven.

Elizabeth is a special angel put on earth, and the day she agreed to take you both and care for you was the best day. I hear how you love her in the way you wrote about her, and so I am giving you to her. She is your mutti *now, and if it cannot be your darling papa and me looking after you, then I could not have chosen a better person.*

Your papa died because he stood up to bullies. Be proud of him, my darlings. He was so proud of both of you. I tried my very best to survive – I pictured your beautiful faces every day and night of my life since I left you – but it wasn't to be.

I love you both with every fibre of my body, heart and mind. Goodbye, my darlings. I wish you wonderful lives.

Your mutti*.*

Xxx

Liesl managed to get to the end of the letter, though she had to pause several times to steady herself. But as she uttered her mother's last goodbye, she crumpled and great racking sobs tore through her slender body. Erich was clinging to Daniel, crying into his chest. Daniel held him tightly, his own tears shining unshed in his eyes. Elizabeth held Liesl, rubbing her back and letting her cry.

CHAPTER 24

*F*ather Dominic was putting his vestments back in the wardrobe in the sacristy after evening Mass when he heard a commotion in the church. It was probably people seeking refuge, but they were usually quiet; the noise and shouting were unusual. He hurried out to find the church deserted but for several Russian soldiers, all surrounding Frau Groenig.

'Stop!' he called, rushing towards them. The old woman was trying to gather her dress around her body, but it had been torn. Their intention was clear.

One of the men shouted something at him in Russian that he didn't understand, but he pressed on. As he approached the group, a man who looked by his uniform to be more senior than the other four or five placed his hand on the priest's arm.

'She Nazi woman,' he said in broken German, then tossed his head in the direction of the soldiers, giving them the go-ahead to continue.

Father Dominic was horrified. Surely he didn't intend to rape Frau Groenig? She was in her seventies at least.

He stood four-square before the officer, towering over him, and spoke slowly in German, not knowing if the man had any idea what he was saying or not. The soldiers stopped and watched.

'She is a parishioner of this church and she works here – let her go this instant.' He tried to sound commanding, to ignore the Mosin-Nagant rifles the soldiers had slung carelessly across their backs and the overpowering smell of alcohol. The man who spoke also had a kind of sub-machine gun.

'No. She Nazi,' the man uttered again, this time more forcefully.

'Please...' Father Dominic realised he held no authority where they were concerned, so he tried to appeal to their sense of right and wrong. Though Stalin, and Lenin before him, tried to eradicate religion in Russia, the grace of God was surely not that easily erased from a culture. 'This is a house of God. Do not send yourselves to hell by committing such a sin in His house.'

'You Nazi priest, eh?' the man asked with a sneer, then translated for his men, and one or two of them laughed. Dominic noticed two of the Russians were young and seemed very uncomfortable.

'No. No, I am not. I hate what they did.' He caught Frau Groenig's eye; he had just confirmed what she always suspected. 'But this woman is not one of them. She is innocent, like most Germans are. Please, you have mothers yourselves, sisters, wives... Show some kindness and let her go.'

The officer gazed at Dominic, his cold grey eyes betraying no emotion. 'You don't know what they do in my country,' he said darkly, his accent very pronounced. 'You do not see what Nazi pig do.' He spat on the tiled floor. 'My family, my sisters, all...' – he struggled to find the words – 'all dead now, bad, bad, dead. You, Germans, not bad. They bad. Bad. She' – he pointed at Frau Groenig and opened his fist to show the NS- Frauenschaft Nazi pin he had pulled from her dress – 'have this, here.' He thumped his chest over his heart. 'She Nazi.'

With an incline of his head, the officer gave the order to his men. As three of the five soldiers descended on her, ripping her dress from her thin body, she screamed. Father Dominic lunged forward to protect her. Her scream, the gunshot and Russian laughter were the last sounds he heard.

* * *

It was no good – she would have to take her chances downstairs. They had not eaten for two days. She and Willi had had words about her going out, but surely he wouldn't just abandon them? Of course not. Something must have happened to him. Frau Braun had said barely a word; it was as if she'd given up completely.

Ariella heaved the trapdoor open. She tried to be quiet, but it was impossible to do it silently. She'd been listening, but amid the explosions, gunshots and screaming that was all anyone could hear these days, it was impossible to tell if there was anyone downstairs.

She took the rope with the knots tied at intervals and prepared to slide down, her limbs aching once more.

Outside, loudspeakers made announcements in Russian, and she was glad that her governess had taught her that language, though at the time, she'd had no interest in it. They were issuing instructions to their own men, not to the citizens of Berlin.

There were no options left. As she always did, she closed her eyes, breathed deeply in and out, and pictured Liesl and Erich. She would get to them, no matter what. She would do it.

She pushed herself off the edge with her hands and scraped the back of her thigh on a rough piece of wood. She was just registering the pain of that when she reached the bottom of the rope. She slumped on the floor. Her hands stung, and every muscle and joint ached, just like before. She dragged herself to her feet. The room swam before her; she was dizzy and weak with hunger. The door to Willi's bedroom was open, the bed unmade. A sour smell emanated from it, but there was no sign of life. She fought the urge to just lie down, to fade away, to stop fighting.

Above her, Frau Braun's face appeared in the trapdoor opening. 'Is Willi there?' she whispered, her voice weak.

'He's not in his room. I'm going to check downstairs,' she whispered back, pulling herself up using the bannister. 'Pull the rope up and slide the trapdoor over again, just in case.'

She crept downstairs, gripping the wall for support. The spring breeze was blowing through the now mostly glassless windows, and the house seemed silent. She gingerly opened the kitchen door and jumped when a rat ran across the floor. There was no sign of anyone having been there for days. She opened cupboards, desperate to find some food, anything at all.

She remembered Willi asking his mother if she still had jars of pickles in the pantry, and Frau Braun had said that there might be. Willi had taken them, she assumed, but it was worth a look. The tiny pantry to the right of the kitchen was shelved, and all the shelves were bare.

Where was Willi?

She left the kitchen and tentatively entered the hallway where the body of Hubert Braun had once lain. There, in the tiny front parlour, she saw him. He was lying on the small settee, his pallor grey. Perspiration prickled his skin.

'Willi!' She ran to him.

He was barely conscious, and the smell was nauseating. She knew instantly – his leg was infected and he was trying to fight the infection but failing. She had to do something.

She ran upstairs and banged on the trapdoor. Frau Braun appeared once more, her eyes like saucers.

'Willi's ill. He's downstairs but he's not conscious. His leg is badly infected. Come down and be with him. I'm going to see if I can find some food and medicine.' She had no idea where she would go or how she would do that, but she could not just let him die.

With more agility than Ariella would have given her credit for, Frau Braun scrambled down the rope ladder. Together, they went down the stairs.

The smell in the sitting room was horrid, so they opened a window but kept the drapes closed, and Frau Braun put a cushion under her son's head, all the while murmuring softly to him that he was going to be all right.

'We'll give him some water and try to keep him conscious. I'll be as quick as I can.'

She stood up to leave but immediately froze. She dared not move – there were voices coming from the street outside. Russian voices.

There were three, maybe four. She could catch the odd word. 'Women, nothing, Nazi bastard.' A crude laugh.

'What are they saying?' Frau Braun whispered.

Ariella just placed her finger to her lips.

The men went on and on, talking rapidly, but she couldn't understand them. Then she heard it. 'Hitler is dead, rot in hell.' Or something like that. And a cheer.

Could it be true? Hitler was dead? Did the Russians kill him? A thought crossed her mind. These soldiers were their liberators, Hitler was dead, the war surely over... Would they not behave properly and give three Jews sanctuary?

Willi's warning rang in her ears; he had told her what had been done to all of the females the Russians came across in East Prussia. She couldn't risk it.

She wished she knew what was happening. The terrible bombing seemed to be a thing of the past, but gunshots and screaming could still be heard frequently. The house trembled constantly at the rumble of tanks moving along the main street that intersected with theirs.

She stood there, trying to decide what to do. Then she crept back to the kitchen and got a cup of water. Giving it to Frau Braun, she said, 'Give him this. Try to get it into him. I'm going to have to go out and see if I can get some medicine or a doctor...'

'They might get you.' Frau Braun's eyes betrayed the terror such a prospect held.

It struck Ariella how the tables had turned. She'd relied for so long on Willi's mother for everything, but now it seemed the formidable Frau Braun depended on her.

'I know.' She sighed. 'But if we don't fend for ourselves, we won't make it. He'll die if we don't get some help.'

'He won't make it anyway, not now. There's no point.'

Ariella was determined not to allow her to go down that road. There was a real chance he would die anyway, but she couldn't let his mother believe it. The prospect of him dying was such a horrible one, for his mother and for their safety, but also for her personally. She missed him in a way she had never anticipated. She missed the feel of his body beside hers at night, she longed to have him to talk to, she missed so much how he could make her smile, no matter how horrific the circumstances.

'And would he give up on you? Would he?' Ariella hissed. 'After all he did to try to save us all?'

Her tone shocked the other woman; she was used to Ariella being much more deferential.

'You won't find any medicine. There is none.' Frau Braun's voice was lead, but Ariella thought she heard a glimmer of hope.

'You don't know that,' Ariella said forcibly.

'Just go. Save yourself if you can, and leave me here to die alone –' the older woman said, but Ariella interrupted her.

'Alone? What are you talking about, alone?' Her temper flared. 'I'm here, Willi is here, and I am sure as hell getting back to my children. I've lasted this long – I won't give up now, not a chance. Liesl and Erich are mine, and Willi is yours. They need us to survive, so let's do this for them, shall we?'

Ariella saw the deep pain in Frau Braun's eyes and softened her tone. 'Look, I know it looks bad, and maybe you're right and there is no medicine, but we have to try, don't we? You saved me, and I will not let you or Willi down now. We are bound together now, and I won't desert you. I'll wait. The order that was just on the loudspeaker was for all personnel to report to their barracks, so hopefully there will be fewer of them on the streets in a while. I'll try to clean his wound in the meantime.'

She went to the kitchen and filled a bowl with water. After tearing a piece off the already torn curtain, she returned to the small dark sitting room.

Katerin Braun sat up straight and gazed in the direction of the small window, beside which hung a framed signed photograph of Adolf Hitler. It was Hubert's pride and joy. As she dripped water into her son's mouth, an armoured wagon passed by, the vibrations causing the photo to fall off the wall. The glass smashed on the tiles of the fireplace.

Frau Braun's laugh startled Ariella. The woman cradled Willi in her arms, mopping his brow as Ariella examined his putrid leg. Gingerly, Ariella started dabbing at it, and Willi groaned.

'I actually believed that jumped-up little Austrian would make our country great again, you believe that? How stupid we were. But back then, at the start, he talked sense. We were destroyed after the last war, the British and the Americans taking everything, our money, our land, even our national pride. Nothing was left. But along comes the führer, and he says to hell with them, they can't treat us like that, and we loved him for it. Nobody will say this now, of course, but for a while, things were better than they were for years. We had jobs and money and holidays and even a car. Imagine that! And he said all this could only get better, German families' lives would get better, we could be proud again, and the only fly in the ointment was the Jews.' She shrugged. 'It made sense.'

Ariella was shocked and confused and wondered if Willi's mother was going a bit funny in the head. But Ariella had enough to worry about and Frau Braun seemed calmer when she was talking, so Ariella resisted the urge to interrupt her again.

'Look at you and your husband, for example. You didn't have to pull heavy bags of letters. No, that wouldn't have been fitting work for a nice Jewish lady. So you got to spend your days teaching your children foreign languages and arranging flowers in your fancy apartment while the rest of us worked like dogs.' Despite the harshness of the words, there was no malice there; it was simply how she saw it.

'All over the city, the Jews had the best houses, the best of everything, and we had to work for them, deliver their letters, mop their floors, clean their toilets. Why you were all so surprised is really the mystery. Jews had no idea how privileged they were and how the rest of us felt about them.' She seemed locked in a reverie.

The seconds ticked on. Ariella had never considered that Frau Braun still hated her because she was a Jew. The woman was talking like she'd forgotten who Ariella was. She tried to quell her feelings of revulsion and pain that she'd spent so much of her life with someone who saw her and her children in those terms.

'So why did you hide me if you felt that way about the Jews?'

169

'Because I thought that if I saved you, then maybe in the law of the universe or something, my boy would be safe.' She shrugged. 'I know it's stupid, but that day I saw you out on the street, I knew that if I didn't take you in, you'd be picked up and that would be that. And so in a split second, I decided.'

'You thought saving me would save Willi?' Ariella finally understood.

'My boy's mother was a Jew, so that made him one. I thought that if I saved one Jew, then maybe God, or whoever is in charge of this mess, would look kindly on my boy and spare him.' She exhaled and her shoulders slumped. 'Stupid, I know, but it was how I felt I had some control over what happened to him. I couldn't bear to lose him, you see. He is so precious to me.' She leaned over him and kissed his clammy forehead.

'And now? How do you feel about Jews now?' Ariella asked. She would do right by this woman either way, she owed her that much, but she needed to know.

'Now I think we are all just victims of a cruel world – you, your husband and children, me, Willi, the people of Germany, of Britain, France, everywhere, all of us – and the sooner we all leave this place, the better.'

CHAPTER 25

'*I*'m going to go,' Ariella whispered. The street was quiet now. She'd rebandaged Willi's wound and cleaned it up as well as she could, and his mother had managed to get some water into him.

Frau Braun just blinked. They were both undernourished. She'd have to find some food and something to fight the infection, but she also wanted to see what was happening.

The dress Frau Braun had given her that first day she sent her out into the world, which felt like years ago, was now filthy and smelly, and the jacket was not much better. She'd not washed properly or changed her clothes in so long, she knew her body odour was pungent and unpleasant.

She thought of the lovely rolltop marble bath in their old apartment, how she used to fill it with hot water, rose oil and bubbles and luxuriate for hours. Or how she would put in toy boats and rubber ducks for the children at bath time when they were little; they would spend hours playing in the soapy bubbles. She could just about conjure up in her imagination the sweet smell of her washed children, their hair soft and fragrant as they cuddled up with her and Peter on the sofa in their pyjamas. Peter would have them giggling, telling them funny stories about talking teapots and the giraffe with the short neck.

They would enjoy a cup of hot chocolate together, then brush their teeth and go to bed. How often did she and Peter stand over their sleeping babies, their hearts bursting with love for those perfect little people? That was a lifetime ago. She could picture her handsome husband easily, but no matter how she tried, she could no longer hear his voice in her head. It was as if he was moving further away. She dreamed of him sometimes at the beginning. She would wake in the attic alone, but for a split second, she would reach for him. Then the reality of where she was, of what she was, would crash over her like an icy shower.

It felt like such a long time since she'd seen Peter. He probably wouldn't even recognise her now, filthy and stinking, a bag of bones. Her curves were gone; her once-lustrous curly copper hair hung limply now.

'Please, be careful, I...' Frau Braun didn't have the words to say what she felt, and Ariella felt a wave of affection for her, the first ever. She'd had a difficult life, and it had made her hard, but underneath was a woman capable of immense love and kindness. To see how she looked at Willi, cared for him, a child that another woman would resent as evidence of her husband's cruelty, reminded her so much of how she looked at Erich and Liesl. They were both mothers, and while Ariella had enjoyed a very happy marriage, the other woman's had been miserable.

The revelation that she had taken care of Ariella because of some belief that her actions would keep Willi safe didn't detract from the bravery of her decision. She had hidden her for so long, and whatever the future held for them, they would face it together.

Ariella reached over and squeezed her hand. 'I'll be fine. I know this city like the back of my hand as I grew up here. I'll stick to the back streets. And besides, I stink so badly, I doubt even the most enthusiastic Russian would risk going near me.' She smiled, and Frau Braun patted her awkwardly on the shoulder.

There was a slim chance that some of Frau Braun's clothes still hung in the wardrobe, but she didn't dare risk it. She thought she might look when she returned. The more disgusting she looked and smelled now, the better.

'Mind yourself.' Frau Braun swallowed.

Ariella knew the other woman dreaded her leaving, but she needed to get to Father Dominic's house. He was her only hope, and he'd surely have something for them to eat and maybe even some drugs. He'd offered to help her once; hopefully he would again.

'I will, don't worry.'

On aching legs once more, the sensation horribly familiar by now, she crept down the hallway and out the back door. She stopped in the little yard, listening intently.

It was probably coming up to 8 or 9 p.m., the summer night sky clear for once of airplanes and searchlights. Berlin was subjugated, she supposed, so no further need to waste valuable bombs.

She looked up and down the deserted street before rapidly walking away from the relative safety of the Braun house. The windows of most houses were broken, an odd lonely curtain some-times hanging limply from the space.

She passed gardens, once an oasis of plants and flowers, now a scene of carnage like everywhere else. The entire city seemed to have been covered in a dusting of ash and rubble. Craters were common-place now where there were once streets and buildings. It was impos-sible to imagine Berlin ever again functioning as a city.

She kept her head down as she hurried through the streets in the direction of the Tiergarten. She would skirt around the actual gardens – they would be dangerous now, she was sure – but she could zigzag her way there by sticking to small residential streets and alleyways.

It was a warm night, and she felt the perspiration trickle down her spine, but still she pressed on.

She stopped when she saw lights ahead, a checkpoint of some kind. Russian surely, but she would have to avoid it. She retraced her steps and took a different route. She passed a few people in more or less the same state – old men, a few children, hardly any women or girls. They were all in hiding.

She couldn't risk being seen on the broad boulevard of Budapester Straße, where the Johanneskirche stood, but she thought she could get to Father Dominic's parochial house behind it by crossing through the primary school at the junction.

The school had taken a direct hit and was almost entirely in rubble, but she kept to the shadows and soon was within twenty metres of the parochial house. She felt relief; she'd made it. She stood in a doorway opposite, watching the house for signs of life. She knew Father Dominic wasn't the only priest living there but didn't know the extent to which his resistance activities were known to his fellow clerics. She didn't want to endanger him further by just turning up, but she had no choice now. Willi was gravely ill, and she desperately needed help.

Perhaps she should try to get into the sacristy of the church, her home for a while, and wait for him there? But what if a different priest came? Or Frau Groenig? Or that Stella woman? The war might be over and the Russians wielding their version of liberation like a club, but that did not mean all the Nazis suddenly changed their minds about Jews. A cornered rat is the most dangerous, as Willi pointed out, so she was not taking any unnecessary chances.

She decided that if she met anyone other than Father Dominic, she would simply use her original cover story: She was from Fallersleben and looking for her aunt and uncle.

When the street was clear, she ran across and up the path to the front door. When she left last time, Father Dominic had let her out the back way, down a narrow staircase and onto the street, and for a second, she considered entering that way. But if she met anyone, her presence there would be suspicious.

She knocked on the door, the large brass knocker making the place sound hollow as the noise reverberated across the tiled floor inside. This house seemed to have escaped unscathed, which pleased her. Poor Father Dominic was doing so much for people; she was glad he still had his house.

There was no answer, and she waited as long as she dared before turning to leave, though what she would do now she had no idea. The priest was her only hope, and roaming the streets in search of food and medicine was looking for trouble. The only other person who knew that she was still in the city was Gretel, but what could she do? She must be worried sick about her three children, because according to Willi, the Russians seemed to be seeking out the more enthusiastic of the Nazis for particularly brutal treatment.

No, Gretel was not an option either.

She racked her brain for a plan. There must be some way to get some food at least. Then she remembered – in the sacristy, Father Dominic kept bags of consecrated hosts, the little discs of bread. They were made in a convent out in the country somewhere, and he collected them in big flour bags and consecrated them at Mass. He'd explained what they were the evening she stayed there. She wondered if Elizabeth was a practising Catholic. Were her children Catholics now?

Would it be a terrible insult to the church that had sheltered her to take the bag of bread? Would it even still be there? It felt wrong. But then Father Dominic had explained that until the point in the Mass when the miracle happens – Catholics believe that the bread and wine are actually turned into the body and blood of Christ – it was just bread. So maybe it wasn't that bad. She'd have to do it anyway; it was their only option.

She knew the sacristy door wasn't locked, though if one tried it, it appeared it was. The trick was to press hard above the brass doorplate as you turned the handle. The lock had been seized for years, but if you kicked the base of the door with your foot at the same time, it would open.

'Best anti-theft system ever,' Father Dominic had joked.

The giant bear of a man, whom no amount of grooming could make look tidy, had been an oasis of calm and kindness for her when she'd needed it most. She'd thought often how sad it was that Catholic priests weren't allowed to marry. He would have made a lovely husband for someone, and she would have liked to imagine him with some nice woman to lovingly mend the holes in his clothes. She hoped he might be at the church. If not, well, perhaps she could leave a note.

She ran as quickly as she dared across the street. It was pitch-dark now, possibly ten thirty or eleven o'clock; it was hard to know. Most of the city was without power, and while the darkness was welcome, it also unnerved her.

There were very few people about. Most citizens who had survived the Nazis or the incessant bombing sensibly stayed in their homes, only venturing out when it was vital.

A Russian army truck containing several soldiers trundled past, but she pressed herself into a doorway and they didn't appear to notice her. She skirted around the church to the sacristy door, pausing only a moment to listen intently for voices from within, though it would be close to impossible to hear anything through the heavy oak door anyway.

Nothing. She pressed her left hand to the door about two thirds of the way up, turned the handle and gave the bottom corner a swift kick. It was worn smooth down there from Father Dominic doing the exact same manoeuvre every day.

The door opened, the swollen timber scraping across the tiled floor. She cringed at the noise but pushed it far enough to slip in. She didn't know if the church still had power, but she didn't risk putting the light on in case she alerted an enthusiastic parishioner, worried about the church.

She remembered the geography of the series of three rooms behind the altar. There was the room where she'd slept; it had a table and a few chairs, and sometimes parishioners met there to discuss church events. There was a life-sized statue of the Virgin Mary in one corner and several icons on the walls depicting various saints. Off that was a room where the vestments hung, different colours for different feast days, and where a bevelled hinged mirror stood, for priests to ensure their vestments were perfect before going out onto the altar. And finally off that, a room where chalices, a thurible and a selection of other gold implements of the Mass were stored in a large mahogany unit. In the base of that unit was where the bags of bread were stored. There was a sink on the wall where the items were washed before they were polished and returned to the cabinet for the next use.

Ariella felt her way, her eyes becoming acclimatised to the dark as she moved from the door through the outer room, then the dressing room and finally into the third inner room.

The almost-full moon was clearly visible through the plain glass window. The stained glass was reserved for the church only; the rooms behind were utilitarian and bare by contrast. She wondered for a moment if Liesl and Erich could see the magnificent moon as well. Were they admiring it, or were they sleeping or busy with their friends or schoolwork?

The pale grey light helped her locate the knob on the bottom section of the wooden sideboard. She pulled it, and to her delight, there was a large cream-coloured fabric bag. And yes, as she opened the cotton ribbon that tied it, she found it did contain a bag of round white discs.

She couldn't help it – she dug her hand into the bag and extracted a fistful. The dried bread was more like wafer than bread, and it tasted of nothing really, but it felt so good to swallow and chew. She sat on the ground, a cup of water from the tap beside her, and ate several fistfuls of the bread.

Once she'd had her fill, she looked at the bag. It was too big and bulky to carry across the city inconspicuously, and she wondered how she could hide it on her person to make herself look less interesting. She took the bag and retied the cotton ribbon, swallowing a last fistful of the wafers.

The bag was around ten by thirty centimetres, so she flattened the contents and wrapped it around her waist inside her dress, using her belt to tie it in the middle. She put the jacket on again. The smell from it of her own perspiration, shed and dried over several months now, caused her to wrinkle her nose. She just about managed to close the buttons. It had been so loose on her before, but now she knew she looked ridiculous, with stick-thin arms and legs yet a plump belly. It would not withstand much inspection – nobody in Berlin nowadays

177

was fat as it was impossible to be. Perhaps she might get away with looking pregnant. She placed her hands on the lumpy bag and was suddenly cast back to a different life, when she sat in their sunny apartment, her baby girl growing inside her, getting bigger with every passing day. She spent her time knitting little jackets and bootees, yellows and creams because she didn't know if it was a son or a daughter. The sheer bliss of knowing she was going to be a mother, she and Peter were going to be parents, was a delicious sensation she never lost the ability to recall. It was no less wonderous with Erich, but possibly less serene as she had her live-wire daughter to care for at the same time. She would never forget the look on Peter's face, first when she introduced him to his daughter, and three years later, his son. Did that really happen? She wondered sometimes if she dreamed it all, but she had the silvery lines on her belly to remind her...the evidence, years later, that once her womb was home to her precious babies.

She considered leaving. The ivory clockface on the wall told her it was now eleven fifteen, and outside on the street there were the raucous sounds of rough men's laughter. She wondered if it would be safer, less conspicuous, to go back to the Brauns' house in the morning. She could spend the night here in the sacristy as she had done before. Frau Braun would worry, but Ariella had a strong sense that her chances of returning unscathed were probably greater if she travelled in daylight. Another advantage of staying was she would surely see Father Dominic in the morning when he came to say Mass. He might have some ideas about medicine for Willi.

She found to her delight that the blanket and cushion she had used before were tucked under the small bench, so she pulled them out and lay down. The blanket smelled unfamiliar, and she wondered as she drifted off to sleep how many people had found sanctuary in the church since she last slept there.

CHAPTER 26

'What do you think?' Elizabeth asked Daniel quietly after she outlined her idea. 'Erich hasn't slept properly for weeks now. And the last sighting of Ariella was nearly a year ago, so we have no way of knowing if she survived or not. Should we suggest it and leave it up to them? Or forget it as an idea? Even if we go ahead, it wouldn't change anything when or if Ariella comes back. She's their mother and she'd obviously be their parent, and anything we would have done would be secondary to that. But it might make them feel less at sea? Or is it a horrible idea?'

Since the arrival of the letter, Erich had nightmares every night, always the same thing – that the Nazis had his mother and were hurting her and nobody would stop them, and that he and Liesl were put back on the train to Berlin alone. She'd hoped the letters would have given them hope, but they instead had unsettled them both, Erich especially. Every night, either she or Daniel ended up sitting beside him, stroking his hair and hushing him back to sleep. He woke each morning exhausted. He barely spoke and ate by rote, despite Elizabeth doing her best to make his favourite dishes.

Even though Liesl had mentioned in the past that her mother might not have survived, Elizabeth knew there was a light of hope inside the girl that somehow, somewhere, her mother was one of the lucky ones. The confirmation in the letter from the priest that she was right to hope was good, but it left so many unanswered questions.

'Is it too soon? Or is it a terrible idea at any time?' Elizabeth wanted so badly to do the right thing; she just had no idea what that might be.

Daniel considered the question, and she gave him time. 'I don't know. Perhaps suggest it and tell them we would love to adopt them but that it would be when and if they wanted it? And that when their mother comes back, then she would take over? But in the meantime, it would make things a bit more official?'

'What do you think deep down? Is she still alive?' Elizabeth asked him.

He sighed. 'I'd love to say yes, and she survived much longer than most so there's a chance, but I'd be preparing for the worst and hoping for the best.'

He sat beside her on the sofa, placing the book he'd been reading on the armrest. 'The way things are looking, I doubt many of them up at the farm will be reunited with anyone.'

The grim reality of the future of the Jewish children was becoming more sickeningly certain with each passing day. Though news of specific families was not common, each day brought new horrors from the advancing troops about the fate of those Jews unlucky enough to have been captured.

'I know. The elation of the war being over didn't last long, did it? The poor little pets. In some ways, the war going on kept hope alive, but now...' She sighed deeply. 'Erich was saying Simon was asking Mrs Simmons in the post office how long she thought a letter would take to come from Bavaria now that the war is over. The poor lad is convinced his father would not have been taken. He told Erich that when his papa left him at the railway station, he explained to him that he had an excellent hiding place for him and his *mutti* and that he wasn't to worry, that they would be fine.'

Tears came to her eyes, thinking of the incorrigible little Simon, such a toughie but soft as butter underneath.

'It was probably the only way he could get the lad to take the train. Erich had Liesl at least, but poor Simon had to come on his own, and he'd only have been seven or eight.' Daniel took her hand.

'I know. But at least they've formed such a bond though, haven't they?' she mused. 'All of them. I think they'll be each other's family for life. I hope so anyway.' She went back to her original question. 'So do we ask Liesl and Erich if they want us to adopt them?'

'I think so. Liesl is older, so it would be more of an emotional thing for her than a practical one. She'll be an adult out in the world on her own before we know it.'

Elizabeth heard the tinge of sadness in his voice and felt her heart warm. By the time she and Daniel got together, the prospect of having a family of their own was well and truly past, but Liesl and Erich had fulfilled their need to be parents in ways they never even knew existed. Daniel adored Liesl, and she confided in him often. He was her champion and regularly supported her in debates. Liesl was an intelligent girl who had lots of opinions, and rather than dismiss her ideas as foolish or immature, as Elizabeth's mother would have done to her, Daniel encouraged her to voice them. His relationship with Erich was just as warm, but he was more of a father figure to him since Erich was just eight when they met. Erich hung on Daniel's every word, and in the boy's eyes, there was nothing he didn't know or couldn't do.

'But I think she would like to be asked anyway. Perhaps we discuss it with her before talking to Erich. She's worried about him these days too, and he'll go with whatever she says anyway.' He smiled because it was true. Erich deferred to Liesl in all things.

'Can you imagine what it will be like for Erich's wife in the future? Every little thing, he'll have to ask Liesl.' Daniel chuckled.

'It won't be a problem.' Elizabeth laughed too. 'Because he would never even consider marrying a girl that Liesl hadn't approved of.'

'That's true,' Daniel agreed with a smile.

'So we'll ask Liesl tomorrow and see how she reacts, and then if she's happy, we'll ask Erich?'

181

'I think so,' Daniel agreed. He let go of her hand and stood up. 'Would you like a cup of tea?'

She smiled. Their lives were peaceful and predictable. They had a cup of tea together every night before bed, sometimes with a thin slice of cake if she'd managed to make the butter and sugar allowance stretch. There was no sign of the rationing abating even if the hostilities had ceased.

'Thank you. There's a quarter of the madeira cake I made left in the blue tin. I used all of the butter ration at Liesl's command.' She grinned. 'She says it's better to use it all and have one nice thing than a scrape you'd hardly see on several slices of bread.'

'I agree with her.' He laughed. 'I'm the same with my secret coffee. I have one full-strength cup a week and savour it. I remember Talia suggesting I make it weaker because it would last, but I'm like Liesl – I'd rather have one good cup than lots of weak ones.'

The casual way he mentioned Talia Zimmerman still made her tense. That he forgave that impossibly pretty girl who had posed as a Jew but in fact was a Nazi spy was a testament to the kind of man he was. Elizabeth tried to be as forgiving as he was, but she found it hard. Talia would have let him hang. She had set the whole thing up that if she were exposed, all fingers would point to Daniel, and if it hadn't been for a chance discovery on Elizabeth's part, the man she loved with all of her heart may well have paid the ultimate price for something he never did.

Daniel saw the shadow cross her face. 'It's all right,' he murmured. 'It's over.'

She nodded. Talia had confessed before taking a cyanide pill, so between the confession and Elizabeth's discovery, Daniel had been exonerated and released. But Elizabeth still found it hard to think about.

'So let me get that tea.' He went into the kitchen, leaving Elizabeth to her thoughts.

Ariella had given the children to her in the event of her death, but she could well still be alive. Elizabeth adored them both and thought that if Erich especially knew he was always going to have a home with her and Daniel, his night terrors might cease. But what if they thought her suggestion to adopt them was insensitive? She wanted to ease their pain, not make it worse.

She knew logically that the chances of Ariella coming to claim the children was remote at best, but she didn't allow herself to even think about that.

She'd examined her conscience on the matter of adopting them. Was there any little part of her relieved, glad even, that there was only a slim possibility that she would lose them? Did any part of her, even the tiniest bit, feel relieved that it was increasingly unlikely that there would ever be a knock on the door, and that Ariella would claim her children and take them away? These thoughts were so dark, she didn't even share them with Daniel. But she was awake most nights at three or four in the morning, these ideas buzzing around her head. She was sure now, after much soul-searching, that her motives were pure. She loved them like a mother, and she wanted nothing so much as the safe return of their beloved *mutti* because their happiness was all she cared about. If she had the choice to wave a magic wand and find Ariella Bannon alive and well, she would do it to fix those precious hearts.

CHAPTER 27

*A*riella woke to the sound of the church door opening. It was still dark outside. She sat up on the hard, narrow bench and listened intently. It couldn't be Father Dominic; he always came in the sacristy. And the church was locked...or at least it used to be. Who was there?

Frau Groenig? No, she kept her cleaning things in the sacristy, under the sink, so she would go in there first. Perhaps the priest had kept the church unlocked as a place for people to go who had nowhere; it was like something he'd do.

Ariella still had the bag of bread under her dress, but as she slept, it had slipped down. She pulled it back up again and stuffed it under the belt. She considered taking it off before sleeping but decided if she needed to get away in a hurry, it was best to have the only food she had easily accessible. She moved silently in the direction of the door that led to the altar and into the church. It was slightly ajar, and she saw to her amazement a Russian soldier sitting in the front pew, his head in his hands. He was alone, and his shoulders shook, and from where she stood, she could see he was crying.

She was torn. Should she just leave, ignore him? Father Dominic wouldn't do that. He would go and see if he could help the man. She had survived because of the kindness of strangers, and though Willi had warned her about the risk to women from the Russians, her instincts told her she was in no danger.

She walked quietly onto the altar, bowing her head as she passed the tabernacle with the exposed sacred heart lamp, and moved towards him. As she pulled the little door in the altar railing that separated the altar from the congregation, he looked up, a hunted look in his hollow eyes. He was young, no more than eighteen or nineteen, she guessed. His head was shaved, and a light stubble covered his cheeks. He was slight of build, and she thought he looked like a boy dressing up as a soldier. Her gut had been right – she was in no danger from him.

'Good morning,' she said quietly in Russian, and he looked blankly at her.

Her governess had taught her Russian at her father's behest. He wanted her to take a course in the Golden Age of Russian Literature. She'd studied Chekhov, Pushkin and Tolstoy as well as the mandatory Dostoevsky. She recalled ploughing through those heavy tomes as a girl, wishing she could read a romance or a mystery just for fun, but her parents wouldn't hear of it.

He blinked at hearing someone other than his fellow soldiers and officers address him in his native language.

'*Dobroye utro*,' he responded.

'Can I help?' Ariella asked. 'You seemed upset?'

His face seemed to crumble and tears shone in his eyes, and though his mouth moved, no sound came out.

'It's all right.' She smiled kindly at him. He wasn't much older than Liesl. 'Would you like a drink? There is some tea in the sacristy. Well, it's not tea exactly, it's some kind of dried leaves, but it is warming.' She smiled at him. 'We could talk if it would help?'

'Who are you?' he asked.

'My name is Mart –' she began, but then paused. 'My name is Ariella Bannon. I am a Jew.'

She had no idea what made her say those words, but something powerful within her felt like she wanted to reclaim her identity.

185

He looked doubtfully at her with eyes that had seen too much for one of such tender years.

'Say the Shema,' he said.

She was taken aback. His eyes bored into hers. It was the prayer she'd taught to Willi and Frau Braun.

'Say the Shema,' he repeated, this time more forcefully.

Ariella began the prayer in Hebrew, the prayer she'd learned as a little girl and recited so many times in her life she'd lost count. Her children knew it, all Jews did. Was this boy Jewish too?

'She-ma yisrael, Adonai eloheinu, Adonai echad.'

He nodded, urging her to continue. He closed his eyes as she continued in an undertone, as was the custom.

'Baruch shem kavod malchuto l'olam va-ed.'

'Shalom,' he said quietly.

'Shalom, shalom,' she replied. He was a Jew.

'How did you survive?' he asked, his voice quiet and gentle.

'I hid with my husband and his mother, and friends helped.' She cast her hand around the church. 'The priest here, Father Dominic, he was one of my friends. He should be here any moment actually, to say morning Mass...'

'Describe him,' the boy said. Something in his voice changed, making her nervous.

'Tall, very tall, wavy brown hair, in his fifties... Why?' she asked.

The boy couldn't meet her eyes. She saw him swallow, his prominent Adam's apple moving in his throat. His eyes were fixed on the image of the crucified Christ hanging behind the altar.

'He won't be coming,' he said slowly.

'What? Why not? What's happened?' What did this boy know?

She sat beside him in the dark church and listened as he told a story of a priest who was trying to defend an old woman as a Russian officer instructed his men to rape her. Only this boy and his friend refused, two Jewish boys from Siberia. His friend was shot by the drunk officer for insubordination.

Roman Grinzaid explained how they were instructed to shoot the priest and how the soldiers accidentally shot the old woman as well while aiming at him. In the chaos and shouting that ensued, he'd slipped away.

Ariella felt numb. Poor Father Dominic, dead in the last days. The war over and still he fell defending someone.

Blood thundered in her ears. How could this have happened? Father Dominic, kind, good man that he was, shot defending a woman who would have betrayed him if she could. She swallowed and forced herself to breathe normally, her grief threatening to overwhelm her.

'What did they do with his body, do you know?' she managed to ask.

He shrugged. 'I don't know. I was gone.'

'So you just went back to your regiment?' she asked.

'It wasn't my regiment. Abraham and I were on a patrol when we were instructed to take part in the attack. I escaped and went back to my barracks.'

'And just carried on?' she asked, incredulous.

'Carried on what?' His brow furrowed in confusion.

'Fighting?' She wondered why he was so bewildered.

'Fighting who? The Nazis?'

She wondered if he was a little shell-shocked as he didn't seem to understand what she was saying. But then he went on, speaking slowly as if she were the one confused.

'But they're all gone, in custody or hiding like rats down a drain now that the war is over and –'

'The war is over?' Ariella repeated his words. She could hardly believe him.

He looked at her strangely. 'Yes, the unconditional surrender happened over a week ago. How could you not know that?' Roman was suddenly suspicious. He looked worried that she might not be as she seemed.

'I've been in hiding,' she said dismissively, focusing instead on the news. 'It's really over?' Her voice sounded strange to her own ears.

'Yes, over. The Germans signed an unconditional surrender, Hitler is dead, and the Allies now control Germany completely. The Soviet Army has liberated you.'

The pride in his voice seemed so out of place in the context of the story he'd just told her. Her face must have registered her thoughts because he went on.

'Some of my countrymen are behaving very badly, very badly indeed, and there must surely be consequences, but please do not think this is how all Russians are...'

Ariella was still trying to process the news that the war was over, the Nazis had surrendered, she was free to go and find her children. The anxiety this boy felt that she not think badly of his countrymen drew her back to the here and now.

'If this war has taught me anything, Roman, it's that there is no one defining characteristic of any nationality.' Her Russian was rusty, but she found the words to say what she felt. 'We are all a mixture of everything – good and bad, brave and cowardly, kind and hateful. No one nation or people has a monopoly on anything. So yes, I know not all Russians are like the ones that killed my friend. Germans have hurt me, exiled my children, but it was also Germans who hid me, who gave me food. So I don't judge people by their nationality, only by their actions.'

He seemed relieved by her words.

'Now, I must leave you. I must go and then begin the long journey to find my children. They are in Ireland, far from here...' she explained.

'They are safe, so that is good.' He smiled for the first time.

'Yes, they are safe, and so will I be hopefully. But I need to get out of Berlin with my family. I need to get to Ireland, but I have no idea how to do that.' She was speaking to herself as much as him.

'You're free,' he said gruffly. 'You have been liberated by the Russian army, and you are now free. But it is difficult to travel. The roads are full of military vehicles and not suitable for civilians, especially women alone.' His face showed his concern. Then he lit up with an idea. 'Can you come with me?'

'Why?' Ariella was suspicious. He seemed nice, but she wasn't going to risk anything at this late stage. 'Where do you want me to go?'

'My commanding officer is a good man, a kind man. He is not a Jew like us, but he will help you. He will give you a permit with a Soviet stamp on it, which will allow you out of the city. I'll vouch for you, and he will give you the papers to get through the checkpoints. You have nothing to fear now.'

She noted the pride in his young voice; his country was liberating her and anyone like her who'd survived Hitler's hateful regime. The behaviour of some of his brothers in arms was deplorable, but he didn't want to dwell on that, and she couldn't blame him. He wanted to help her, and her gut instinct was to let him.

'One moment.' She made a split-second decision. She ran into the sacristy once more and went to Father Dominic's bureau. It was never locked and contained only his prayer book and a small lighter. He was a chaplain in the First War, he'd told her, and though he didn't smoke himself, he kept the lighter and a few loose cigarettes in his pocket. Sometimes it was the only comfort he could give those wounded, dying men. She knew he had no siblings and his parents were dead, so she took both the lighter and the book. She would keep these things, so precious to Father Dominic, for the rest of her life. If she got to Ireland, she would have a Mass said for him; that was what was done in his religion to remember and pray for the souls of those who died. She would ensure her children knew about this kind, gentle man who risked everything to save others.

She emerged back into the church once more. Roman still stood where she'd left him. Was it safe to go with him? She knew he would not attempt to assault her, but could he control his countrymen? Was it foolish to risk wandering into the lion's den? But then a Russian pass would be invaluable. She'd need one for herself, Willi and Frau Braun; it might be the only way she would get out.

She thought quickly. 'Can you get papers for my husband and mother-in-law as well? We need to go together.'

He hesitated, glancing at his watch. With an impatient sigh, he said, 'Very well, go and get them.' He seemed glad to be doing some good.

'They are on the other side of the city, and my husband is sick. I'll have to walk, but if you tell me where your barracks are, I could come there...'

He thought for a moment. 'That's not safe. I'll have to accompany you. The sun is coming up, and I need to be back at my barracks soon, but if we hurry, and I explain to my commander why I was late...' He gazed intently at her, noting her doubt. 'Don't worry, you will be safe with me. I'll protect you.'

Together, they slipped out into the street as dawn streaked across the sky. It was quicker to skirt along the railings of the Tiergarten and up to the Brandenburg Gate, so she led him on the main streets. Despite the early hour, there were people about, all looking dishevelled and destitute. An old woman and a little boy entered a house that bore a large sign that read, 'By the authority of Herr Police President of Berlin, this house has been covered in rat poison. Do not enter.' But either the old woman couldn't read it or she didn't care. A boy picked up a man's shoe and put it in his bag; even a single shoe would be worth something on the black market, she supposed.

She turned a corner and stopped. Right on the pavement in front of her was a body in a green uniform. Herman Glos. His handsome boyish face was unmarked, but the back of his head was a mess of bone, blood and tissue. People ignored him – dead bodies no longer shocked anyone – everyone scurrying about in the early morning like rats.

'Please, we must hurry,' Roman urged, and she mentally shook herself and walked on. She offered up a quick prayer for Herman's mother, the woman who raised her precious boy to be polite to ladies, just one of millions who would grieve forever.

The few buildings that still stood – those that survived first the Allied bombings and then Stalin's organs, the slang term for the deadly Katyusha rockets – were exposed. Whole walls were missing and she felt voyeuristic as she tried not to stare at living rooms and kitchens laid bare for all to see, mostly looted of their contents now.

An old man passed them on Tiergartenstraße, pedalling an ancient bicycle with no tyres, and children and adults alike scoured the gutters for cigarette butts. Willi had told her that butts had become a commodity as nobody had been able to buy cigarettes for so long. Black market cigarettes were getting enormous money from those who might still have some currency.

The Brandenburg Gate was still standing, a miracle considering all around it were rubble and vehicles in various states of destruction. Twisted metal and stone, shattered glass and despondent people were all she saw as she picked her way through the chaos. The Red Army had draped their flag, the red with the hammer and sickle, from the Reichstag.

She should have felt relief – no more dreaded swastikas – but all she felt was a deep bone-weariness. More flags, more men deciding the fate of others. What was wrong with people that they were so intent on control? If she never saw another flag again in her life, it would be too soon. All flags did was separate, show difference, one group rallying to one flag, another group rallying to another, all of it based on nothing more than what patch of earth you happened to be born on. It was all so stupid.

Draped on the gate itself was a home-made looking banner that read in Russian, 'Long live the Soviet armies that planted their victory standards in Berlin.'

She and Roman shared a look, his a combination of pride and embarrassment, as a girl, no more than twelve or thirteen, saw him and bolted down a side street, clutching her thin dress around her.

Eventually, they arrived at the Brauns' house. It had taken so much longer than it used to, as clambering over debris was unavoidable now. She pushed the front door and turned to him. 'Please wait here. My mother-in-law is nervous, and I'll have to convince her to come out of hiding. Please wait for us. I'll be as quick as I can.'

He did as she asked, and she went into the sitting room, the bag of communion hosts still around her waist. She would give Frau Braun some of those to eat.

She knew Roman didn't speak much German, just a word or two, and she spoke rapidly. 'Frau Braun, listen carefully. The war is over. There is a Russian outside. He's all right – he won't hurt us. I'm going to get us out of here. I've told him you are my mother-in-law and

Willi is my husband. His commanding officer is a good man, so he is going to help us. Is Willi any better?' She rushed to Willi's side, and his eyes opened. His fever appeared to have abated, and while he was in a lot of pain, he seemed a little better. She looked into his eyes and he smiled.

'Willi, now is the time. You and your mother are Jews – try to remember what I taught you. All right?'

He nodded with difficulty and took their forged papers out of his pocket.

'Good idea,' she whispered, and stuffed them under the cushion of the couch. They did not need them any more, and it would only complicate things further if they were found with them.

With their help, Willi managed to stand. Sweat ran down his head, but he was determined. Between them, they got him out onto the footpath outside where Roman stood waiting.

'Is everything all right?' Roman asked, taking in Willi's deathly pallor.

Frau Braun looked terrified.

'Yes, we'll be fine. Thank you, Roman. This is my husband, Willi, and his mother. And we are Jews.'

CHAPTER 28

*E*lizabeth and Daniel sat close together, waiting for the elderly judge to finish dealing with a black marketeering case in the small district court. The last time they'd been in a courtroom together, Daniel had been in real danger of being sentenced to hang for treason, and while the circumstances couldn't be more different, they were both tense. The judge seemed particularly cranky into the bargain. So far he'd dressed down a policeman who didn't have the correct paperwork and was most acerbic with a man who had four previous convictions for brawling with his brother when drunk. He'd sentenced both brothers to two weeks in jail to make them think about their stupidity and wasting police time with their nonsense. He was not a person to be trifled with, that was for sure.

Erich and Liesl sat behind them, both in their best outfits. Daniel wore a suit and tie, and Elizabeth dressed in her navy dress and jacket. All around were people with all kinds of reasons to be there, from fines for lack of dog licences to dangerous driving. She had hoped there might be a small family law court, something a little less public, but it wasn't to be. The district court sat in Bangor once a month, and all legal matters were dealt with there.

The clerk called their names. 'Mr Daniel Lieber and Mrs Elizabeth Lieber.'

They stood and were ushered to the front of the room. The clerk handed the judge a sheaf of papers. He shuffled through them and asked the clerk some questions, which neither of them could hear. The clerk seemed to answer in the affirmative.

'Approach the bench,' the judge commanded. All around them, people were coming and going, the doors constantly being opened and closed as policemen, wigged barristers, suited solicitors and members of the public mingled.

'This is an application to adopt two German children, I believe?' He gazed down at them over half-moon spectacles, his intelligent pale-blue eyes fixed on them.

'Yes, Your Honour,' Elizabeth confirmed. 'My husband and I –'

But the judge held up his hand to stop her. 'And are their parents dead?' he asked. 'You're sure of that?'

The matter-of-fact way he asked made Elizabeth cringe. Poor Liesl and Erich were still very raw.

'No, we don't know. But as I submitted with the application, I have a letter from the children's mother...' she said, hoping they couldn't hear her.

'Have I seen that letter?' the judge asked the clerk, who directed him to the bundle of papers in front of him. The clerk approached the judge and spoke in his ear for quite a long time.

'Ah, yes, I'm sorry – I had forgotten. Yes, I'm familiar with the case. You outlined your reasons in your letter very well, Mrs Lieber. And they were left in your care by their mother, is that correct?' He rifled through the papers. She'd submitted all the necessary paperwork weeks before.

'Yes, Your Honour. You have copies of the letters there in your file, I think.'

He found them and read them again, taking his time to take in each word. After what seemed like an age, he took off his glasses, laid them on the bench and observed her and Daniel. Eventually he spoke.

'Under normal circumstances, this would not be sufficient

evidence. It would be necessary to perform a legal search to ascertain if the parents had wills, which might indicate their plans for their children in the event of their death. In normal circumstances, I would also need death certificates to even consider the application.' He paused, wiped his glasses with a cloth and replaced them on his nose. 'But these are anything but normal circumstances, and I fear many more European children will find themselves in similarly precarious situations as time goes on.'

He perused the letter again and sighed deeply. 'And are the children here?' he asked as he looked up, a new softness to his eyes.

'Yes, Your Honour,' Daniel replied.

'Can you go and get them please, Mr Lieber? I would like to speak to them.'

'Of course.' Daniel turned and made his way through the packed courtroom. He beckoned Liesl and Erich towards him, reassuring them that nothing was wrong.

'The judge just wants to speak to you both. It's fine,' he whispered, walking forward with them, skirting around groups, a hand on each of their shoulders.

As they joined Elizabeth, she gave them an encouraging smile. Their faces were drawn and worried, and she hoped she was doing the right thing. They had both agreed immediately to her and Daniel adopting them. They wanted it, but it was happening because they had no hope of ever seeing their parents again, so it was all tinged with deep sadness.

'Liesl, Erich, come up here to me,' the judge said, removing his glasses once more and leaning forward on the bench. They stood immediately in front of him, a few feet away from Daniel and Elizabeth.

'Firstly, let me say how sorry I am that your daddy died. It is a very hard thing to bear even as an adult, but for a child, it is something you never really get over.' He paused and looked at each of them in turn. 'I lost my father in an accident when I was a little younger than you, Erich, so I know. It was a long time ago now, but it still hurts. So you won't ever get over it, but it does get easier to bear after a while. You'll never forget him, nor should you, but I am sure he would want you to get on with your lives and make him proud. That's the first thing.' He smiled gently at them.

'The second thing is this business of your mammy. You know the situation is that we don't know, and she could turn up any day. We hope that she will, of course, but Mr and Mrs Lieber think it might make your lives a bit less up in the air if you were adopted by them in the meantime. It might be until your mother comes, or it might be forever, you understand? What we do know is that your mammy wanted Elizabeth to take care of you, so we are following her wishes.'

Elizabeth knew he had to make crystal clear to them what was happening, and he was being as gentle as he could, but the reality was he didn't think there was much chance of Ariella being alive either.

'Now, this is an unusual case, and I need to make a decision. So to do that, I'm going to ask each of you a question, and if there is any doubt in your minds, any doubt at all, then you must tell me and we will figure it out. Do you understand? Don't worry about upsetting anyone. We all have your best interests at heart here.'

Both of them nodded.

'So I'll start with you, Erich. Do you understand what adoption means?'

Erich looked back at Daniel, who gave him an almost imperceptible nod.

'It means that Elizabeth and Daniel would be our mother and father from now on, and Liesl and I would be their children. But if our mother comes back, she would be our mother still.'

'Exactly. So are you sure you want Elizabeth and Daniel to be your new parents?'

The hubbub in the courtroom seemed to quiet down, though people were still occupied with other cases. Elizabeth found she was digging her nails into Daniel's hand.

'I'm sure,' Erich said, loudly and clearly.

'No doubts? Because this could be forever. They will be your mum and dad, just as much as your real mum and dad, if we approve this application today.'

'No doubts,' Erich said. He looked over at Elizabeth and Daniel and grinned. 'It feels like they are my mum and dad now anyway. I love them.'

Tears pricked at Elizabeth's eyes, and she felt Daniel's arm go around her shoulder. He gave her a squeeze.

The judge went on to Liesl. 'So, Liesl, you are almost an adult, so you don't have to do this if you don't want to. Please answer the same question. Are you happy for Mr and Mrs Lieber to adopt you, to become Liesl Lieber?'

They'd talked about the children's names, and both she and Daniel said that if they wanted to continue to use their Bannon name, then that was absolutely fine. But they both said they wanted to change to Lieber. Their reasoning was it would feel like they were a proper family if they all had the same name.

'I am.' She smiled.

'Well, then, that's the really important people taken care of.' He winked at Erich and Liesl and then beckoned Daniel and Elizabeth to stand beside the children.

'So, Mr and Mrs Lieber, this is a very serious undertaking. I hope you both understand that. I know you have been acting *in loco parentis*, that is, in the place of their parents, as we say, for several years now, but nonetheless, this is different. Do you both give me your word of honour that you will love these children as if they were your own flesh and blood? Daniel?'

'I already do, Your Honour, so yes, I give you my word.' His voice was strong and clear, his Austrian accent still there, with no doubt in his words.

'And you, Elizabeth, do you promise the same?'

Elizabeth let go of Daniel's hand and stood between the two children she had come to love as her own. 'I am their mother now, and I will be until the day I die. I hope Ariella comes back – we all do – but in the meantime, and forever, I love them from the bottom of my heart.'

The old judge nodded and handed the sheaf of papers to the clerk, muttering something to him. The clerk nodded and scurried out of the courtroom.

'So your application to adopt these children has been approved by this court. The papers will be ready for you to sign in the clerk's office. I wish you all luck and happiness.'

'Thank you, Your Honour,' they said in unison, and arms around each other, they left the court.

'Now we have one last job to do,' Daniel said as he led them to the car.

'What?' Erich asked.

Elizabeth had promised they would be going out for their tea to a fancy hotel and that they could order whatever they wanted to celebrate, and he was anxious to get there.

'It's a surprise.' He and Elizabeth shared a look, and both children were confused.

'A good surprise?' Liesl asked.

'I hope so,' Daniel responded as he started the engine. They were going to Belfast for their tea, but they took the road back to Ballycreggan, pulling up outside their own house.

'What are we doing at home?' Erich asked, frustrated that his delicious meal was being delayed, but Liesl shooed him inside ahead of her.

Daniel led them to the back garden, where the vegetables and a few flowers were flourishing. In the back corner, where the compost heap used to be, was a small wooden bench, with beautifully carved arms and a gold plaque screwed to the backrest. Beside the bench was a hole.

Daniel went into the shed and took out a bare-rooted tree. They watched expectantly, and Elizabeth could tell he was nervous. He'd worked day and night on the bench since they got the letter from Ariella, and she knew how much it meant to him that they were happy with it.

'This is a cypress tree. It grows in Israel, but also here in Ireland, and we will call this our Etz Chaim, our Tree of Life. So we'll plant it today to commemorate two things – in honour of Ariella and Peter, your *mutti* and papa, and to mark the day we four officially became a family.'

Liesl took Erich's hand and led him to the bench, admiring the beautiful carvings on the backrest of two couples with two children between them. Screwed to the back was a brass plaque, and Erich read it aloud.

'*Ata lo bokher et ha'mishpakha shelkha hem matnat ha'el lekha, kmo she ata lahem*. It means you don't choose your family. They are God's gift to you and you to them,' Erich explained to Elizabeth, his eyes bright with tears.

Liesl moved to Daniel, and his arm went around her shoulders.

'Thank you, Daniel. It's so beautiful, and when we want to feel close to them, or talk to them, we can come out here?'

'Of course you can.' He kissed the top of her head.

Erich took the tree and gently placed it in the freshly dug and watered hole. He dug into the pile of earth beside it and shovelled it in on top of the roots, then he handed the shovel to Elizabeth. They each took a turn, and soon the hole was full. Liesl took the watering can from the shed and filled it, sprinkling the tree's new bed with water.

CHAPTER 29

*A*riella, Willi and Frau Braun walked most of the day away from the city towards the west, part of a huge procession of the destitute, the injured and the bereft. True to Roman's word, his commanding officer had taken care of them, got them a meal, had Willi seen by a doctor who gave him some medicine and arranged a lift in a military truck as far as the city boundaries.

He had also issued all of them Jewish identification cards, stating that they were victims of National Socialism and asking that they be afforded any help they needed. How meaningful those slips of paper would be in the streams of people, each searching and trying to find loved ones or get home, was unclear, but they were free. And though they were filthy and tired, it felt good. In the absence of any better ideas, they were, like everyone else, walking towards the advancing British and American Allies in the hope of getting help.

Rumour had it that Germans who'd settled beyond Germany's borders were being summarily dumped back into the defeated and destroyed country as the victorious Allies made plans to carve up and administrate what remained of the glorious 1,000-year Reich. Millions were displaced, and with no effective communications in operation, it was hard to envisage how the European continent would ever be anything but a chaotic mess of people all trying to get somewhere else.

Mile after weary mile they trudged. They didn't talk much but stayed close by each other all the time. They'd eaten all of the little discs of bread she'd taken from the sacristy, and they drank from streams. Ariella carried a small hessian sack containing the identity cards issued by the Russians and Father Dominic's prayer book and lighter.

There were no road signs – they'd been removed in case of an invasion – but they knew from their fellow travellers that they were on the road to Leipzig. A kind old man said that someone told him the Americans had set up a station at a town a few kilometres away and were trying to help people. Perhaps if she could get a message to Elizabeth, she could find a way to get to Ireland. She explained her plan to Willi and Frau Braun, who she'd taken to calling *mutti* now, not only for safety but also because it felt like they were family.

They covered themselves in their coats as they slept on the side of the road when they were too tired to go any further. Willi urged Ariella and his mother to rest more than him; he usually stayed awake and watched over them. He seemed to need very little sleep. The pain in his leg was still there, though the infection was clearing. He regularly hobbled off into the fields, re-emerging with some vegetables and, once or twice, a few eggs. They hated to steal – people were in such a bad way – but they needed to survive. It felt good to have him beside her; he was her strength. And eventually one night, while Frau Braun slept, she told him about what had happened to Father Dominic. She'd sobbed in his arms, the first time she'd cried in months.

On and on they walked, part of a procession of the desperate and traumatised. German military vehicles lay abandoned, twisted wrecks of metal mostly, on the sides of the road.

They came to the small town and immediately saw the lines. Her heart lifted. It wasn't the dreaded swastika, or even the hammer and sickle, but the stars and stripes flying merrily over the makeshift station in the bright sunshine. She mentally took back her earlier feelings about flags – as she hurried towards it, she'd never been so happy to see a flag in all of her life. She urged Frau Braun and Willi on, showing them the American flag. They hurried to the line. The crowds were all the way down the street and around the corner, but Ariella didn't care. They joined the back of the line and waited. Each slow inch forward was an inch closer to her children. Willi stood beside her in the line, while Frau Braun sat on the pavement and waited. As night fell, they maintained their place in the line, listening as everyone did for reports from those who'd made it to the top.

It would seem what was being offered was minimal, but then the whole situation was so overwhelming it was hard to know where to even start. Food and water were dispensed, and some trucks had been provided to transport people, but the reality was most people had nowhere to go. They'd had their houses bombed, their families had dispersed, their men were gone, presumed dead at the front, and now there were sightings of emaciated victims of the many camps making their way back to home, wherever home might be. Each story was as tragic as the next; nobody had the monopoly on heartache. But Ariella kept her spirits up with the knowledge that her request was imminently doable. She needed to get to Ireland.

'Come with me,' she blurted, surprised at herself.

'What?' Willi asked. 'Where?'

'To Ireland, come with me. We can...I don't know, start again or something... I can find my children and you and *Mutti* could get a house...'

He smiled. 'If we can get you to Ireland, we'll be doing very well. Besides, my mother is too old. She wouldn't go that far, and I can't leave her.'

Ariella's face flushed. He was right of course; she was being stupid. But just the prospect of being apart from him was horrible.

The next morning, as she finally got near to the top of the line, she saw a harassed officer in his fifties. He'd been walking intermittently down the line handing out pieces of paper, asking people to fill out their name, address and next of kin. Seeing the confusion caused because people didn't know what he wanted, she began to translate.

Once the news that she could speak both English and German came out among her fellow refugees, she was inundated with requests for help. She offered her services willingly, and this seemed to endear her to the authorities. By the time she reached the top of the queue, she'd filled out so many forms she'd lost count.

Eventually it was their turn. The weary officer beckoned her forward. 'Thanks for your help. It's so difficult with all the different languages, and everyone is so...' He ran a hand over his thinning grey hair. 'I'm Lieutenant Jeff Golden.' He stuck out his hand and she shook it.

'I can imagine. Have you been here long?' she asked.

He seemed surprised that anyone would ask about him; he was clearly used to people wrapped up in their own problems.

'Well, yes. In the Battle of Leipzig, I commanded a platoon of machine gunners. We set up covering fire to protect the infantry crossing the bridge. The last battle of the war, I believe. Anyway, what can I do for you?' His kind blue eyes showed he wanted to help but doubted that he could.

'I need to get to Ireland. My children went to Ireland in 1940. A relative is caring for them there, and I need to get there as soon as I can.'

She knew everyone's need was as urgent as hers, but she hoped because hers was a simple request really, it could be done. The rumour mill among the gathered crowds suggested that the Allies were using military vehicles and vessels to move the millions of displaced people around Europe.

She saw the doubt on his face. 'I'm happy to stay here and translate until then if that would help? I speak German, Russian, Italian, French and a bit of Dutch as well as English.'

'Well, I won't refuse your offer of help, and I can organise some food for you and whoever is with you and find you a safe place to sleep, but I honestly don't know when I could get you out. They are sending transports, but the volume of people and the number of vehicles, well, it's going to take months at least to get people where they want to be, and that's the people that have somewhere to go.'

'Well, I'll stay and help, and if any transport becomes available to anywhere west, then I can get on it?' she asked quietly. There were lots of people before her, but she had to get back to Erich and Liesl.

He shrugged and sighed, and she saw the lines of weariness on his face. 'I'll see what I can do, but I'm not promising anything,' he said, and pulled up a chair beside him. 'Have a seat. It's going to be a long shift.'

All that day and into the night, she worked, hearing stories of such horror and heartbreak she wondered if they were real. Willi helped hand out food and water, and he checked regularly on his mother. He spoke reasonable English – she'd taught him during the long nights they'd spent at Walther's, knowing it would be useful after the war – so he also helped people fill out their forms.

As midnight approached, Lieutenant Golden said they would have to close the line for a few hours and sleep. He showed them where they could get mattresses and blankets, and they found a corner in the local town hall to lie down.

She lay her mattress beside Willi's, Frau Braun on his other side, and used her hessian sack as a pillow. She felt like she would be able to sleep on a bed of nails.

She must have drifted off immediately, and when she woke to someone shaking her shoulder and whispering her name, it took her a few seconds to realise where she was.

She blinked as her eyes acclimatised to the darkness. It was still pitch-black so it must have been the middle of the night, but Lieutenant Golden was urgently insisting she wake up.

'Ariella, quietly please, come with me.'

He stood, and she saw a few people stir. Every spare inch of floor was occupied. She got up, took her bag and followed him, trying not to step on anyone.

Once outside, he turned to her. 'It would help me enormously if you stayed, of course.' He gave her a small smile. 'But this vehicle is taking these officers back to France. I've asked them to take you, but there's not much space. It will be a squeeze.'

Ariella saw the military truck, covered in khaki tarpaulin. The engine was idling, and a man in uniform was crossing the street opposite and heading to the driver's door.

'I need to get going – is she in?' he called to the lieutenant, and Ariella stood, torn.

Willi appeared. 'You're getting out? That's wonderful.' He smiled and something crossed his face. Regret? She couldn't tell.

'But I can't just leave you and –'

'Of course you can. Go, Ariella, find Liesl and Erich.'

'But what about you and your mother? You both did so much for me. I can't just abandon you... I don't want to...' She was so torn.

'We'll be fine,' he said. He was about to speak again when the driver called.

'Look, ma'am...' He checked his watch. 'I shoulda been gone forty minutes ago. I got delayed and Lieutenant Golden here asked me if I could squeeze in one more. I've got casualties and servicemen and everything back there.' He jerked his thumb at the back of the lorry.

'Please, just one minute.' Her eyes filled with tears and she clung to Willi.

'Goodbye, Ariella. Take care.' His voice was choked with emotion.

'Willi, I...' She had no words.

'Just go and find your children. You did it. Against all the odds, you made it. Well done! I'm so proud of you, Ariella.' He smiled sadly.

The driver opened the door and called again. 'OK, ma'am, let's get you outta here.'

She climbed up into the truck. There was a metal box beside the driver's seat, so she sat there.

'Write to me,' she called to Willi, but amid the roar of engines, she didn't know if he heard. As the truck pulled away, she gazed out the window, tears blurring her eyes. Willi was standing there, his arm raised in a wave.

She waved back, her heart breaking.

CHAPTER 30

$\mathcal{E}$lizabeth waited at the school gate. It was coming close to the holiday break, and the children were in high spirits. School these days was an endless hive of activity – plays, sports days, art exhibitions – and everyone was counting down to the holidays.

In a hail of chatter and laughter, the children piled out of the school bus, driven by Daniel as it always had been. He waved at Elizabeth and she returned the wave, though she'd seen him only an hour earlier.

Erich and Liesl had received a letter that morning from Bud, which put them both in high spirits. He explained how he was in Italy and had met a girl called Gabriella who he was determined to marry and bring back to Biloxi with him. When he'd been stationed at Bally-halbert, the RAF base just out on the coast, he'd fallen badly for the duplicitous Talia Zimmerman, so Elizabeth was glad to hear he was in love again. He deserved someone decent.

The children had expressed hope they'd get to see him before he went back to the United States. Elizabeth explained that the army didn't take friendships into consideration when dealing with their enlisted men, but she hoped the same. Bud had joined the British army before the Americans entered the war and would be repatriated to Britain rather than America, so there was a chance they would see him again. Elizabeth was just relieved their young American friend had made it through unscathed; they would have been devasted to lose him.

Elizabeth saw Liesl chatting animatedly with Viola as the children from the farm poured out of the bus. The girls spoke in Polish as they got their books ready for the first lesson. In reality, there was little else Elizabeth could teach them, but they were a huge help with the little ones. Liesl wanted to matriculate and go to the university to read languages, so she was studying hard. She wanted to be a translator, and Elizabeth thought she would have great aptitude for it. Though neither of the children spoke German regularly any more, she knew Liesl hadn't forgotten it, and the young woman was also fluent in French and Italian. Elizabeth often heard her practising to herself as she walked past the girl's bedroom. Liesl had asked Viola to speak to her in Polish, so she was getting a handle on that very difficult language as well. In a post-war world, when the huge undertaking of reconstructing Europe began, there would be much need for linguists, and Elizabeth saw a bright future for her girl.

The war was horrific beyond measure, and no advances in society could ever make up for the pain and grief, but Elizabeth was glad that Liesl was coming of age in a world where women were going to be taken seriously in the workplace. The expediency of the last six years saw women doing things unheard of before, and there was no way that the fairer sex were going to be happy to trot back to the kitchen and the nursery and let the men dominate industry, engineering and commerce as they did before. Women had proven they were as good as – and often better than – the men they replaced, and she hoped her gender would fight to keep their position.

That can of worms had been well and truly opened, and already she heard grumblings about women taking men's jobs, jobs that would be needed for the returning soldiers to support their families. Mr Bell, the local butcher, was one of the proponents of that view, but Elizabeth had pointed out to him as he was airing his opinions in the packed butcher shop that in fact wives were not being supported by their husbands. Quite the opposite! Women were supporting their husband's careers by caring for their children and running their households, and there was no reason whatsoever that the situation could not be reversed. Why couldn't the returning men stay at home and care for the little ones, and allow their wives to continue in the roles they were filling so adeptly? After all, they were bound to be exhausted after all that fighting. Wouldn't staying at home with children and cooking and cleaning be so much easier? She'd smiled sweetly at him.

He had blustered and silently fumed at being challenged but had no answer, and Elizabeth had given a smirking Bridget Rafferty, who was working as a forewoman in a munitions factory, a conspiratorial wink as she left with her pork chops.

Liesl was growing into a modern woman and didn't see her gender as a limitation. The romance with Ben was ongoing. He was a perfect gentleman, but already Elizabeth could see her darling girl would need something more. She was a complex and extremely intelligent young woman now, and Ben was a nice lad, but she would be surprised if it lasted long term.

Kitty Livingstone from the village was casting admiring glances at Erich as she and a few others watched the pre-lesson football match, but she might as well be howling at the moon for all the interest he had in girls yet. She was sure it would happen, and when it did, he would be a boy the girls would like, but for now he was only interested in airplanes and playing football. He was saying these days that he wanted to be a pilot, and while she didn't discourage his dreams, she thought of all the pilots lost in this last war and vowed silently that she would steer him in another direction when the time came. Unlike his sister, the books held no lure for Erich, but he was good with his hands and always helped Daniel with projects. The chances were he would follow in his adopted father's footsteps, which would suit Elizabeth just fine. She'd love both of the children to stay in Ballycreggan, but in the case of Liesl at least, that wasn't likely. The young woman had an adventurous spirit, and much as she'd love to, Elizabeth could not clip her wings. Erich, on the other hand, was a home bird.

Daniel parked the bus and jogged across the school yard. For so long, he'd done that each morning while neither of them was able to make their feelings known to the other. Though his trial for treason was horrific, in many ways, it was what forced her to admit to herself her feelings for him, and him for her. She could never have imagined being happy again, but the Bannon children and Daniel had rejuvenated her cold broken heart in ways she would never have thought possible.

He gave her a surreptitious wink as she gave her charges the warning of the first bell. It put them on notice that in ten minutes, lessons would begin and they would be expected to be at their desks ready to start the school day.

The square in Ballycreggan was busy: deliveries for the butcher, people on their way out of first Mass, Bridie from the sweetshop passing the time of day with Mrs Bell as she swept the pavement outside in anticipation of the children appearing after school with that week's sweet ration coupons. They'd heard she got a big jar of bullseyes, clove rock and toffees delivered, and excitement was high.

Nobody took any notice as the bus from Belfast rounded the corner into the square as it did every morning at that time, and nobody saw the tiny woman who alighted. She was only about four foot ten and weighed no more than a hundred pounds, with flaming red hair and wearing a cornflower-blue dress. She had no luggage except a small hessian bag.

She stood on the street as the bus pulled away from the kerb. Elizabeth rang the school bell once more, and Daniel went to get his toolbox – there was a leak in the girls' toilets that he needed to see to. The mothers who were delivering the little ones into the junior infants class moved away, going about their business knowing that their precious children were safely at school. Within moments, the schoolyard was empty, the ball kicked into the goal in a last-minute score for the locals, waiting for it all to begin again at small break at eleven o'clock.

Father O'Toole crossed from the parochial house to the chapel in preparation for the next Mass, and the mothers of the village popped in to the butcher's and the greengrocer's to get supplies for the evening meal. Johnny O'Hara, of O'Hara's Inn, purveyors of fine wines and spirits, rolled the empty beer barrels consumed over the weekend out onto the pavement; the brewery lorry would be by that morning.

The woman just stood and observed the peaceful, industrious little village. Ballycreggan seemed to her like a village from a storybook. No craters, no uniforms, no 'Keep Out' signs, none of the things that she'd seen on the long journey from Germany, through France and eventually to England, where she'd had to cross the country to get to a ferry port from whence she could get to Ireland. The journey had been long and exhausting, but people were kind and each weary mile brought her closer to Ballycreggan. War was a strange thing, she noted. Undoubtedly it brought out the worst in people, but it also brought out the best. When people saw her alone, they'd given her food and put her up in their houses, and she'd contemplated how such kindnesses, the great and the small, restored her faith in humanity.

She walked in the direction of the school. She knew Elizabeth was a teacher, so that was the best place to look. She'd sent a telegram from England, but the man in the post office said some telegrams were getting through and others weren't, and that she'd just have to take a chance.

Daniel was taking his stepladder out of the bus when he saw her marching up the hill towards the school. He froze and stared. It couldn't be?

She stopped when she saw him staring at her. For a long moment they stood, and then he approached her.

'Ariella?' Daniel asked, and she smiled.

CHAPTER 31

*D*aniel introduced himself, explaining who he was and as he extended his hand to Ariella, she walked into his arms as if she'd known him all of her life. He felt her relax against him, and a deep shuddering sigh emanated from inside her. He held her as she cried tears of relief and joy, and he simply murmured over and over, 'It is all right, you're safe now. It's all right, your children are here, they're fine, you're home.'

Eventually she pulled away from him and looked up into his face. 'Did you get my telegram?' she asked.

'No.' He looked dismayed. 'We didn't.'

She sighed. 'I sent a telegram from England saying I hoped to arrive today, but the man said the wires were not working properly so perhaps it would not go. I suppose it didn't.'

'No, we got nothing, but they will be... Well, I can't tell you how happy and relieved they'll be to see you.' Daniel was struggling to find the right words.

'They're in there?' She pointed at the school.

'They are, just starting lessons.' He had a thought. 'Look, would you mind coming to our house? There are lots of children in there in the same position as our two... I mean your two...' He coloured. He was so used to thinking of Liesl and Erich as his and Elizabeth's.

'Our two.' Ariella smiled and put her hand on his arm. 'They are ours, not just mine now.'

He smiled, realising she was not there to whisk them away instantly at least.

'Thank you.' He exhaled. 'I don't think they'd want the reunion in front of everyone, and, well, for the others too...' He didn't want to say it outright, but witnessing a happy reunion would be hard for the other children.

'Of course. Is it far?' She smiled. She'd waited this long.

'No, just up the street there. You see that big house with the yellow door?' He pointed to their home. 'It's open, just turn the handle and go on in, and I'll bring Elizabeth and the children in a few minutes.'

'Thank you, Daniel,' Ariella said calmly.

The schoolyard was deserted, all of the children at their desks. He went in to Elizabeth, interrupting her class, and as he told her the news, he watched as the colour drained from her face. She recovered quickly and sent him to get Mrs Morris to take over her classroom. She called Liesl and Erich out, and told them they needed to go home right away.

'What? Why?' Erich asked. 'School's only just started.'

'I know, sweetheart, but there is something at home you need to see.' She caught Daniel's eye over their heads, and he nodded. It was better for them just to see their mother.

Erich had been angling all summer to get a dog, and Elizabeth heard him whisper to Liesl, 'Do you think it's a dog?'

'I don't know.' Liesl was puzzled but relaxed when she saw the radiant smiles on Elizabeth's and Daniel's faces. It wasn't going to be a bad surprise.

All four of them walked out of school and up the street, Erich badgering them all the way to tell him what the big surprise was. It must be huge to take them all out of school.

Daniel opened the front door and led them into the sitting room, where Ariella stood.

The children stopped in the doorway, not believing their eyes. Ariella opened her arms wide, her beaming smile and bright eyes lighting up the whole room.

Then Erich yelled, 'Mutti!' and threw himself into her arms. She embraced him, bringing Liesl into the hug at the same time. The girl was speechless, silent tears pouring down her face as she clutched her mother. Ariella touched their faces, kissing them and marvelling at how big they'd grown. Daniel put his arm around Elizabeth's shoulder, and together they stood and watched as their beloved children were reunited with their mother. They left them to the reunion, and Daniel took Elizabeth to the kitchen.

'It's going to be all right,' he whispered. He told her of the exchange and how Ariella had called them 'our children'. Elizabeth visibly relaxed. Like him, she was both delighted and terrified.

They stood together, unsure for a while, and then decided it would be best to leave them to it. They looked in on the reunion and explained that they were going back up to the school and would see them all later.

Erich jumped up from the sofa where he'd been sitting beside his mother and hugged Daniel and Elizabeth. 'Can you believe it?' he asked them, his eyes bright. 'Even better than a dog!' He laughed.

'It is the best news in the whole world.' Elizabeth chuckled as Ariella took Liesl's hand. 'We're so happy.'

'And we can all stay here together, can't we?' A frown of worry crossed his face.

'We'll work out all of that later, but yes, everyone can stay here for as long as they want,' Elizabeth reassured him, and gently pushed him back to his mother. 'See you all in a while.'

'Thank you, Elizabeth. See you later.' Ariella spoke gently and quietly, and she was different to how Elizabeth had imagined her. She was tiny, like a little bird, and her hair was not red like some Irish people's – it was more of a burnished copper. She had sea-green eyes and an intense gaze. She was so petite and so ladylike, she reminded Elizabeth of a little porcelain bird her mother had had on the mantelpiece. But she clearly was tougher than she looked.

The rest of the day was a blur, and Elizabeth just kept busy. She tried not to think about Ariella taking the children away, and she hoped Daniel had interpreted the conversation correctly. Did Ariella really see them as Elizabeth's too? Or was that something she just said in the moment?

It was entirely her prerogative of course, but facing the stark reality of losing the children made Elizabeth feel sick. She knew that despite his assurances to her, Daniel felt the same way. He'd come in a while ago looking for a bandage because he'd sliced his thumb with a screwdriver. It was something he would never normally do, but like her, he was miles away.

They walked home together, neither even able to voice their fears. There were so many things to be ironed out, so many conversations to be had… It was hard to know where to begin.

The children were out when they got home. They were showing Ariella all around the village, so proud of their little place it nearly broke Elizabeth's heart.

Elizabeth longed to talk to Ariella, to find out her plans, but there would be time enough for that. For now though, mother and children needed just to rediscover each other.

The Morrises had assured her they would handle her class for the rest of the week if she wanted to take some time off. It was kind of them, but she needed to work. She didn't want Ariella to feel she was looming over her and the children.

She popped out and shopped and bought food with the ration books to make as celebratory a dinner as she could. Daniel brought vegetables, butter and eggs from the farm, and she baked a cake.

Ariella and the children let themselves in through the garden gate, and the children showed Ariella the bench Daniel had made and the tree they planted.

'Well?' Daniel asked as he stood behind her while she stirred the soup. Elizabeth knew exactly what he meant.

'I couldn't be happier and that's the truth,' she said, leaning against him as she felt his arms encircle her. 'Look at their faces.' She pointed out into the garden. 'How could I feel anything but joy at seeing that?'

'You are a remarkable woman, Elizabeth Lieber, do you know that?' Daniel murmured into her ear.

'She's the remarkable one, not me. To endure all she did, to survive against all the odds.'

'What now though?' he asked.

'Well, we'll have to see. It's up to Ariella really, and Liesl and Erich, what they want to do.'

'Well, there is nothing to go back for, so hopefully she'll be happy to stay here. Do you think?' he asked, and she saw the vulnerability there in his eyes. He loved them too much to let them go.

'Let's hope so. I've made up the spare bedroom for now anyway, so I suppose we just have to take one day at a time. But yes, I really hope she is happy to stay here.'

Elizabeth knocked on the window to beckon them in for dinner.

As the children went to wash their hands before gathering in the dining room, Ariella came into the kitchen to offer to help Elizabeth. It was the first time the two women had been alone since her arrival. Elizabeth found that her mouth was dry. She smiled as she cut the soda bread she'd just taken out of the oven, the aroma filling the large kitchen. Ariella was hard to read, and while Elizabeth longed just to ask her straight out what her plans were, she decided to let Ariella take the lead. There was a serenity to her, a kind of stillness that Elizabeth felt could be restful in other circumstances but for now was disconcerting.

'Can I help?' Ariella asked.

'Thanks.' Elizabeth smiled. 'But I've got everything under control, I think. Daniel was here, so he did a lot of it.'

Ariella just nodded, then inhaled appreciatively. 'What an incredible sensation.' She smiled and her face lit up; there was something otherworldly about her. 'I can't remember the last time I smelled home cooking like that. We've been eating whatever we could find for so long, but fresh-baked bread, home-made soup, and here, in your house, with my children... I wonder if it's real. Sometimes I think I'll wake up in that little attic again and it will be just another day.'

215

She smiled at Elizabeth's incomprehension. 'But I haven't told you that story yet, have I? It's a long one, but I'll get to it.'

'Take your time. It must be hard to adjust,' Elizabeth said.

'It's not hard, it's just a bit, I don't know, surreal, I suppose. I had so many days when I could have given up hope, but knowing they were here with you, happy, safe, loved – it kept me going.'

'I'm so glad you did. They've been so sad.' Elizabeth was anxious not to say the wrong thing.

'Elizabeth, I wanted to say something to you. Well, I want to say lots of things, but this is the most important for now. Liesl told me about the letters from Father Dominic and the adoption.'

Elizabeth felt the lump in her throat that had been there since Ariella got off the bus. 'We would never have done it if we'd known –' she began.

'Please,' Ariella pleaded, her voice gentle. 'You adopted them to make them feel safe. Poor Father Dominic hadn't heard from me in so long, he assumed I was dead – not an unreasonable assumption in Berlin these days, I can assure you. He's dead himself now, poor man. He was so kind. So please, do not apologise for adopting them. I gave them to you in that letter. I will never be able to thank you enough. You loved my precious children when you didn't even know me or Peter, you took them in, and I can see how much they love you and Daniel. Before coming here, I had no plan. I was just going to see how it all went. But now I know for sure I cannot take them from you, from this community. It would be too hard on them and on you. I stayed alive all of this time to be reunited with them, but not to take them away. So I have a proposal.'

'Go on.' Elizabeth's heart thumped loudly in her chest.

'I was thinking I could stay here in Ballycreggan, if that would be all right, and that we could both be a home for our children. They told me all about the farm and their friends there, and everything is so up in the air in Germany. I used to think we would live there after the war, but now... That is no place for anyone, especially Jews. It would be too hard.'

She sighed, thinking of her beleaguered homeland. 'Anyway, Peter and I made some investments in America. I don't have the share certificates, but I met our American broker a few times and he has copies. So if I contact him, he should be able to sell those shares, and I'll have some money at least to maybe buy a little house or something, and I can get a job... Also there is money in an account in Germany, but I don't know –'

Elizabeth interrupted her. 'You're family now, Ariella, and please don't worry about things like that. We have this huge house with more bedrooms than we need, so if you are happy to move in here, either temporarily or permanently, then that would be what we would all want, I'm sure.'

'Thank you, Elizabeth. That would be lovely. But I promise it won't be forever. I feel like I just want to be near them all the time, but I won't take them from you and Daniel, so that would work for all of us.'

Elizabeth felt the same way. She would never deny them their mother's love, but losing them was a heartbreaking option.

'I can never repay you.' Ariella's eyes shone with unshed tears. 'I honestly don't know how –'

'Ariella, you owe me nothing. I lost my first husband in the Great War and miscarried our child shortly after that. I never imagined for one second that I would ever love again, and I shut myself down. But because of Liesl and Erich, I had to open up my cold frozen heart. They needed love and so I loved them, and they loved me in return. I would never have come back here were it not for them, never have met Daniel, never have set up the Jewish school. So my life now, this life I love, is all down to you. If you hadn't sent them to me, having no idea what kind of person I was, well, I don't know what would have become of me. So you see, I may have saved them, but in more ways than I can even explain, they saved me too, so there is no debt to be repaid.'

'So we can share them?' Ariella asked with a smile.

Elizabeth was blinded by tears. This was the best possible outcome. 'Yes, let's share our wonderful children,' she said as she walked into Ariella's embrace.

CHAPTER 32

*T*he following weeks flew by, and gradually Ariella filled the Liebers in on the process of getting to Ireland. She told the children with gentle sensitivity how bad things were in Germany and all of Europe. She told them of displaced person's camps with hundreds of thousands of people trying to find their way home, and she urged them to tell their friends to not give up hope but also to not be impatient.

Her stories of how Frau Braun hid her in an attic, of Father Dominic, who took such risks to help those who were hunted, and about the people who worked for the White Star organisation soothed their troubled minds. Not everyone was bad; not everyone wanted their families dead.

A Mass was said for Father Dominic, and everyone attended, even the Jews. Father O'Toole gave a very moving sermon based on Ariella's recollections of the man, and on the goodness of people and how little acts of kindness were like little acorns that grew into mighty oaks. The rabbi asked Daniel to make a plaque in Father Dominic's memory to be placed in the synagogue, and Ariella was so moved when she saw it. Daniel had carved a beautiful Star of David and underneath inscribed, 'In memory of Father Dominic Hoffer, who, through his bravery and compassion, saved many Jews during Europe's darkest days.'

In the evenings, Ariella told them of Roman, of Willi and Frau Braun, of how they got by, and she managed to make it all sound more like a gigantic adventure than the gruelling terror-filled nightmare it was. Even Stella Kübler took on the characteristics of a storybook witch.

After tea one evening, Elizabeth and Ariella were in the kitchen washing up, as Daniel had to go back to the farm – the ancient boiler had breathed its last apparently, and there was no hot water.

'It would be great to hear that the Brauns were all right. You must worry,' Elizabeth said.

The two women had slipped into an easy friendship, and while at the beginning it had been a little tricky, the children not sure who the authority figure was, they soon realised they thought the same way about things. A definite no for Erich who wanted to leave school, get an apprenticeship and then join the air force, a no for Liesl who wanted to go to Belfast with a gang of boys and girls from the village to a dance at the big American base, a maybe to them getting a dog and a reluctant yes to Erich joining the big boys in jumping off the big Hangman's Rock into the sea that summer. It was an unwritten Bally-creggan rule that nobody under fourteen was allowed to cliff dive off the protruding rock that towered over the glittering sea below, and Erich had been plaguing them since the start of summer to allow him.

'I would dearly love to hear from them. I thought he – they – might have written by now, but...' Ariella shrugged, but Elizabeth could see the disappointment there.

'Tell me to mind my own business if you like, but do I get the impression there might be more than friendship between you and Willi?' Elizabeth asked with a smile.

'Oh no...' Ariella coloured. 'He's much younger than me, and besides... No, it wasn't like that. We were just all so hell-bent on getting out alive, we didn't think...'

'But in another life, when things were calmer?' Elizabeth probed gently.

'Look, it doesn't matter now anyway. I just hope they're all right. His leg never fully healed, you know? A botched job in a field hospital, and then back in Berlin there was nothing. He never complained or anything. He took care of us, his mother and me, and he was always joking and laughing through it all.'

'He sounds like a wonderful man,' Elizabeth said.

Ariella smiled sadly. 'He is.'

* * *

THE LONG SUMMER STRETCHED ON, and soon Ariella became part of the fabric of Ballycreggan. She offered her services to the rabbi as he began the long search for the families of the children at the farm, writing letters, searching reports, making contact with the Red Cross. She didn't need to be paid, and she was glad to be of some help. The American broker had expressed his deep condolences at the loss of his friend Peter. He sold her shares easily and had deposited the proceeds in her new Irish bank account. There was more than enough to buy a house and to live off for the rest of her life. He also mentioned that the process of recovering her money in a German bank account could be done. It would take some time, but he would vouch for her and use his connections to help her in any way that he could, so she was financially secure.

She'd purchased a lovely house with four bedrooms at the other end of the village, and Liesl and Erich came and went between both houses. It was a period house, built in the 1700s some time by a merchant, and it retained a lot of the old features. Daniel and Erich had done an incredible job in decorating it and furnishing it for her, and she, Liesl and Elizabeth had made curtains and bedcovers. It was now the loveliest and most bright and welcoming home she could imagine. The children often slept over, and she loved that they and their friends felt welcome there. It was a fairly fluid arrangement that suited everyone.

She'd bought an old bicycle that Daniel fixed up for her, and now the sight of Ariella Bannon whizzing by on her bike was an everyday feature of Ballycreggan.

She closed her front door each night and sat in her bedroom, brushing her hair. She missed Peter, and seeing Erich growing so like him was bittersweet. Sometimes she was sure it was her husband when she glanced at her son, just for a split second, but Peter was gone. Like so many others. There was more bad news than good when it came to the families of the children at the farm. She tried to stay busy all day, but at night, his face swam before her eyes. She prayed he was all right.

Willi. His name hurt her heart. She was sure he would have written by now. He knew where she was going – surely he would have got in touch?

But why would he? His plan was to take his mother back to the Black Forest, and then whenever she died, he would go to America. There was no reason for him to contact her, except that she hoped he would.

She'd looked through the Red Cross lists that the rabbi had received, and there was no mention of them. She'd even written to the mayor of Ludwigsstadt. Frau Braun's father had been the former mayor, so perhaps if the Brauns turned up, he'd know, but she'd heard nothing.

She'd survived, she was reunited with her children – what more could she want?

She got into bed and gazed out at the dusky sky. It amazed her how in summertime in Ireland it never got really dark. It was bright until ten or eleven at night and then became dusk for a few hours before the sun rose again very early. She liked to look at the sky after seeing nothing for so long in the attic; it was something she never took for granted.

Eventually, she dropped off to sleep.

The next morning, the sunlight woke her early. She pulled the pillow over her head and tried to go back to sleep. Two birds outside her window were having an argument, and the exchange was reaching a crescendo. Finally admitting defeat, she pulled her robe on and went downstairs.

The children were up at Elizabeth's but were coming down in the afternoon to take her to the beach. Today was the day Erich was going to jump off the cliff. She'd confided to Elizabeth that she'd rather not watch her darling son's body hurtling at speed into the ocean from such a great height, and Elizabeth agreed that she was dreading it too, but Daniel just laughed and told them if they really thought it was the first time he'd done it, they were very naïve indeed. Erich and Simon had been secretly practising for the last two weeks so they wouldn't look foolish in front of everyone.

She was going to spend a few hours with the rabbi this morning. She could see how the revelations were taking a toll on him, and the fact that she'd lived through it and he didn't need to temper his words with her seemed to help. She knew first-hand the horror that was Germany. He was courteous and grateful for her help, and she felt a deep connection to him. He'd offered to say Kaddish for Father Dominic and Peter, and she accepted gratefully. Though neither man was a Jew, she knew they would both appreciate it.

She thought she would have a light breakfast – she found she ate so little now compared to before the war – and then cycle up to the farm. The rabbi would be at his desk no matter what time she arrived; he was so driven to find out what he could for the children in his care.

She was standing at the kitchen window looking over her little garden when she heard the letterbox rattle at the door. She pulled her dressing gown tighter around her. Her hair was flowing freely. Normally it was pinned back, and she'd allowed it to grow again since Frau Braun's haircut. She was barefoot as she padded out her front door.

She bent to pick up the letter. It had a Zone Francaise stamp with a coat of arms she didn't recognise. Heart pounding, she opened it and pulled out the single thin sheet, sinking onto the stairs to read its contents.

Dear Ariella,

Thank you so much for your letter. I can't believe you thought to write to the Mayor of Ludwigsstadt – he's actually a cousin of Mutti's. Good old German nepotism still at work even if nothing else does! Her cousins run everything here, just as her papa did, and they were very happy to see us. They welcomed us back with open arms, and I can see her blossoming in front of my eyes. She laughs now, actually laughs!

Ariella smiled, thinking of him joking. She could hear his voice as she read, and she realised how much she missed him.

I was so glad to hear you'd been asking after us. We are both fine and have settled, at least temporarily, here in Ludwigsstadt. Mutti sends her regards.

Ariella, I regret nothing so much as not having the courage to say something that night you left. I don't know why – well, I do. I was afraid you'd reject me, or worse, take pity on me feeling like you owed us something, and I couldn't bear that. But I've been so sad since we parted. And then we got the message from the mayor... Well, it seemed like a good sign. So here goes, and please don't feel like you have to respond to be nice to the poor old cripple – I'd rather you just told me the truth.

I love you. I don't know when I fell in love with you, but it was a long time ago, and I have never stopped loving you. Watching you drive off in that truck, not knowing if I'd ever see you again, was like a physical pain, much worse than the leg, I can assure you. I know all the reasons you might think this is an audacious proposal – I'm too young, I've only one leg, I've no money – and you'd be right, but here I am nonetheless.

So if you want me – and I have no idea if you do or not – then I'm yours. Wherever, whenever. I promise, if you agree, I would love you forever, I would try to be a good role model for Liesl and Erich, I'd take care of you all, and I would never again allow you to eat a bowl of porridge.

Ariella pealed with laughter. Even at his most serious, he couldn't stop his natural exuberance from bubbling up. In a world of such doom and misery, she needed his optimism and fun. More than that, she needed him.

You can reach me at the above address. We are in the French Zone of Occupation, and remarkably, things are going back to normal, or some version of normal anyway.

I'll wait to hear from you.

JEAN GRAINGER

All my love,
Willi

EPILOGUE

rau Braun fastened the last of the buttons on the back of Ariella's dress and stood back to admire her handiwork.

'Your hem is crooked,' the older woman said, pulling her sewing basket towards her once more. 'Though it is nice,' she muttered.

'Well, you made the dress, so if I look nice, it's down to you. Remember that dress you gave me, the one with the flowers? I knew then you had style, even if you had no occasion to wear it.' Ariella smiled at her soon-to-be mother-in-law.

Frau Braun had smiled more in the six months since she and Willi arrived in Ballycreggan than in all of the years before. Apparently she was the one who'd admonished her son for letting Ariella go, and she was also the one who insisted he write to tell her how he felt.

She was living now with Ariella and going daily to the farm as a much-needed volunteer, and the children saw her as a grandmother. She was warm and kind to all of the children, and the volte-face was remarkable. She could be just as acerbic as she always was, however, when it came to adults, but they were getting used to her. Her heart was in the right place, but she didn't suffer fools.

'Well, Rabbi Frank isn't one to put up with brides being late, so I'll just fix this as best I can,' Frau Braun said sardonically. She and the old rabbi were wary of each other, but there was the beginning of a thaw there.

Willi had introduced himself to the rabbi the day he arrived, three weeks after receiving Ariella's telegram that read simply, 'Come to Ballycreggan. I love you too.' Willi had explained to the rabbi how he was in fact a Jew. Like Daniel, he knew nothing of that part of himself, but also like Daniel, it fascinated him.

The rabbi had been happy but not surprised either, and he even commended Frau Braun on raising a good Jewish boy, who, like her, had done the right thing when needed, even if he had no idea what he really was. Willi had begun his official instruction and was, with the rabbi and Daniel's help, well on the way to being a full member of the Jewish community in Ballycreggan. In lots of ways, Willi said, it made sense.

He worked on the farm and spent all the time he could with Ariella. It wouldn't be proper for them to live together until they married, something that made them both laugh considering how many nights they'd slept together in Berlin, but she was so looking forward to him moving in.

She introduced him to the children, and to her amazement, they remembered him as the paper boy and the teenager their papa used to tease about football. They warmed to him instantly, and Frau Braun delighted them with her remarks about the adults. She was always on the side of the young people, and they loved her for it.

* * *

THE LADIES WERE in Ariella's new house, and Willi was getting ready at the Liebers' with Daniel and Erich to make sure he arrived on time and looking suitable. They were getting married at the synagogue on the farm, just as Elizabeth and Daniel had done.

'Right, you're as good as we can get you.' Frau Braun stood up, taking some pins from her mouth. Ariella smiled. Never one for extravagant compliments, her mother-in-law, but she felt such affection for her all the same; they'd been through so much together.

'I know it was you who made him write. Thank you,' Ariella said sincerely.

'Well, it was either that or have him going about like a sick calf, day in and day out. I couldn't endure that long face a second more. Come on now, we'll be late.'

That was as much as she was going to get, so Ariella suppressed a giggle and walked through the door Frau Braun held open for her, down to the kitchen below.

Liesl looked beautiful in a pale-blue dress with navy trim; she and Elizabeth had worked on it for weeks. She and Elizabeth both stopped what they were doing and gazed at Ariella as she entered.

'Oh, *Mutti*, you look so beautiful,' Liesl said.

Elizabeth beamed at her. 'You really do.'

Ariella's red curls were tamed, and Frau Braun had twisted them into an elegant chignon, just allowing a few tendrils loose to frame her heart-shaped face. Her sea-green eyes shone with happiness, and the fitted ivory dress complemented her creamy skin perfectly.

Her connection with Willi was there for everyone to see. There was an age gap, but that didn't matter. Willi adored Ariella and she felt the same. They'd endured so much together; it gave the entire community such joy to see them finally get married.

A beep outside told them Levi was there with the school bus. He was charged with getting the wedding party to the synagogue on time.

'Papa would be so proud of you,' Liesl whispered to her mother as they walked out to the bus.

'He would be proud of all of us,' her mother replied with a smile.

The End.

I SINCERELY HOPE you enjoyed this book. If you did, it would mean the world to me if you would consider leaving a review on Amazon.

If you would like to continue this series and return to Ballycreggan with Erich, Liesl and the gang, the next book is called

The Hard Way Home
Here are the first 2 chapters to get you started

THE HARD WAY HOME
Chapter 1
Dublin, Ireland, 1950

Liesl sat behind the podium, focusing her attention entirely on the speaker from the other team, mentally noting his points, formulating her rebuttal. The crowd was respectfully listening to her opponent, so despite the ornate hall being packed to capacity, his voice was the only sound. Ancient books rested behind grilles the length of both walls, and the entire place smelled of a rich cultural and academic heritage dating back centuries. Liesl loved it. Trinity College Dublin were proposing the motion today. Not her chosen position at the best of times – she preferred arguing against – but it was the luck of the draw.

It required all of her analytical and oratory skills to argue in support of this motion – 'that this house supports Irish neutrality in the period 1939–1945' – something she personally vehemently disagreed with, but the Irish Varsity debating finals held no place for sentiment.

She allowed herself a quick glance down at the audience in Goldsmith Hall, where Elizabeth, Daniel, Ariella, Willi and Erich were sitting, proud as punch. She'd warned them in advance that she would be saying things she fundamentally disagreed with, but they said they understood and insisted on coming to support her. She made them promise not to look at her, as it was going to be difficult enough without seeing them there: her *mutti*, who hid in a Berlin attic for years; her mother's husband Willi, who'd lost a leg in Russia but didn't let it stop him; her adopted mother, Elizabeth, who lost everything when the Germans bombed her house in Liverpool; tall, dark, handsome Daniel Lieber, her adopted father, who as a Jew had escaped Vienna only by the intervention of a friend in England; then her brother, Erich, tall as Daniel almost and filled out too, who looked so much like she remembered her father it took her breath away sometimes. Arguing that anyone should have been neutral in the face of the evil that killed their father and forced her and her little brother on a train and into the arms of strangers was going to be hardest of all.

She risked a glance at her brother. She was ten and Erich seven when they left Berlin, and they were very close. His sleek dark hair was a little longer on top now as was the fashion, and his dark-brown eyes gave him a soulful look. How she loved them all. She was delighted they'd finally made the trip down to Dublin together, though it was time enough for them since she was in her final year of her degree programme, majoring in international relations with a minor in French and German. Elizabeth and her mother visited sometimes, taking a day trip on the train, and Erich visited often because he loved socialising with her college girlfriends, but the men were always busy with something. Normally, she caught the train to Belfast every few months and Daniel picked her up from the station and brought her home to Ballycreggan for a visit.

She missed them all, and though returning to the bosom of both of her mothers, her brother and her father was wonderful, she loved her life in Dublin.

She looked around the room. She liked Trinity. It felt nice to be part of something, but like always, she wondered when, if ever, she would feel like she truly belonged. Her teammates were Irish, born and raised, as were most of her fellow students. Those who weren't had left home, wherever that was, to study at the famous Dublin university. As a German Jew, raised first by her parents in Berlin, a Jewish mother and a Gentile father, and then cared for by a lapsed Catholic, Elizabeth, and moved initially to Liverpool and then on to Northern Ireland, she struggled to feel that sense of belonging. Ireland was divided; the North where her family lived was part of the United Kingdom, and here she was in the Irish Republic. It seemed like nowhere ever felt like home.

She focused on her opponent. If she caught the eye of anyone in the family, she'd lose focus. Her team had come so far; it would be a shame to lose now. The final speaker from University College Dublin was mesmerising. He spoke with such passion against neutrality, his argument being that it was not the time for politicking and that it was a moral question. The defeat of Hitler and the Nazis was imperative, and Ireland should have left her own issues with Britain aside and done the right thing.

The tall young man with a lilting accent that suggested he was from the south of the country held everyone enthralled as he painted graphic pictures of concentration camps, death marches and the relentlessly cruel and ruthless suffocation of human rights perpetrated by the Nazis across Europe. His eyes blazed with venom for an Irish administration that refused to allow Jewish refugees into Ireland, and he railed against those who put religious dogma and bigotry ahead of humanitarianism. Liesl found herself falling under his spell. He pushed his reddish-brown curls out of his eyes. She didn't dare make eye contact, choosing instead, as she'd been taught, to look nonchalantly into the middle distance while taking in every word.

He finally sat down, and she could feel the backing for him, even from the Trinity supporters, those from the Protestant college as it was seen in Ireland. The reality of the war, and in particular what was done to the Jews and other marginalised groups, was becoming more and more apparent every year as survivors gave testimony, wrote books and allowed the world to hide no more behind a curtain of ignorance.

But Liesl didn't need books or diaries of Jews who'd been victims of National Socialism to know what it was like. She knew on a deeper, more personal level. But that would not be apparent from her speech. She was determined to remain true to her argument, even if she didn't believe a word of it.

This was it, her chance to win the coveted trophy. Her teammates had done a solid job – they had been clear and committed to defending the motion – but she knew she was the one who would make or break it.

Though she'd warned her mother before the debate about the topic, to say what she was about to with her mother in the room felt so wrong. She mentally shook herself. This was not about her or her family, or what they'd experienced. This was just a college debate, and while it wasn't life or death, she would like to win. She could do this.

'Mr Chairman, distinguished guests, fellow students, the motion for debate this evening is the question of Irish neutrality during the last war.' Liesl looked around the room, making eye contact here and there, establishing a connection with her audience. 'And the proposition have done a thorough job outlining where the Irish government went wrong. They have brought us close to tears at the fate of the Jews of Europe, and indeed, one would need to have a heart of granite not to be moved. But I put it to you that hindsight is perfect vision.'

She wondered if the audience could hear the trace of a German accent in her voice, a slight lingering even after ten years in Ireland. She looked Jewish, she knew that. Her first name was German but her surname was Irish, so while her friends and family knew who and what she was, this audience and the judges did not.

'This country was at war with Britain since the arrival of the Anglo-Normans in 1169. Think about that, ladies and gentlemen. Eight hundred years of armed resistance to subjugation, mistreatment, abuse and even genocide that was perpetrated on the Irish people by our next-door neighbour. The Irish were forbidden to speak our language, to educate our children, to own land, to enjoy our culture. Every single human right, every aspect of human dignity, was denied the Irish people by their oppressors.' She paused and looked around, her voice low and determined. 'They didn't force the Irish into concentration camps, it's true, and they didn't exterminate them with poisonous gas, but they killed, they beat and tortured, they exiled, and they spread fear and hatred throughout the entire country. And when we finally achieved freedom, through centuries of Irish blood being spilled for the cause, the demand was made from London, the birthplace of every decree of misery for this nation, that we forget our old silly grievances, put aside our petty harking back to the past and join up with them to fight a people with whom we had no quarrel.'

231

She could sense the room shifting. The next few moments were crucial.

'Why should a young man from Carlow or Kerry don a British uniform, the uniform that had struck fear and loathing into every seed, breed and generation of his family for centuries, and go to Europe to shoot Germans, who had never harmed a hair on their heads?'

She could see a few slight nods at the rhetorical questions – she was winning. The opposition had brought up that de Valera, the Irish Taoiseach, or prime minister, visited the German ambassador in Dublin in May of 1945 and expressed his condolences on Hitler's death, but to that she had no answer. Nor could she bring herself to try to vindicate such an action, so she chose to ignore it.

'When Winston Churchill accused us of "frolicking with the Germans and the Japanese", it was with the knowledge that the Irish people had, in so many ways, assisted the Allied effort. This country fed Britain during those years, we gave radar and weather information, we returned Allied airmen and tried to repair and return their crashed aircraft – all facts, ladies and gentlemen, of which Mr Churchill was well aware.'

She took a sip of water.

'We did what we could, and what we should have done in support of the cause of what was right. But allying ourselves to an enemy as tenacious and duplicitous as Great Britain proved herself to be was unconscionable. Historians are doomed, ladies and gentlemen, for they are trying to analyse the actions of those in the past, with the benefit of knowing what comes next. We know now what Hitler and his followers did. Of course we do. But we didn't know then. Mr de Valera was dignified in his response to Churchill, who described so eloquently how Britain stood alone against an occupied European continent, when our Taoiseach asked, and I quote, "Could he not find in his heart the generosity to acknowledge that there is a small nation that stood alone not for one year or two, but for several hundred years against aggression; that endured spoliations, famines, massacres in endless succession; that was clubbed many times into insensibility, but that each time on returning consciousness took up the fight anew; a small nation that could never be got to accept defeat and has never surrendered her soul?"'

The words that had so rallied the Irish people in the face of Churchill's criticism sank in around the room. Liesl stayed silent, allowing their impact to resonate fully before going in for the kill.

'Should we have taken more refugees? Yes. But should we have thrown away the sacrifice of so many dead generations who fought to free our island from British oppression? Never. We were neutral. And we were right to remain so. Thank you.'

As she sat back down, she caught her brother's eye. Erich was a strapping eighteen-year-old now, but to her he would always be her little brother, entrusted into her ten-year-old care by her mother on the platform of Tempelhof station in Berlin in 1939.

Unlike her, Erich wasn't studious and couldn't wait till he left school. They'd been educated together in Ballycreggan Primary School, with Elizabeth as the teacher. It was an incredible stroke of luck that Elizabeth's home town was the location of the only Jewish refugee camp in Northern Ireland, so they'd grown up with Jewish friends, boys and girls from all over Europe who'd been brought to the farm on the Ards Peninsula in County Down to escape the Nazis.

Erich and Daniel had a business going. Daniel was an engineer, and Erich was serving his time as a carpenter. They were father and son, in every way but blood.

He made a face at her, trying to make her laugh. She gave a hint of a smile but looked away. The judges had yet to decide, and she didn't want to throw it all away.

The judges withdrew to deliberate, and the volume in the hall rose with the hum of conversation.

Beside her, Val and Jerome, her teammates, were equally inscrutable. They'd done their best, but it was a hard motion to support. However, as Professor Kingston was constantly reminding them, the judges were not making a moral judgement; they were judging the standard of oratory and rhetoric and the debaters' ability to adapt and reply.

Liesl glanced across at the UCD team and flushed when she was caught staring at the lad with the brownish-red curls. He looked back at her, his green eyes dancing with merriment, the earnestness of his performance moments earlier seeming dissipated. He was tall and muscular, and now that the debate was over, he loosened his tie and collar rakishly. He joked with his teammates, and they seemed to hang on his every word. She risked another glance, and again he caught her, this time giving her an almost imperceptible wink while simultaneously listening intently to the studious-looking teammate beside him.

The chairman of the judges led his fellow presiders back into the room, and both teams stood. He made all the usual remarks, praising both the Trinity and UCD teams for an excellent debate. He singled out Val and the last speaker from the UCD team, the young man with the curly hair, for particular praise. It was impossible to tell how he was going to vote. She was sure he was finished and was about to make his judgement when he paused and looked at her.

'I must make exceptional mention of the captain of the Trinity team. Not only is it wonderful to see our female students represented, but to see a debate so ably argued and with such passion is something unprecedented, even in these hallowed halls. Therefore, I and my panel of judges find for the proposition and Trinity College Dublin.'

The crowd burst into thunderous applause, and Liesl caught Professor Kingston's eye. He was over the moon, accepting handshakes and congratulations coming from every direction.

The chairman invited the dean of students onto the podium to present the trophy, and Liesl went forward to accept it. Val and Jerome were beaming, and Liesl looked down to see her family standing and applauding vigorously.

Eventually, the photographs were finished, and as she walked backstage, she felt someone grab her hand. In the darkness and the crush of people trying to get out of the small exit, it was impossible to see who had done it, but a note was pressed into her palm.

She felt a surge of excitement – was it from the UCD captain? He was only a few feet away, but when she risked a glance, he was deeply engaged in conversation with someone. She wouldn't read the note until later, not wanting to be caught looking too eager if it was from him.

She put it in her pocket and went downstairs, where she was immediately enveloped in hugs from her friends. Daniel and Elizabeth stood to one side, looking so proud, and Erich was trying to make room for Willi and Ariella to get in to greet her.

Once all the hugs and congratulations were complete, Daniel announced, 'Everyone, to the Shelbourne! The drinks are on me.'

Chapter 2

LIESL'S FRIEND Abigail linked her arm through hers as they sat in the corner of the Shelbourne bar. They were both Jewish, so had gravitated to each other on the first day of university and had been inseparable since.

'Did you see the UCD dreamboat making eyes at you?' Abigail whispered. She giggled, sipped her lemonade and nudged Liesl to look towards the bar, where the UCD team had also congregated. She was right; he was looking over.

'I...I don't know who you mean,' Liesl objected.

Something about his gaze was disconcerting. Was the note from him? She was dying to find out but needed to be alone to read it.

Erich sidled up beside them. Every time he met Abigail, he flirted most amateurishly, but she was always nice to him.

'Erich Bannon, so good to see you again,' Abigail said. 'Join us!' She patted the seat beside them.

'Hello, Abigail, you look lovely tonight,' Erich said, trying to sound suave and sophisticated.

Liesl fought the urge to laugh.

'Thank you, Erich, so do you. I like your tie.'

Erich blushed to the roots of his dark hair. He had grown up to be handsome, Liesl supposed. It was hard to tell when it was your little brother, but according to Elizabeth, all the girls in Ballycreggan had an eye for him. But he was after someone a little more exotic than the girls of a small rural village.

'I was just asking your sister if she noticed her admirer from the UCD team. He couldn't keep his eyes off her.' Abigail nudged Liesl again.

The two girls were as opposite as chalk and cheese. Abigail was short with a rounded figure and had what she called mousy hair, though in reality it was light brown. She constantly bemoaned the fact that Liesl was so pretty compared to her, but Liesl thought her friend was lovely and told her so frequently. However, Abigail had yet to have a boy ask her to a dance or the pictures, and they were in their final year.

'The lad with the curly hair? Aye, he seemed keen, right enough.' Erich grinned.

Erich was pure Ballycreggan these days and, unlike her, showed no trace whatsoever of his German identity. He looked, spoke and dressed like an Irishman, and that's how he saw himself. He was proud of her, Liesl knew that, and they were very close. But he couldn't understand her studying German of all things, the language of the people who killed his father and tried to kill his mother and who snatched him and his sister from the happy life they had in Berlin before the war.

Things had worked out well for them. Elizabeth was their father's first cousin and had agreed to take them from the Kindertransport, but for so many others, the future had been much less certain at the time.

'He wanted to get inside my head. That's what debating is all about, rattling your opponent. He was so fiery in his delivery, he would have wanted to put me off. That, my dear Abigail who sees the romance in every single thing,' Liesl teased, 'is what you witnessed.'

Later though, when she went to the ladies, she took the note out of her pocket. Her heart pounded. Something told her it was from him.

The writing was rushed and scrawled, and Elizabeth would have had a fit if she'd seen it. As a schoolteacher, she insisted on neat hand-writing.

Liesl, you are the most incredible woman I've ever seen or heard. I have to get to know you. You intrigue me. Will you meet me in Bewley's tomorrow at eleven for coffee or tea or any beverage of your choosing? I'll throw in a cream cake to sweeten the deal. I'll be there, waiting impatiently.
Jamie Gallagher

She smiled. He was as confident in his note as he was in his speech.

She put the note back in her pocket and left the cubicle. As she washed her hands, she took a moment to think. Winning the debating final had been all she'd thought about for the last few weeks, and she'd spent her time researching and writing her speech and collaborating with her teammates every evening. But now that it was over and they'd won, she had some free time. Her final exams were not until May and it was only October now, so she could probably allow herself a little diversion. And there was something fascinating about him.

'Jamie Gallagher,' she whispered, then caught herself in the mirror. 'Ah, would you catch yourself on,' she muttered as she gazed at her reflection.

Abigail was like a broken record telling her how pretty she was, but she didn't think it was true. Her dark hair and brown eyes combined with creamy skin that took the sun just made her look unusual in Ireland, but she was nothing special. Anyway, she didn't go on dates; she wanted to focus on her studies, and that was what she had come to do. She'd had one boyfriend, Ben, back in Ballycreggan, but he'd been hurt when she said she wanted to come to Trinity and so the relationship kind of fizzled out. She missed him. He was a nice boy, but they wanted different things from life. He'd accused her of being restless, of never allowing herself to be happy, and maybe he was right. She was searching for something – she just didn't know what it was. Since then, she couldn't be bothered with boys.

Even her mother had suggested that she socialise a bit more. Because Ariella had survived the war by hiding in Frau Braun's attic – Frau Braun was Willi's mother and also now lived in Ballycreggan – she wanted everyone to really appreciate life, to take joy out of being alive. Liesl remembered how her *mutti* used to walk up to the Bally-creggan National School every morning to hear the children singing the *Modeh Ani*, a prayer of thanks, in Hebrew. Rabbi Frank taught it to everyone, and all of the children, Jewish and Christian, sang it together each day, first in Hebrew and then in English. It reminded them all of how wonderful life was and how lucky they were to be alive.

She pushed her way back into the crowd and saw Daniel buying more drinks for her friends at the bar. Her stepfather, Willi, was good-naturedly passing them back. Daniel was such a generous man. She loved him, and he was the patriarch of their family. She sat down with Ariella and Elizabeth, who were both sipping whiskey and soda.

'Oh, darling, I'm so proud of you! You were incredible up there. I could hardly believe this poised young woman was my little Liesl.' Ariella squeezed her hand, her face suddenly wistful. 'When I met your papa, he was at university and he too was a debater. He was excellent, and I went to some of them just to see him in action. He would never argue for or against things he didn't believe, though, which was ridiculous of course. I mean, you had to fight that Ireland was right to remain neutral, when I know you don't believe that. But he was young and pig-headed and stubborn.' She laughed at the memory, a lovely sound that always reminded Liesl of a little bell ringing. 'He got thrown off the team in the end, but oh, how proud he'd be of you, Liesl. Erich looks so much like him– sometimes when he steps into the room, for a moment I have to do a double take – but you are the one who really takes after Peter.'

'Do you think I shouldn't have argued –' Liesl began, feeling like she'd betrayed her father's memory. He'd always done what was right; he'd died doing so.

'Oh, of course not, darling! That would have been ridiculous, and it's why you will succeed.' Ariella smiled. 'You're passionate but also pragmatic. I often wonder if Peter had been less rash, maybe if he'd not been as forceful that day he intervened with that Jewish lady in the street, maybe he could have stopped those Nazis abusing her a bit more diplomatically, then perhaps things would have been different. But that's how he was, all or nothing.'

'But I'm afraid I sounded like I was forgiving them...' Liesl wasn't convinced.

'Liesl, my love, it's peacetime now. That's what all those millions of people who fought back died for. Of course we must move on, try to put it behind us. Otherwise it was for nothing if we are going to relive it every single day and hold onto grudges and hurts.'

Liesl nodded but knew her mother wasn't practising what she preached. She would never return to Germany and could never forgive them, and Liesl didn't blame her.

'Your papa would be bursting with pride if he could see you.' Ariella took her hand and kissed it.

Liesl loved to hear about her birth father, but her mother rarely spoke of their lives before. Liesl knew that any happy memories had been obliterated by the way their country turned on them, what Ariella had endured during the war years and the horrors she saw in those final months.

'You were so impressive, Liesl, honestly. We knew you'd be good, but the judge was right – you were exceptional. Especially since we knew you didn't believe a word of it.' Elizabeth chuckled. 'You are a worryingly convincing liar, Miss Bannon.'

Liesl grinned. 'Ah, yes, what else am I lying about?' she said dramatically, and her mother and stepmother laughed.

'We were just saying on the way down how we wished you did a little more of the things girls lie to their mothers about,' Ariella said wryly.

'*Mutti*, believe me, you don't. If you heard some of the shenanigans the girls in my halls get up to, you'd never sleep a wink with worrying about me. I've told you before, I want to get first class honours, and they don't hand them out like sweeties, so I need to work hard.'

'We know you do, sweetheart, and I'm sure you'll pass with flying colours, but a little fun isn't going to do you any harm, you know. You're young, free and single in a big city – you should be enjoying it, not stuck in books from dawn to dusk.' Elizabeth patted her hand.

It was as if she'd always had two mothers, and in every way that mattered, she had. She and Erich had not seen Ariella for six years when their mother arrived in Ballycreggan, undernourished and over-whelmed. But she'd stayed alive as a Jew in Berlin for the entire war, determined to be reunited with her children. Elizabeth and Daniel had cared for them, had even adopted them because they had all assumed that Ariella was dead, and what could have been an awkward or fractious reunion turned out to be the complete opposite.

Ariella married Willi Braun, Frau Braun's son, and since there was nothing for any of them back in Germany, staying in Ireland seemed the sensible thing to do.

'I am enjoying it here,' Liesl insisted. 'I love Dublin, and I really appreciate that I'm studying at Trinity. The fees are huge, and I just want to make the most of the opportunity – it's not one many people get.'

'Your papa would have wanted it for you,' Ariella said with a sad smile. Luckily, Peter Bannon had made some investments in America when he saw how things were going in Germany, which Ariella was able to recoup after the war. The money from those investments allowed her to rebuild her life with plenty to spare.

'So tell me, how is everything at home?' Liesl asked, changing the subject. 'How are Frau Braun and the rabbi and everyone? I haven't heard from Viola for a while – how is she?'

Elizabeth and Ariella shared a glance that Liesl caught.

'What? What's happened?' she asked.

'Did Viola not write?' Elizabeth asked.

'No. I've written to her three times but got no reply. I was getting worried.' Liesl raked their faces for a clue. 'Do you know something?'

'Liesl, Viola and Ben are together.'

'Oh.' Liesl struggled to find words. 'Together?' She swallowed. 'As a couple?'

'I think so,' Elizabeth said.

So that was why her friend hadn't written. Viola and her sister, Anika, had been Liesl's best friends growing up, and Ben was her old boyfriend. She'd tried to keep the relationship with Ben going when she came to Trinity – he was from Dublin but was working in Belfast now, having moved up to Ballycreggan to be with her as a boy of seventeen – but it was impossible. Finally, after many fraught letters and a few disastrous weekend visits, Liesl broke off the relationship. Ben was hurt and angry. He said he loved her and had moved up to Ballycreggan to be with her, and now that she had a much more exciting life, there was no room for him. She hated to admit it, but he was right.

At university, she met all sorts of people, with exciting ideas and plans for the future. Ben had been her first boyfriend – well, her only one – but he didn't fit in her new world. She'd told Viola all about it last time she was home, and now that she knew about Viola and Ben, her friend's reaction made sense. She'd said that Liesl was too sophisticated for them all now, and the conversation had ended awkwardly, something she'd only once before experienced with Viola.

'When did this happen, that Viola and Ben started going out together?'

'A while ago,' Elizabeth said gently. 'Look, I told both of them they should tell you themselves, but…'

'They didn't,' Liesl said dully.

It felt like betrayal, but she knew she had no right to complain. She'd broken it off with Ben, and she was the one who'd left Ballycreggan and Viola. The one weekend her friend had come down to Dublin was a disaster. A friendship that worked in Ballycreggan just didn't seem to translate to Dublin. She found her friend prickly and hard to talk to. Perhaps something had been going on with Ben at that stage; she didn't know.

'Will it last, do you think?' Liesl asked Elizabeth. She had no right to feel hurt, but she did. Viola and Ben were both free to go out with whomever they chose, but she wished they felt like they could tell her.

'I don't know,' Elizabeth replied. 'Though they seem quite serious.'

'I'm happy for them.'

Liesl's heart was heavy. She inhaled. Ballycreggan as she knew it was changing – she and Viola, Erich and his friends, school, the synagogue on the farm. It had felt almost like where she belonged, but each time she went back, things were different, and it was hard not to feel sad.

'So how about everyone else? Anything else exciting happening?' she asked, trying to insert some brightness into her voice. She could see by their faces that Ariella and Elizabeth were worried about her.

'Oh, nothing,' Ariella said. 'Rabbi Frank is fine – he sends you his blessing and good wishes. And Levi and Ruth have decided to go to Israel. Some of the children – well, they are all growing up now, but some of the older ones are going with them.'

'To live, you mean?' She was surprised.

'Yes, they want to live in their homeland, and they see Israel as that. It's both sad and exciting. The rabbi and I have exhausted almost every avenue in trying to find the families of the children of the farm, and in most cases, there is nobody left. But we've been lucky a few times. Remember Benjamin?'

Liesl nodded. Benjamin Krantz was only a toddler when he arrived and so had been in the kindergarten group, but she knew him; they all knew each other.

'Well, incredibly, his grandfather and one aunt survived Bergen-Belsen, so he's going back to Prague to be with them. Though he cried, the poor child. He's thirteen now and Ballycreggan is the only life he knows, but we hope it works out. I tried to teach him whatever Czech I knew, but it is going to be hard. They might be family, but they are strangers.'

'Poor Benjamin. I hope he'll be all right. He's just a little older than I was when I left Berlin, but at least I had Erich. I suppose he could always come back if he hated it?'

Ariella nodded. 'We will give him some money for the fare and keep in touch by letter until we're sure he's happy, although I'm not sure legally we have the right to take him back. Rabbi Frank has corresponded with the grandfather and he seems very anxious to reunite with him, so we can just hope.'

Liesl nodded. 'What about the Schultz boys? Last you told me, Dieter and Abraham were waiting on a letter?'

'Yes.' Elizabeth nodded. 'Their older brother is married in Vienna and has asked them to go to him. They're thinking about it, but they are sixteen and eighteen now so they can choose for themselves. They and Erich and Simon spend a lot of time together playing football. Dieter is going to the technical college in Strabane to study motor mechanics and Abraham finishes school this year, so they are going to see how they feel.'

'Maybe they should go for a visit first, see how it works out,' Liesl suggested. 'I keep trying to imagine what it would be like to go back to Berlin. Would I feel at home or like a stranger? It's hard to know until you actually do it, I would think.'

'The Berlin I left in 1946 was nothing like the one you remember, darling,' Ariella said sadly. 'It's up to you of course, but for me, if I never see that city again, that is fine. It was just rubble and suffering, and so many people just wandering, lost. Willi and Frau Braun feel the same. They speak English all the time now, never a word of German.'

'I can understand that, but you know, studying German and reading Max Weber, Thomas Mann and Chekov is good – it reminds me that Germany was once a place of culture and learning and art and that it can be again. The Nazis might as well have won the war if we allow them to rewrite our future as well as our past.'

'I'm glad you see it that way, darling. It's right that young people should be optimistic and forward looking,' Ariella said with a sad smile.

'You always try to see both sides. It's one of your many talents, Liesl.' Elizabeth smiled.

'And so who is going to Israel with Ruth and Levi?' Liesl asked, and she saw that look pass between Elizabeth and Ariella again.

'Well, originally it was just Max, Rosa, Gretchen, Paul and Anika...' Elizabeth paused. 'But I think Viola and Ben are considering it now as well. There's been a huge take-up of people going now, from all over the world, I'd imagine, since the Law of Return was passed. Levi has always been a Zionist at heart, so he is happy to go. Ruth is nervous though. And the children who have nobody left are drawn there too. They want to be with people who understand. So now Michael is going, Malek and Katarina, Josef... Who else, Ariella?'

'Anika is gone already – she went straight from Poland. She wanted to go back. She knew there was nothing left in Warsaw, but she wanted to see for herself. Viola said she'd rather remember it as it was. So the sisters will be reunited.'

Liesl was lost in thought as her mothers talked. After years of upheaval and chaos, everyone seemed to be finding where they were meant to be. Everyone but her. Erich was going to stay in Ballycreggan, that was for sure. Her parents were all secure and happy there too, and now her oldest friends were leaving for Israel.

Something told her that Israel was not her calling. She might go someday, for a visit, but she had no desire to live there. Was it because she was German? Or because her father was a Gentile? She didn't think that was it. She just didn't feel that connection to the homeland so often talked about in her faith. The trouble was, she didn't feel that connection anywhere else either.

To continue reading click here
The Hard Way Home

ALSO BY JEAN GRAINGER

To get a free novel and to join my readers club (100% free and always will be)

Go to www.jeangrainger.com

The Tour Series

The Tour

Safe at the Edge of the World

The Story of Grenville King

The Homecoming of Bubbles O'Leary

Finding Billie Romano

Kayla's Trick

The Carmel Sheehan Story

Letters of Freedom

The Future's Not Ours To See

What Will Be

The Robinswood Story

What Once Was True

Return To Robinswood

Trials and Tribulations

The Star and the Shamrock Series

The Star and the Shamrock

The Emerald Horizon

The Hard Way Home

The World Starts Anew